Healing Time

"This book will have you laughing a completely *loveable* and crazy character. Her quirky thoughts are fun to read and her adventures in dating (or lack of) will have you giggling until your sides ache. It's ...anteed to make you giggle and feel good — what ...could you want in a book?" — *Kidzworld*

...ndromeda Harmony has two beautiful best ...ppie dad who still lives in the irresponsible 60s, ...sh on JT, a bad case of hickeys from some ...gives her chicken pox, a total self-absorption ...o an inferiority complex, and a compulsion to ...n every detail of her life. Rivers presents Haley ...n a list of catastrophes that grow increasingly more ...s until Haley ends up in the hospital near death with ...gitis. Not so funny? Rivers pulls it off." — *VOYA*

...y is a bright, realistic, and appealing protagonist, ...ose wry wit and brilliant naïveté help her transcend ...r situation. The journal covers September through New Year's Day, leading teens to anticipate another installment. All will want to know the outcome of TGYML." — *School Library Journal*

"Sixteen-year-old Haley Harmony is ... much more than a self-described obsessive compulsive with bad hair. She's a likeable, grounded soul, despite the fact that she spends an awful lot of time hyperventilating ... A pleasure from start to finish." — *Quill and Quire*

Cure for Crushes

"I can't help it. I'm a sucker for Bridget Jones and I'm a sucker for Karen Rivers's ongoing series based on the star-crossed life of Haley Harmony. We first met the unfortunately named Harmony (hippie parents, home-schooled, deck stacked against her socially) in *The Healing Time* *Hickeys*. It's refreshing that Haley, told through v. f[...] diary entries, is not entirely likeable; nor are her [...] endlessly patient. And without her brother's sho[...] lean on, Haley finds herself alone more this time[...] wondering, like all of us, if she really is capab[...] ness and how to make the good hair days o[...] bad." — *The G*[...]

"Haley has a lot going on during part two of Th[...] Year of My Life (TGYML): she has a boyfrien[...] she keeps avoiding; her bestish friends, flawless Jule[...] sympathetic Kiki, are getting on her nerves — no, th[...] not — uh, yes, they are — well, sometimes, anyway; an[...] does not, absolutely not, still have a crush on JT (the[...] that gorgeous Jules wound up with, of course!). Her pe[...] nially jobless, hippie Dad has, ugh, an MYG (Much Young[...] Girlfriend)! If all that weren't enough, a party faux pa[...] weekend mishaps, birthday-party bungee-jumping, broken[...] limbs, devastated self-esteem, over-dyed hair, and non-cooperative horoscopes all conspire to make Haley's TGYML an ongoing disaster." — *School Library Journal*

"We've all had our fair share of *red-faced moments*, and that's why it's so easy to relate to the accident-prone Haley. Her quirky accidents and comical thoughts are the best part of the book cuz they'll make you laugh until your stomach hurts!" — *kidzworld*

The ~~Cool~~ Quirky Girls' ~~Aimless~~ Guide to ~~Parallel Parking~~ Rest Stops and Road Trips

The ~~Cool~~ Quirky Girls'
~~Aimless~~ Guide to
~~Parallel Parking~~
Rest Stops
and Road Trips

KAREN RIVERS

POLESTAR
An Imprint of Raincoast Books

Raincoast Books gratefully acknowledges the ongoing support of the Canada
Council for the Arts, the British Columbia Arts Council and the Government of
Canada through the Book Publishing Industry Development Program (BPIDP).

Edited by Elizabeth McLean
Cover art by Monika Melnychuk
Cover design by Teresa Bubela
Typesetting by Tannice Goddard

NATIONAL LIBRARY OF CANADA CATALOGUING IN PUBLICATION DATA

Rivers, Karen, 1970–
  The quirky girls' guide to rest stops and road trips / Karen Rivers.
  ISBN 10 1-55192-907-4
  ISBN 13 978-1-55192-907-1
  I. Title.
PS8585.I8778Q57 2006   JC813´.54   C2006-901511-2

LIBRARY OF CONGRESS CONTROL NUMBER: 2006924083

Polestar/Raincoast Books   *In the United States:*
9050 Shaughnessy Street   Publishers Group West
Vancouver, British Columbia   1700 Fourth Street
Canada v6p 6E5   Berkeley, California
www.raincoast.com   94710

Raincoast Books is committed to protecting the environment and to the
responsible use of natural resources. We are working with suppliers and printers
to phase out our use of paper produced from ancient forests. This book is printed
with vegetable-based inks on 100% ancient-forest-free paper (40% post-consumer
recycled), processed chlorine- and acid-free. For further information, visit our
website at www.raincoast.com/publishing.

Printed in Canada by Webcom.

10 9 8 7 6 5 4 3 2 1

I'd like to dedicate this book to every actor who thinks she would make a great Haley, and every producer who thinks this book would make a great movie, and all the directors who think they could turn it into a smash hit film. Thank you, in advance.

And to you of course, for reading it. Thanks!

CONTENTS

"One's destination is never a place, but a new way of seeing things."   — HENRY MILLER

"I have found out that there ain't no surer way to find out whether you like people or hate them than to travel with them."   — MARK TWAIN

road trip

    noun: any journey made by car, bicycle, bus, etc.; a series of games played away from home.

    verb: (road-trip) go on a road trip.

                      — THE CANADIAN OXFORD DICTIONARY

AUGUST

Monday, August 11

Dear Junior:

I have news! I've got a Plan.

Ready?

Here it is.

I am going to write a book. Don't tell anyone. It's Top Secret. I would die if anyone knew. (Like you'd tell, anyway.) (Like you *could*.) But you, Junior, my closest friend (or laptop computer, as the case may be), know what I mean. Because you *are* me. I mean, you aren't a "you." You are just a journal.

Not JUST a journal, I don't mean that. You're a computer, actually. Named after the famous JT, of I've-had-a-crush-on-you-my-whole-life-but-not-anymore fame.

Never again.

What I'm trying to say is that I have to write it down — the thing about writing a book — so that I believe it myself, so it looks like a "goal" (see: Melody's Ongoing

Lectures About Goals And Writing Them Down). It's going to be a travel book, but funny. *Really* funny. The kind of book that 20th Century Fox (or somebody) will option to turn into a movie starring Hilary Duff or one of the Olsen twins (are they ever in movies separately?) or Lindsay Lohan or whoever the It Girl of the moment is, unless it's Jules, in which case I'll opt to poke my left eye out with a fork instead.

Let's hope it doesn't come to that. I'm clumsy enough without the threat of only having one eye and reduced depth perception.

I think I can do it. Write the book, that is. Not the fork thing. Obviously that's just a figure of speech; I don't think I could actually bring myself to do it. It's very hard to hurt oneself, unless one is a cutter, which is a whole different thing. Come to think of it, I'd find it pretty hard to poke out someone else's eye with a fork too. Even if that person was attacking me, I think I'd find it too squinchy to actually go for the eye. Besides, what are the odds that I'd have a fork with me?

As I was saying, I'm almost sure it shouldn't likely be a problem to write this book. I was reading a book *about* writing books and it basically said that if a bunch of stuff happens to you, you can write it down, and likely it will be funny, though presumably only if the things that happen to you are funny. It wouldn't be true if, say, you were the last survivor of a nuclear holocaust.

Not that you'd bother to write a book if you were. I mean, who would read it?

It went on to say that you shouldn't write a book about anything outside of your own experience, such as writing a travel book about a trip down the Nile in an inflatable tube, although that has a lot more room for peril and catastrophe and humour and/or intrigue than a trip down the coast in a lime-green Volkswagen van. But, whatever. It's good advice. No doubt someone somewhere in Africa would read my Nile book and point out all the things that were wrong with it, which would be millions, if I'd made it all up.

I'm going to stick to the truth. Maybe only a teeny bit embellished, if nothing actually happens to me while I'm away.

Anyway, I may not have actually finished reading the book. It's possible that I was reading it quite happily when a tiny worm crawled out of the spine of the book and I was forced to burn the book and scream and dunk my hands in bleach and then panic about why all the skin on my hands turned a dead white colour and took ages to go back to normal.

I also may not have taken a billion years of writing classes at college (I've never set foot on a college campus), but how hard can it be? (*NB*: I did not actually get around to applying for college, so likely will not get in or go.)

To make a long story short (or no longer than necessary), my dad and his new girlfriend (actually, his fiancée) Melody (whose newest favourite hobby is lecturing me on The Rest of My Life™) gave me a VW van for a high-school graduation present. Seriously.

A VW VAN.

I can't think of anything much cooler.

And what else to do with it but drive ... somewhere?

Question to Self: Wasn't buying me a van a bit like buying someone luggage? Isn't it basically an invitation to leave? MMMMelody is pregnant, after all, and starting a new family with my dad. This is something to contemplate. Seriously, WHAT WAS THE MOTIVE BEHIND THE VAN? But must not overthink this.

It's a remote possibility that they are trying to get rid of me to start fresh with their less flawed baby who is likely not going to be the massive screw-up that I am.

At least I hope not, for his/her sake.

Maybe they are planning to have several babies. Maybe they want to just pretend I don't exist.

Mustn't think about it too much because is making me sad.

The tiny hitch in The Plan is that I haven't exactly passed my driver's test yet. Not for lack of trying. It took a few tries to pass the written part. I had no idea that driving was so complicated. To be honest, I'd be surprised if most people who actually drive could have passed the written stuff, but in any event, it's done now.

The driving part of the test is a whole other story. I can't seem to pass it. BUT THIS IS NOT MY FAULT. I'm sure everyone says that, but in my case, it's true. For one thing, on the horribly rainy day that I first took the test, I had a terrible pain in my side, very close to my belly button, but deep down. It got worse when I poked at it, or more accurately, when I stopped poking at it, which I know is a bad sign. After I pressed and released for a while, I almost threw up. To make matters worse, I had a fever and I was really cold. My teeth were chattering.

And I was sweating.

Not a good start.

Then when I got into the driver's seat to take the test, there was a guy in the passenger seat AND a woman in the back. Who was she anyway? I was not prepared for two passengers and/or testers. I'd never even heard of this. Everyone I knew who had taken the test had just gone for a drive with a friendly person and had said I had nothing to worry about. Nobody had mentioned this possibility. I was paralyzed with fear and with pain.

The woman was wearing a puce-coloured macramé sweater that was not at all flattering to her skin tone. I think she had rosacea, her skin was very pink. The man was completely covered with freckles. (I love freckles, but this man did not look quite right.) His breath was furry and the rest of him smelled like rank foot sweat.

The conditions were not favourable. My horoscope had been terrible that morning. Not to mention the fact that The Bird had crapped on my favourite T-shirt and I didn't notice until I got into the car.

The whole time Macramé Sweater Woman was writing stuff down and glaring and NO ONE EXPLAINED WHO SHE WAS. *Very* distracting, to say the least. Unusually Sweaty Guy was so nervous that he was shaking and mumbling, and the more nervous he got, the more nervous I got. You know how dogs sense people's nervousness and get all agitated themselves? Not that I'm a dog, but you know what I mean.

In all this mayhem, there is a possibility that I forgot to take off the emergency brake when we left the parking lot. The hideous screeching noise should have given it away, but it didn't. I *heard* it, I just didn't know what it was, or that it was coming from my car. The billowing smoke, however, did make me stop. In traffic. Facing the wrong way. When the fire trucks came, I knew it was probably not going to be a pass.

So.

It's a technicality. I'm sure I'll pass next time. I won't bore you with the three other attempts. Needless to say, none of them were my fault. Especially the time the wind knocked a massive branch off a Douglas fir tree and dented the hood of my car and I drove up onto that man's lawn.

It wasn't much of a lawn anyway.

The point is that I have to pass this thing. Kiki says it's just a mental block and I can get past it. Kiki is usually right, so I'm concentrating on visualizing myself passing the test.

This isn't actually helping. But don't tell Kiki. For some reason, I don't like to disappoint her.

The travel book is my best idea for what to do after graduation, after ruling out, say, working at Dairy Queen or joining the Hare Krishnas or winning American Idol (which I'd love to do if only I could sing and if I was an American).

So. I have these two best friends (as you know): Jules (who is a model) and Kiki (who is going to Harvard).

I also have a boyfriend, Brad[1] (who is a hockey star and was just picked up by a team called the San Diego Gulls. Don't ask, I don't know who would name a hockey team after a seagull, either).

Everyone is just so ... busy. And they have PLANS. I need a PLAN, too, and that's where the book idea came from.

I want to surprise people. Secretly, I'd like to win an Academy Award or something equally amazing and have everyone freak out at my success, but that might be a little out there. I can't act, for one thing. But I can write.

At least, I think I can.

And I need to prove something to ... everyone. I think they think I'm just going to work at the mall for the rest of my life and live with Dad and Melody and The Cat and The Bird (and The Baby, due in December) and eventually just grow old and die, boring and lonely and probably grossly overweight and maybe bald.[2]

People (except Melody, who barely qualifies in the category due to her sheer annoyingness) don't expect much (anything) from me because I'm not a superstar athlete and I'm not gorgeous and I'm not particularly smart or funny or shining in any other way. You know what I mean by shining, right? I mean like Jules or Kiki. Supernaturally pretty or supernaturally smart. I'm just not. And I tend

---

[1] More on Brad later.

[2] See: Hair Damage. As in overdyed, overstressed, overstraightened, overcurled.

to fall down, fall over, or fall off edges of things. I catch rare diseases. Sometimes, like this morning, a handful of hair falls out of my head in the shower for no discernible reason.

I guess you could say that Kiki is the Smart One, Jules is the Pretty One and I'm, well ... I'm the Clumsy One. Or the Unlucky One. Or the Quirky One, if you're feeling nicer. Which is kind of like drawing the short straw, if you think about it. But there you have it, what can I do? I don't want to just sit around waiting for *something* to happen. This is my *life*. And I'm going to start trying to be a better person. More ME and less ... I don't know. Less trying to be everyone else. And just less worrying all around. As part of that, no more horoscopes (someone else telling me what kind of day I'm going to have) and no medical websites (someone else telling me what's wrong with me).

OK, the second one was my friends' idea. They claimed it was driving them crazy. I'm trying, OK?

The point is that I'm me. And I'm going to drive.[3] To something or somewhere. And I'm going to write stuff down. And it *will* be funny. Really. And everyone will be surprised when I get published and win prizes and go on book tours and get into *People* magazine. Maybe I'll be the Famous One.

Ha.

I'm not going to tell anyone, though. I swear.

Love,

Haley Harmony, Girl Explorer

---

[3] See: Passing Driver's Test, lack of success at.

3:30 p.m.

"You can't write a book," said Jules rudely. "You wouldn't know how. Your grades in English sucked. Didn't you get a *negative* mark on your Shakespeare paper? How did you even graduate?"

"Of course I know how," I said. "And *English* isn't the same thing. That's grammar and such. And that paper was a fluke. I misunderstood the question."

"You need GRAMMAR. And you can't *call* it that," said Jules, flicking my title page with her perfectly manicured index finger. "That's just a *lame* title." She dangled the piece of paper between her fingers like it was a largish dead rodent with a bad smell carrying an incurable plague.

"It isn't lame," I said, grabbing it before it dropped on her SPF 500000 suntan-lotioned face. It already had her greasy fingerprints on it. (It took a long time to think of that title. You have no idea. "The Cool Girls' Guide to Parallel Parking" was my best option. What's wrong with that?)

"It is so lame, it's worse than lame," she said. "No one says 'cool.' It's *awful*. It's the *worst*." She flipped her blonde hair back over her shoulder (hair extensions) and fixed one aquamarine blue eye (contact lens) on me. "Seriously." She turned over. "Do you think I'm getting a zit?"

"I don't care what you think," I said. "I think it's catchy. Yes, you have a huge zit. A boil, really. It looks infected. It looks like a second head growing out of your cheek. It could develop a life of its own."

"I never get boils," she said. "I've never even heard any-one call them boils except you. Besides, you can't write.

What have you ever written?"

"Um," I said. "A journal."

She rolled her eyes. On the plus side, this caused one of her too-bright contacts to slip, revealing her real eye underneath.

"It's not like your dad will let you go on a road trip by yourself anyway," she said, blinking furiously. "Who would let their kid do that? You'll be killed by some creep at a rest stop. Even *your* dad wouldn't let that happen. You're going to have to lie, and you're a terrible liar. Or you'll have to make it all up."

"Shut up," I said, pithily.

"Shut UP!" she laughed. "That's mature."

"What," I said. "Ever." I was feeling ever so slightly hostile.

Let's be realistic: Jules is moving to New York, Kiki is moving to Boston. If they can do that, what's the difference if I drive to California so I can write a book, and then come home? It's educational, but it's *real*. It's travel with purpose. Why would I be more likely to get killed just because I'm travelling than they will be?

I mean, if you think about it, none of those choices is any scarier than the next. If anything, they are all the same — they involve going somewhere to learn something or to become someone. I flipped *my* hair in response. Which did nothing, as I have to use so much product in my hair that it barely moves. Also, I should mention that it's slightly lavender. I'm not sure what happened, so don't ask.

I should explain some stuff here, even though these are just my notes and will never see the light of day and I'm probably just explaining this to myself and not to anyone reading The Book, which I plan to make really good — polished and impressive and prize-winning, with just the right amount of hilarity and adventure — and not lame, like these notes. I might use these notes, but just a bit, mostly they'll be edited within an inch of their lives by someone smarter than me. Like, say, an editor with a college degree.

It might be a good idea to start the book with a section about Jules. That way, if she does become famous, people might be more drawn to my book to read the scoop on her.

Must remember to include some of Jules' scarier secrets, but nothing too personal, like the time her mom made out with her boyfriend. Or that whole thing with the drama teacher that was creepy and awful.

Hmm, come to think of it, I don't think I *could* spill her secrets. That would be wrong. I couldn't live with myself.

"You're getting blotchy," she observed. "You really should avoid the sun."

I glared at her. Maybe I *could* be convinced to tell the world about that waxing accident she had. I shifted away from her and tilted Junior out of the sun so I could type some notes.

Background Notes for Groundbreaking Book
1. Introduce self and other potential characters.

Jules is my best-ish friend, and I'm Haley. We just graduated from Sacred Heart High (SHH) in June, and now it is August. The summer went by so fast, I can't believe it. Although I have a theory that time works differently as you get older. When you are six years old, for example, the two months of summer vacation are a huge percentage of your whole life. When you are seventeen, two months is a much smaller percentage of your life, so it goes by relatively quickly.

By the time you're fifty, two months is nothing. It will be like a weekend when you're five. Think about it.

It's a pretty weird feeling to have graduated and to have no particular place to go in the fall. That in and of itself isn't weird, but it feels weird when it's happening to you. It's sort of *aimless*, after a lifetime of having an aim — to get through the next grade to the next and the next. The worst part (one of the worst) is that now I don't have any reason for buying new school supplies, back-to-school clothes (invariably cords, jeans and sweaters), or getting a fantastic new hairstyle. And frankly, I like an excuse to buy a good pen. I have very specific pen needs. For example, it has to have a felt tip, but not a wide one. And it can't make noise when it moves on the paper, not that terrible newspaper-styrofoam noise that sets my teeth on edge, for example. And I like new paper. There's something about blank paper. It's like a fresh start, just sitting there, waiting for you to mess it all up.

Usually, I spend the entire summer making plans for the Best School Year of My Life™, or dieting and experimenting with new hair such that I look good (or at least almost normal) when school goes back, or stalking JT (or my crush of the moment) (not that I have crushes anymore now that I have a boyfriend).

JT is such an old crush that he's not even worth mentioning. He certainly won't be in my book. He always smells so good, though. And I heard he got a job as a fitness trainer this summer and has developed a lot of muscles and a (fake) tan. He has very nice eyes, but that's all I'm going to say. The boy is an idiot. He has the IQ of a diseased rodent. He has the moral turpitude of a ... well, a rabbit, I guess. Or some other animal that likes to have a lot of girlfriends.

And then there's Brad.

Brad. Brad. Brad.

Crushes are for single girls. Not for girls wearing rings.

OK, it's not a *ring*, per se, it's a bracelet, but any jewellery is *like* a ring. Not that I wear the bracelet, but I would if it weren't so ugly. Not that it's ugly. It's really lovely. Maybe it's *too* lovely to wear because it's so fancy that it looks silly with my lame clothes. Or maybe it's something weird, OK? Like when I wear it, I feel like there isn't enough air in the room to fill up my lungs.

But enough about that. I'd rather talk about my hair, which is practically a character unto itself.

As in, if I do anything more to it, it will continue to leave my scalp in record numbers and eventually I'll be bald, à la Sinéad O'Connor, who anyone born after 1980 has never heard of, unless their father is an '80s music aficionado, which mine happens to be at the moment due heavily to the influence of Melody. Before The Fiancée entered the picture, he was only into things you could watch, a.k.a. '80s movies and daytime talk shows. The music is a new tangent. It's fine, I guess. It could be worse. A lot of old hippies (my dad is totally a '60s throwback) get stuck in the '60s or '70s. I'm probably lucky that dad somehow, mysteriously and without explanation, fell in love with the '80s. I've seen *The Breakfast Club* a few too many times by now anyway.

It's still my favourite movie of all time. I probably shouldn't admit that, but it's true.

2. Establish a setting, although is a travel book, so setting will change, but start with the here and now.

So it's August, and it's too hot to move or really even argue like you mean it. We live in a city called Victoria, which you may or may not have heard of, or at least maybe you think you've heard of it but you don't know why. Trust me, you don't have much of a reason to have heard of it, other than the fact that it has some nice scenery. It's pretty. But it's also really hot, although it's Canada, so let's keep it in perspective.

It's not hot like the desert. It's not hot like Hawaii. It's just sticky. Not that I'd know what to compare it to because I've never really been very many other places, except California with Jules last year. And Hawaii when I was a kid.

Jules travels. Kiki travels. I just don't travel.

Except for camping with my dad, which doesn't count. That's more about hunkering down in the woods in a smelly tent and hoping he remembered to bring junk food.

Jules is just back from New York — she's commuting, or so she says, like she knows what that means — where she got a contract to do some kind of modelling for a catalogue I've never heard of, wearing clothes I wouldn't be caught dead wearing. Secretly, I'm thrilled. I think she thought she'd walk in the door of Ford Agencies and come out on the cover of *Vogue*. I love Jules, I do. But sometimes I think that Jules loves Jules enough for the both of us. I'm not a model, but I know that CATA-LOGUE MODELLING is not in the same universe as *Vogue*. It's not even as cool as *Jane* or *Seventeen*. You wouldn't catch Maggie Rizer doing catalogues.

Never mind that if *I* walked in the door of Ford, some-one would probably ask me for a cup of coffee or I'd end up fixing the jammed copy machine or I'd just get thrown out the door by security for not even being close to pretty enough.

OK, that's not really about setting. My attention is wandering.

Darn.

This is harder than it looks.

Um, setting.

Well, it's going to start here, OK? In Victoria, B.C., Canada. Look it up on a map if you aren't sure where it is.

I guess I can't write that because it sounds rude.

I flipped Junior off. His batteries were dying anyway. Jules snored. For a pretty girl, she isn't very dainty. I poked her with my foot and she muttered in her sleep. I'm pretty sure she said, "Lame."

I should not have told Jules about the book. What was I thinking? She may be my best-ish friend, but she is not very nice (i.e. she is just jealous). But Kiki is too busy and Brad is, well, Brad. Besides, he's away playing hockey. As usual. Big Surprise. I mean, it's not like he ought to be hanging out with me and going to the Thrift Shop to buy clothes and wandering around town with no purpose, fantasizing about passing my driver's test or anything. Of course he has better things to do, and besides, he's going to maybe be a big NHL star and then I'll be glad to have stuck it out with him. Not that I'm shallow. I'm not.

Don't tell anyone, but secretly I'm afraid that I am. But I'm afraid of a lot of things. I'm trying to get over that, I really am. I turned Junior back on again and he beeped obligingly.

Other Things That I'm Afraid Of (same old stuff, I'm sure you know this already):
1. Dying of some terrible unknown disease, such as Ebola.
2. Dying of some known disease, such as cancer or kidney failure.
3. Dying in a fiery crash.
4. Dying after falling off an edge/building/cliff.
5. Dying.
6. That I'm shallow.
7. That I'll never really like myself.
8. That I'll be stuck here forever with my dad, Melody, The Baby (who will certainly grow up to be Somebody) and

The Cat and no one will notice or care.

9. That I'll be stuck here forever alone.
10. Rickets.
11. Scurvy.
12. Alopecia.
13. Ghosts.
14. Movies that feature anything to do with cults and/or the paranormal.
15. Getting fat.
16. Yellow teeth.
17. Animals with rabies.
18. Michael Caine's rheumy eyes.

I have to take this road trip. It would solve so many of my life's problems and probably knock some of those things off the list. It's not like I can avoid the first five anyway. I think maybe when your number is up, it's just up. I try not to think about it too much. Death, I mean. Although sometimes I think that if I knew how I was going to die, I could just relax and enjoy my life building up to that moment. For example, if you knew you were going to die from pneumonia when you were eighty-three, and it was an absolute fact that nothing could change, you could stop worrying about cancer and participate in more dangerous sports, such as hang-gliding or rollerblading.

After graduation, my friends made me promise to stay away from all medical websites and stop analyzing all my unusual symptoms (like when my toenail suddenly fell off for no reason and I became convinced I had either gangrene or diabetes) on the internet. And I promised.

I'm trying not to obsess about my health. I realize that it gets boring, mostly because Jules told me about fifty-five times in the last week alone. Which in and of itself is boring.

So.

What was I saying?

Oh, right.

Look, I miss Brad. Sort of. I miss the *idea* of him. Actually, to tell you the truth, I'm kind of glad he's away. I love him. Well, I like him. I mean, he's really nice and it was good to have a boyfriend in the twelfth grade and stuff but I'm kind of wondering ... I mean, sometimes I just have a hard time breathing, like I mentioned before. It's possible that I'm allergic to the metal in the bracelet he gave me. It may be nothing to do with him. It could even be that I have undiagnosed asthma and am seconds away from collapsing on the ground gasping through my blocked bronchial tubes with no inhaler in sight to save me. (But I'm not going to look it up! I'm not!)

I know that doesn't make sense — not the undiagnosed asthma, which is always an outside possibility — but feeling like Brad takes away my air, and not in a good "take my breath away" kind of way.

When he's away, I miss him. When he's here, I can't wait for him to go.

"Have you heard from Brad?" Jules asked, abruptly waking up, sitting and lighting a cigarette in one elegant gesture. The fact that Jules smokes drives me crazy. Think about it — it's something that will give you cancer, causes wrinkles AND yellows your teeth. Not to mention triggering asthma.

I cannot abide yellow teeth. Not that Jules has yellow teeth. She has very small, even, white teeth. Like Heather Graham or a chihuahua with a good dentist.

"Put that out," I said. Thinking about Brad (or the second-hand smoke) was giving me a tiny pinch of pain in my lung. Probably I was growing a tumour from being best friends with a smoker for too long.

"We're outside," she pointed out. Which was true. The sun had moved over a bit so we were now sitting in the shade of the school field. It was a bit strange for us to be there, if you think about it. We don't even *go* to this school anymore. Also, the grass was making me sneeze and irritating my lungs even more. I took several big huge breaths and got dizzy. Jules gave me a look and rolled her eyes.

Jules knows me really well.

"Stop it," she said. "You'll hyperventilate again and I don't have a bag for you to breathe in."

"Brad called last night," I admitted, mostly to change the subject back again. I'm very suggestible and if I thought about hyperventilating, I probably would. What I didn't say was that all I could think about since last night was breaking up with Brad. But I know I *shouldn't*. He's nice. I like him a lot.

Other people like him.

People say things like, "What does HE see in YOU?" as though it's a miracle that someone like him would choose me. (OK, it was just one girl in a washroom at a café, but if she is thinking it, likely other people are as well).

It's just I have this idea that I should break up with him. And I've thought about how to do it and it's like I can hardly stop myself from doing it, even though I don't really want to. I love Brad.

Sort of.

"Oh," she said. "So you're pining away for him?" She smirked.

Jules is currently "between boyfriends." Which means that about a million people ask her out every week but she says no. I think she thinks that now that she is a "model" she will have the opportunity to date "rock stars" and "famous actors."

"He's in San Diego," I told her. "It's so hot there. He's busy. I'm not pining."

"It's hot *here*," she said. "I'm so bored, I could cry. I can't wait to go back to New York. Although everyone leaves there for the month of August, you know." She waved her hand about airily and somehow managed to make herself look even more pretentious than before. "The city is *deserted* in August."

"Uh huh," I said.

I tipped my head back. Every once in a while, my stomach just dropped, like I was going down a really fast elevator. Probably to do with my circulation. Not that I'm overanalyzing it, I'm just saying.

"Well," I added. "I'm leaving pretty soon myself to do my research."

"Right," she said, rolling her eyes and flicking her cigarette across the dead, dry grass.

"Nice," I said, and stood up to stomp it out. She could light the whole place on fire just by being an idiot.

"I've got to go," she said, and she walked off without even offering me a ride. I lay back down on the grass and watched her drive away in her brand-new Jeep Liberty that she got for a graduation present. Why did her mom give her a car? It's not like she needs one in New York.

The heat and the grass combined to make me prickly and uncomfortable. Sometimes I wonder why I'm friends with her. What's wrong with me? For some unaccountable reason, I felt like crying. I cried a bit just because I could. It felt weird to be lying on my back on my old school field crying, kind of like when you go outside in the middle of the night in your pyjamas. Like all the things separately (being in your pyjamas, being outside) were normal, but combined together they made something strange.

Once I started crying, I felt even sadder. Maybe I have PMS or some other irrational mood disorder, perhaps triggered by a tumour in my adrenal gland. I sniffed. Which is what I was doing when I heard a voice saying, "Haley?"

And of course it was my arch-enemy Izzy Archibaud (ugh) and my former crush JT (sigh ... ugh).

"Are you totally crying?" she said, sitting down next to me. Her blonde curly hair bobbed up and down. Isn't heat supposed to make curly hair frizzy? Even the whites of her eyes seemed whiter than humanly possible. I stifled the urge to poke her in them. For some reason, I wouldn't have a problem doing *that*.

"I have allergies," I said, sneezing smoothly.

"Oh," she said. She sort of cringed and pulled away.

"They aren't contagious," I pointed out, sneezing again. It sounded fake, but who cared? Why was I even bothering to fake my allergies?

There was a really awkward silence.

I felt like I should say something. JT, who I had a crush on from the third grade (or thereabouts) onwards, was standing two steps away from me, smelling good, but looking like an idiot (obviously). What was I supposed to say to some boy who broke my heart by dating Jules and then turned out to be a jerk anyway?

Nothing, that's what.

In lieu of talking, I blushed like crazy. The fact that he's Brad's cousin is, well, just a horrible coincidence. Possibly the worst coincidence of all time. I don't still have a crush on him, it's just that my facial blood vessels haven't got that memo yet.

"You're sunburnt and stuff," he observed. "You should get out of the sun. You'll get wrinkles and look gross."

"Yeah," I said, getting up so fast I nearly fell over again. "Right. I wouldn't want to get skin cancer. Ha ha!"

He looked at me oddly, or at least I think he did. From what I could see. Sometimes when I get up, I see these little drifting lights and my vision blurs. I thought that happened to everyone, but then I mentioned it to my eye doctor when I was getting a new prescription and he let me know that it didn't happen to everyone. In fact, it usually only happened when your retinas were detaching. He reassured me that when the retinas actually DID detach, it would close my vision like blinds shutting. I must remember to NOT verify that on the internet when I get home. Perhaps I have inoperable eye problems and will be blind in a month, thus solving my problem of what to do when I grow up. I wonder if I can get a nice seeing eye dog. I like dogs. Then I can walk around with my dog and people can admire me for being brave and I won't need an actual career. That would give me the Tremendous Sense of Accomplishment (or TSA) that Melody is always referring to, I'm sure.

"How's the Bradster?" JT said, squinting at me. I wish he wasn't so cute. When he squints, his whole face looks like it's smiling. Which is irrelevant because he really *is* an idiot. I don't know what I ever saw in him. Being blind will be good for me. I'm too visually driven. It's like the fact that he has green smiley eyes eradicates all the other facts against him, such as his small furry animal mentality.

"Good," I said. "So, yeah. Then. Anyway. Right. I've got to go." Which I'm sure you'll agree was extremely articulate.

"Call me sometime!" called Izzy after me. "We can hang out!"

"Yeah," I said. I didn't turn around. I should explain that I once caught Izzy and Brad together at a party and she's been my arch-enemy ever since. Together, together. It was ...

I don't want to talk about it.

Come to think of it, she was my arch-enemy to begin
with, in that I never liked her and she dated JT a long time
ago. She's too pretty. And one of those people who always
does everything right. She's unbearably *happy*. Happy
people depress me. She's like a human pep rally. I bet she
had all her Brownie badges and sold more Girl Guide
cookies than anyone else. She's just that type of person. If
we lived in Texas, she'd probably be one of those scary
beauty pageant girls with giant hair and a permanent gri-
mace and the misguided belief that a ribbon across her
chest might help the cause of world peace.

I belatedly stuck out my tongue, but I'm sure she didn't
see. I would have flipped her the bird but that would have
been offensive to my pet, The Bird, and Izzy wasn't worth
even that.

The pavement was so hot, it burned my feet through
my horrible dollar-store flip-flops. It took ages to walk
home, and when I finally got there, I had a blister between
my toes. It was bleeding. Great. Likely, it will become
infected and cause untold havoc. That's something to
look forward to now, isn't it?

Note to Self: Getting my licence may save my life, i.e. if I
    got my driver's licence, I wouldn't have to walk and
    would get fewer blisters. Ergo, I would get fewer infec-
    tions.
Conclusion: GET LICENCE. Or else.

Oh, I should mention that on the way home, I stopped at
the library and got some books and atlases so I could map

out my trip. I have this idea of stopping at all those weird roadside attractions, like giant dinosaurs or big mushrooms or whatever and taking pictures for the book. There is something inherently funny about The World's Largest Marshmallow or The World's Smallest Hockey Stick or whatever random item towns celebrate to disguise the fact that their town is really dull.

At least, I think there is.

I've just realized that there will only be a market for this book if everyone has the same sense of humour as I do. And what are the odds of that?

Friday, August 15
10:37 a.m.
Notes for CGAGTPP (The Cool Girls' Aimless Guide to Parallel Parking):

1. Lose the word "aimless." It's too ... aimless. No one wants to read an aimless guide. It sounds too meandering and pointless and depressing. And there is no opposite word to aimless, unless it's "aimful," which sounds made up.

2. Stop telling people about this book. They will criticize your title and your idea in general. It's not good for your self-esteem.

3. Find some way to earn massive amounts of money in the next two weeks (legally) so as to be able to leave at the beginning of September, when normally would be going back to school, if in fact was still in school.

4. Figure out route, budget, etc.

5. Figure out how long it will take.

6. Plan route to go via Disneyland as have always wanted to go and even though was in Anaheim (or L.A., as Jules insisted it was) last spring (across the road from Disneyland), did not go. Although don't like rides, like the idea of national theme park with giant stuffed (creepy) mascots running around hugging people against their will.

7. On second thought, no real reason to visit Disneyland.

8. Possibly find someone to travel with. People who are NOT possibilities include Jules, Kiki and Brad. Maybe will take The Cat for company and add The Cat to title! The Cool Girls' Guide to Parallel Parking AND Driving Cross-Country with The Cat!

9. Nah. How would you like to drive all the way to California with a litter box in the car? Gross. The Cat wouldn't like Disneyland. Besides, that title is WAY too long.

10. Get new pens.

5:17 p.m.

Dear Junior:

Disaster! I've failed my driver's test *again*. There is something wrong with me. Seriously. Thank God I didn't get into college. I'd be a laughingstock. I mean, look at all the people who drive. My DAD drives. Jules drives. JT drives. That's proof: Any idiot can do it.

Except, apparently, me.

I swear, it looked like I had miles between myself and that grassy knoll. Also, when they are building cars, why don't they build enough clearance underneath them for concrete barriers? How was I supposed to know? Once I was headed that way, to avoid the king-sized poodle that lurched into the road (king-sized poodles should be illegal), I felt committed and thought I should follow through.

ARGH.

This is The Worst Day of My Life™. I can't retake this stupid driver's thing for another two weeks and by then, it will be September and it will be Too Late for my Plan to properly start. Not to mention the fact that I haven't saved enough money yet. I may as well start writing up resumés and dropping them off at the mall, where I'm doomed to work at Foot Locker for the rest of my life, selling over-priced running shoes to sweaty-footed morons while everyone else moves on and grows up and leads glamorous and exciting lives replete with tropical vacations, shopping sprees at Sephora, an innate ability to walk in high heels, and impressive degrees leaving a string of initials after their impressive hyphenated married names.

Or else do what Jules suggested, which is to make the whole book up. I mean, she's right. Who would know?
Love,
Fated-to-be-a-Loser Girl

Saturday, August 16
9:30 a.m.

I *hate* family breakfasts. I'm sure that Family Game Night, which I've seen advertised on television but never witnessed in my own house, is worse, but I'm beginning to think eating should be a private thing. Something you do alone. Something you don't have to watch other people doing.

Like Melody.

I hate Melody. Well, I don't HATE her, but I strongly dislike her. (The eggs, I definitely hate.) For one thing, the only two things she talks about are The Baby™ and How To Get On With The Rest Of My Life™. I'm not sure which of these two topics is the more irritating. I'm going to vote for HTGOWTROML because The Baby is just The Baby. He hasn't had time to mess anything up yet so I can't take anything out on him (or her — I mean, you hear stories all the time where they get it wrong, right?). In truth, I'm a bit excited to meet him (or her). I hope he's more like me than Melody. He'll be my half-brother, so maybe he will be at least sort of like me.

Not that he'd want to be.

I just hope he's OK and not born with two belly buttons or six thumbs or whatever else people fear about unborn babies. It's possible that I may have sneaked a look at this horrible book that Melody swears by called *What to Expect When You're Expecting*, which is a million times worse than all the medical websites put together as far as instilling fear is concerned. Seriously, if I ever get pregnant, I'm just going to bunk down in a hospital for the entire time in a sterile room and allow no visitors. But I'm not going to get paranoid on her behalf, although I did have to remind her not to eat deli cheeses because they might contain listeria (never mind what else is in them), which might hurt the baby. Somehow from this, she's decided that I'm her best friend, hence her favourite third topic, How We Can

Do More Things Together.

Trust me, that's the worst one.

Today, she's on the other Worst One (see: HTGOW TROML).

All she needs is a whiteboard, and she'd be able to draw me out an actual map for my future, I'm sure of it. I wonder if it would contain a maze and riddles. It would certainly be done precisely. She's more than a little anal-retentive about straight lines. Unfortunately, her first straight line leads to either getting a job or going to college, neither of which appeals to me necessarily.

"More Froot Loops?" Dad said, pushing the box toward me.

"No thanks," I said. "I'm getting fat." The Bird squawked in agreement from where he was perched on my (fat and meaty) shoulder. "Get off me," I growled.

"I'll kill you," he said. This used to be creepy but now, seeing as it's pretty much all he says anymore, we're all used to it. "Pretty pretty," he adds.

"See?" Dad said. "You're beautiful." Dad smoked a lot of drugs in the last thirty years, I should remind you. His opinion is all but meaningless as his brain likely looks like a fried egg that's been dried and then reconstituted in an egglike shape. I hate eggs, but I love my dad. I glared at him lovingly.

"You just need to exercise more!" chirped Melody. (She doesn't talk, she chirps.) "What you need is a workout schedule! You should come with me to Pilates."

"Isn't it prenatal Pilates?" I said pointedly.

"Well," she said, looking down at her mountain of

eggs. I swear, she eats ten eggs at a time, all scrambled into one barfy big heap. I'm sure that *What to Expect* would warn her away from that. Don't eggs have salmonella or something? I should check. She, apparently, is expecting a Baby Who Loves Eggs. "Yes. But they wouldn't mind! I'm sure they'd let you in as a special case!"

"I'm going for a run after breakfast," I said sourly. I wasn't planning on it, but I needed the escape. If I were being completely honest, I might admit that I don't really like running. I mean, I *do* like running, but it was something that Kiki and I always did together (i.e. she made me do it) and now that she's all busy with leaving for Harvard and being hyper-intelligent, she hardly has time to run with me and I don't like it enough to do it alone.

Also, it's dangerous. I should know. I once got two black eyes by running into a particularly skinny tree that I didn't see that hit me right in the nose.

"Great!" said Dad, looking from me to Melody and back again. Honestly, sometimes I feel sorry for him. It can't be easy living with both of us because we couldn't be more different, i.e. she's a freak, and I'm not.

I should mention that there is something about Melody that makes me feel mean. It's not even that I don't like her; I think it's that I don't really have a mother. (I do, but she's a nun and not exactly a part of my life except when I walk by the nunnery and wave at the flower garden on the off-chance that she's there and might see me. Not that I *do* this, but I could if I wanted to.) And Melody is sort of confused between being my mother and my best friend, and both these roles are already filled. I want her to be my ...

...

...

Oh, I don't know. I want her mostly to leave me alone.

I sort of wouldn't mind her *being* my mother, but she just isn't. She's too young and I'm not a baby and she's not very good at it. I hope she's better at it with her own baby, my brother/sister. I'm torn between feeling sorry for her and being mad at her. As usual.

I wish I ...

Well, never mind.

I should mention that she plans to give birth to The Baby in the living room in a wading pool. The wading pool is in the backyard right now. It has a picture of a huge octopus on the bottom and one of those tiny slides for toddlers on the side. Over the course of the summer, it's been filled with water and emptied by evaporation so many times that it's developed a weird algae-like film on it. I certainly hope she figures out how to sterilize it prior to the Big Event.

Then I notice that she's wearing my sweatpants and stretching them all out of shape. I glare at her with all my might.

"Running is SO hard on your joints," she said, helpfully. "They've done studies. Swimming is SO much better."

"I like it," I said. I shoved my cereal bowl away. "I hate swimming. It dries out my hair."

She looked dubiously at my hair. I mean, I could see where she was coming from. It's not like it could get worse.

"Want to practise driving later?" Dad asked. "I have some more tricks about parallel parking that you could use." He winked.

I shuddered. Winking was an entirely new thing that he'd begun since hooking up with The Fiancée.

"Sure," I said. "Thanks." I looked at the clock. It seemed like it was moving backward. My life was moving backward. As in, down the drain.

"Don't forget to tie your shoelaces!" Melody yelled.

I screamed.

But only inside my head.

It wasn't too hot outside yet. To be honest, it wasn't usually terribly hot here at all. I think global warming has something to do with the fact that it's thirty degrees in the afternoon lately. Which is like ninety, I think. I'm not good at metric/non-metric conversions. Believe me when I say it's hot.

I run up the street and back and I don't throw up or pass out, which is a good sign, so I go a little farther. At the top of our street, there is an intersection of five roads. Don't ask. Road design obviously wasn't much of a priority here — nothing goes in a straight line, everything is very windy and pointless.

Much like my life.

ANYWAY, I just ran for a while. If by "ran," I mean "jogged." I guess people who really RUN differentiate between the two things, but as far as I'm concerned, if my feet are moving, it counts. I was trying to stay on the shady side of the street, so I kept turning and turning and then going farther and farther. As usual, I brought no water and didn't remember about planning to have reserve energy to get home. When I started getting tired and my vision started to go weird, I slowed down (which is funny when you consider I was moving pretty slowly to begin with) and that's when I noticed, out of some weird coincidence, that I was really near the nunnery where my mom lives.

Which was weird. I swear, I didn't plan it. I slowed down to a walk. OK, I hunched over and dry heaved into a plant, but don't tell anyone. I may have gone too far and the Froot Loops weren't sitting well.

I stood there for a bit and stared. It's not like my mother might be taking a stroll around the grounds. I think she might even be away somewhere, saving flood victims in South America or building a school on a cliff in Peru or something because that is what she does in lieu of mothering me. I think it's penance because she messed up my life.

I'm not bitter, it just sounds like I am.

I sat down on the sidewalk, which was really gritty and uncomfortable. Someone had carved the initials LP into the sidewalk. Not in a heart, not anything else, just LP. Maybe they weren't initials. Maybe the person really just loved old records.

I stretched my legs out. They were hurting from the running.

Watching the nunnery wasn't as interesting as it sounds, and it doesn't even sound interesting. It looked empty and just basically like a big ugly building. I don't know what I was expecting. Honestly, sometimes I don't even understand myself.

My point is this:

I swear, I didn't see that kid on the bike. And anyway, he wasn't hurt at all. How could he not have seen me there? Also, aren't kids supposed to ride on the road and not on the sidewalk? It hurt me a lot more than it hurt him. I don't know this for sure, but I'm guessing that when a 100-kilogram kid (number may be exaggerated for dramatic effect) runs over your legs on his ridiculously over-equipped mountain bike, it more than just pinches a little.

"SHIT!" I yelled. I don't usually swear. Not very much, anyway.

The kid tipped over as soon as he hit my legs, but I guess he was scared of me, and he just pulled himself up and cycled off like he was being chased by a rabid horse. I wasn't even up off the ground and he was GONE.

I sat there for a few extra minutes and inspected the tire tracks on my legs. How were my legs not broken? Was that even possible? I poked my calf to make sure there was no gross piece of bone sticking out or something. Believe me, I've been there before. But there wasn't. Just some leg stubble (*note to self:* shave legs) and the tire mark.

I stood up and nearly fell over, but I think that's just because I stood up so fast. I have very low blood pressure. My legs felt OK. They felt like they had been run over by a bike, but OK.

I limped home. It's a good thing that my right leg took the brunt of the impact, I guess. It would be hard to limp on both sides. You know, it took an hour to get home. And by the time I did, it was hot. Probably I have heat exhaustion and will be dead by morning.

On the plus side, I lost four pounds. I guess there's something to be said for exercise after all.

Tuesday, August 19

Note to Self: Stop writing in journal. Everything must be about the book. Say you only get to write 1,000,000 words in your life that are any good. And you waste them writing your journal? That's just dumb.

TCGGTPP: Chapter One

Practical Packing and Planning for Your Road Trip
1. Remember to pack the following:
2. Always take …

Forget it.

It's possible that I have NO IDEA what one should pack for a road trip. I'll start with obvious things:

1. First aid kit, including sutures and bandages
2. Merck Medical Manual
3. Laptop computer with wireless internet
4. Shiny silver blanket with HELP sign on reverse
5. Cellphone
6. Gas card

Argh.

This is impossible. For one thing, everyone knows those

things already. If they don't, they are just begging to die of exposure on the side of the highway in the snow bleeding from the head and starving with no one to talk to and no internet access.

Oh my god.

I'm having a panicky realization.

The fact is, I can't do this. Who am I to write a book? Other people do it, but that doesn't mean I can. What a ridiculous idea. I've probably mentioned this before, but I saw this movie once where Anthony Hopkins (or Perkins, I get them mixed up) killed this bear with a stick, saying, "What one man can do, another can do!" I think about that sometimes to cheer myself on. And I really do, I actually envision it in Anthony Hopkins/Perkins accent and everything. "WHAT ONE MAN CAN DO, ANOTHER CAN DO!"

And then I think, pffft. That's *ridiculous*. It's downright *absurd*. What someone can do, another *can't* do. If we could all do the same things, we'd all be on the Olympic gymnastics team on our breaks from performing life-saving brain surgeries in between solving impossible mathematical equations and whipping up perfect lemon mousses in our restaurant kitchens. If there was ever a scenario involving me, an angry bear, and a stick, I'm guessing that the bear would win.

SO JUST BECAUSE OTHER PEOPLE WRITE BOOKS DOES NOT MEAN THAT I CAN.

Focus.

Focus, Haley.

Don't panic.

Breathe.

I'm not going to give up. I'm just going to write stuff as it pops into my head and then later, I'll *edit* it. In the book I almost read about writing books, the author said, "Give yourself permission to write a really bad first draft."

Wednesday, August 20
Really Bad First Draft

[Must remember to leave instructions for my dad in case something terrible happens to me so that he deletes Junior and all my notes before anyone reads them (i.e. Jules) and laughs hysterically about what a bad book I started to write.]

Maybe I should write an outline. I've forgotten whether the book said to write an outline or not.

Nah.

Outlines are difficult. I hate outlines.

Maybe I should just write. But have nothing to write about yet as haven't left yet.

ARGGGHGHGHGHGH.

Maybe I should write resumé to hone skills and also to get job. But in order to get a job, I'll have to somehow make myself look presentable, i.e. have normal colour hair. Ideally, I'd be thinner too.

Maybe should start popular French diet.[4]

Or go to France.

---

[4] There's a book about how French women never get fat and this is (apparently) because they eat only high-fat food and they don't fill themselves up with the empty calories of diet crap. Which makes me think of ice cream. Will get French diet full-fat ice cream and then will come back to resumé and RBFD.

Friday, August 22

Dear Junior:

I've run into an obstacle with The Book, i.e. I can't seem to get started or find the time to continue once I have started. Not that I'm doing anything interesting, like saving the world or building houses for Habitat for Humanity (which is actually what Kiki is doing in these last couple of weeks before going to Harvard) or learning how to cook Indonesian food (like Melody) or undergoing thigh liposuction (Jules).

On the plus side, my hair is fixed (sort of). (I rinsed it through with red, and although it's a little bright, at least "red" is a normal-ish colour, although I must admit it's a bit of an unusual tint.) It was Melody's idea. I don't know what I was thinking to let Melody touch my hair, but I did. It worked out OK. So, whatever. Don't get excited. It doesn't mean we're best buddies.

She used henna (definition: putrid-smelling rotting plant root with uncontrollable results). I don't recommend it. But because she is pregnant, she can't use real dye. I can't say I blame her. I don't want my brother (sister) to be born with two heads or even an extra toe. She was doing her own hair and I let her do mine because the lavender made my pimples show too much. THIS DOES NOT MEAN ANYTHING.

I'd rather be friends with Izzy Archibaud than with Melody, frankly, which will happen on the fourth of NEVER.

I spent the day running around the mall delivering my resumé to every place on earth, ranging from the Gap (which would be mildly cool and they had a bag there I would have been really happy to own, except the part where I don't have a spare $78) to the bookstore (very cool and owned by a man who looks like Hugh Grant in *Notting Hill*) to McDonald's (I have no pride). I never thought that I'd be thinking a job at Orange Julius was a good idea, but people change.

Last summer was SO much more fun. I almost wish that I'd flunked grade twelve just so I could go back and do it again. And I didn't even LIKE high school. The idea that *that* was actually the best time in my life makes me want to hurl or cry or both.

Maybe they only say that about people who actually enjoyed high school. I might have enjoyed it more if I hadn't missed most of it due to nearly dying from chicken pox/meningitis, and the unspeakably bad Hickey Incident, which I won't even talk about, but suffice to say that no one likes the nickname "Haley Hickey" or "The Hickey Girl." Trust me.

Strangely, the mall looked so much bigger when I was in school and it was the cool place to hang out. Now it just looks small and brown and pathetic. All those people who get their exercise by wearing jogging suits while they window shop make me sad. Can't they exercise outside? I'm sure they pump stuff into the air here that makes you want to shop. There is also something weird about the lights that makes everyone look greenish-tinged. Or maybe I need new contact lenses.

In other news, did you know there was a store there that sold both edible underpants and fake poo? I drew the

line at that one. I will NOT apply there. I mean, seriously.
I'd rather work at New York Fries.

I think.

Love,

Future Mall Worker of America (FMWA)

7:07 p.m.

Oh no. I've got a job.

How could it happen so quickly?

They didn't even interview me. How could they not
interview me? I was fully prepared to be an excellent
interviewee. I'd even got a book from the library called *Job
Interviews for Dummies*, although I hadn't actually read it
yet. However, picking it up was the important first step. I
had every intention of reading it while lying in the wading pool in the backyard sipping cold lemonade.

But instead, there was a message when I got home from
the mall (on the bus, where I had to sit next to someone
who was coughing so much that I probably should go
ahead and dip my entire body in bleach to avoid getting
TB) saying that I could start tomorrow. I've listened to it
several times.

Transcript of Message:

*Hi, uh, Haley? Can you, uh, start tomorrow? Because we're,
like, desperate? And someone here said they knew you and you
were, uh, OK? So, OK. Good. See you.*

It's probably not a good sign that they are desperate
and that they admit it. I'm wondering if I should wait and

accept a better offer. What if the Hugh Grant look-alike bookstore owner suddenly realizes that when he said, "We don't hire anyone, I work here alone, it's a small shop," he meant, "I simply must give you the job as you clearly would sell books better than anyone"? What if the Gap suddenly has an opening?

But then I'd end up spending all my money on Gap clothes. Or I'd develop a completely inappropriate crush on the bookstore guy, even though he's at least ten years older than me.

Not that ten years is a lot.

But what if he never calls?

I could wait.

On the other hand, if I hang out at home too much more, Melody is going to turn me into a hippie and/or my brain will rot from watching too much TV and pro-crastinating writing The Book. My Top Priority™ MUST be to make money, quickly.

Furthermore, since the henna incident, Melody's begun working on me to stop shaving my legs. I mean, seriously. Just because I may have nicked my shin last time and woken her up while she was napping because I thought I was going to faint from hemorrhagic blood loss does not mean I should take such extreme measures.

It doesn't much matter because it is possible that in the throes of an argument with Melody over which TV show to watch, I may have hurriedly called back the number and accepted the job.

What was I thinking?

I'm not a waitress, I'm a writer! I'm writing a book!

Saturday, August 23

11:30 p.m.

I'm a waitress. My feet hurt. My head hurts. My body hurts. I never want to see chicken fingers again.

But I have a bunch of money in my pocket.

TIPS. Tips are going to save my life.

Maybe being a waitress isn't so bad, after all. Not as a career choice, certainly. It's just temporary. Don't worry. I'm just postponing The Plan, I'm not calling it off.

11:32 p.m.

"It's just temporary," I said. I was talking to Brad on the phone. I liked him *so* much better when he was out of town. Even I knew that was weird, don't worry. I'm not that crazy.

I twirled the cord around my finger and watched it turn purple. "I miss you. When are you coming home?"

"I just never thought of you as a waitress," he said. "I don't know about coming home. You're a waitress, really? You?"

"Yes," I said.

"Weird," he said. There was a silence. "A waitress? You're not really the type. Aren't you worried about ... I don't know. The danger?"

"What is THAT supposed to mean?" I snapped.

"Nothing," he said. "I just thought ... well, sometimes you trip."

I hung up.

Maybe I don't like him better when he's not here, after all.

Maybe I don't care when he comes home, or even IF he comes home.

11:47 p.m.

Me: I don't even care if you come home.

Brad: You called me back to tell me that you don't care if I come home or not?

Me: Yes. In fact, I don't like you better when you are away.

Brad: Er, OK.

Me: I thought I did, but I don't.

Brad: Haley, don't be weird.

Me: I'm not weird!

Brad: You're being weird.

Me: Don't you miss me?

Brad: Not right now.

Me: What does THAT mean?

Brad: Uh, nothing.

Me: I don't want to see you anymore.

Brad: Fine.

Me: I take it back, I don't mean it. What do you mean, "Fine"?

Brad: I meant, "Fine." You're giving me a headache.

Me: Whatever, sorry. Forget it.

Brad: Which part?

Me: All of it! [panicking] I'm really sorry!

Brad: It's not a big deal. I insulted you. I'm the one who's sorry.

Me: Well, I'm still sorry.

Brad: Look, I have to go, I'll call you tomorrow.

Me: Hmmph.

11:55 p.m.

> **Summary of Day, not related to Book, but Practice Writing, such as suggested writing exercise re: describing your school lunches when you were a kid, but Totally Different.**
> *Hefty Hoovers is an inexplicably popular restaurant, home to all-you-can-eat ribs and orange vinyl booths and real sawdust floors. If you close your eyes and breathe deeply, you can smell fermenting ... um, meat? The light casts long shadows on the diners' animated and mysterious faces.*

Well, except it doesn't. It's fluorescent and there are no shadows and the diners tend to be other mall workers (e.g. Hot Bookstore Guy — HBG) on their lunch breaks.

It just seems like all descriptions are better when there are "long shadows" and "mysterious faces." Or "short shadows." And "animated faces."

Writing descriptions is harder than you might think.

Hmmm.

OK, let me try again.

> *The view from Hefty Hoovers out across the food floor of the mall is of The Gap. The Gap has a great sweater this season, pink with a dark stripe that I would buy if I ever bought things that weren't on sale or from the Thrift Store. The Gap has really good sales, I don't care what Jules says about the quality.*

Ooops.

Hefty Hoovers is …

Oh, forget it.

Reasons to Not Bother Practising Writing:
1. Am not a writer.
2. Am a waitress.
3. Am too tired.
4. Am kidding myself about writing a book.
5. Don't have time to both WRITE book and PRACTISE writing book, might as well just dive right in and do the actual WRITING.

Will get to the book in a minute.

I guess the good news is that I made some tips. The bad news is that my feet are bleeding and raw. And the worst news of all: the uniform. I kid you not when I say that no one needs to have the word "Hefty" emblazoned on their chest in giant letters.

And to make matters worse, working in a restaurant apparently means serving the enemy. Or in this case, the arch-enemy. Yes, today, at 2:12, I had to bring a tossed salad (with dressing on the side) (and no tomatoes) to Izzy Archibaud. And an iced tea with no ice and a slice of lemon. She was alone. Even as I moved around the restaurant, I could hear her talking to other people — she has a particularly piercing voice — including, but not limited to, HBG.

I mean, honestly. He's WAY too old for her.

As she was leaving, she was all, "Thank you SO much, Haley! That was SO nice of you."

"Whatever," I said. "It's my job."

"I know!" she said. "That's SO great!"

If there's anything that makes me insane, it's falsely sincere people.

"Well, it was SO much my pleasure," I said as sarcastically as possible.

"Really?" she said.

"No," I said.

She gave me a blank confused look, which was to be expected. Sarcasm was often lost on people like Izzy.

Weirdly, she gave me a five-dollar tip. On a four-dollar salad?

I don't get it.

Question: What does she want from me? Why is she being so fake-nice?

Sunday, August 24
7:00 a.m.

That settles it. In order to not become a career waitress, I must crack down and get writing. So here goes. I'm just going to do it.

I am.

Really.

I even set my alarm for 7:00 a.m. (and got up!) so that I'd get a bright and early start.

Oh, just a minute, The Cat wants to go outside.

7:42 a.m.

The Cat has ruined my favourite pants by using my leg as a scratching post. I have no idea why we have pets, particularly a cat. Cats are vicious and also purveyors of disease. My leg is bleeding. Probably I'll get rabies or the dreaded Cat Scratch Fever.

Hang on, The Cat wants to come back inside again.

7:50 a.m.

How am I expected to get anything done with the sound of Melody barfing in the bathroom next to my room? Remind me never to get pregnant. It seems really vile. In addition, it's making her grumpy and difficult to get along with, not that she was any treat before. As she pushed by me to get to the toilet, she actually snapped, "Get out of my way!" in a really unpleasant voice, as though her body had been possessed by a particularly scary clown with a homicidal streak.

It almost makes me miss Perky Melody.

Well, not really.

Actually, I like mean people better.

8:01 a.m.

It's clear to me that the only place I'll get any work done is in The Van, which I'm going to use as an office. Just am going to run down to the store to get some office supplies! I'll be back. Don't worry. Today is Serious Writing Day.

8:50 a.m.

The store doesn't open until ten. I'll just kill some time having coffee at Starbucks for an hour and then will get supplies and rush home to accomplish at least twenty pages of writing, possibly more if things go well. I can type at least 100 words a minute, which means that in two hours of good writing time, I should be able to write 12,000 words, which is a lot of pages. I don't know how many, but will find out.

9:41 a.m.
OMG.

Have bumped into HBG at Starbucks. Actually, I accidentally took his coffee (caramel macchiato) instead of my own and took a sip of it before I realized it wasn't mine and then nearly choked to death on it (sweet, horrible nightmarish drink).

"That's my coffee," he said.

It was difficult to tell if he was angry or not due to the English accent, which was so Hugh Grant it was impossible to see it as anything except charmingly rakish.

Swoon.

"Uh!" I said. "Uh!"

"I'll let you buy me another one," he said.

"That's OK, sir," said the annoying barista. "I'll make you another one."

He winked at me. Which was almost like flirting.

Of course, I have a boyfriend. I cleverly ignored his flirting, grabbed my coffee (extra-hot, extra-shot, fat-free latte), and fled.

I wish Kiki was available for a long discussion on morals and values. Am going to call her.

9:50 a.m.

Kiki: Haley, I'm just hanging off a roof right now. Can I call you back?

Me: Sure.

Kiki: OK.

Me: Remember when ...

Kiki: [interrupting] Haley, I have to go!

Maybe I'll call Jules. Jules used to be a much better friend before she was almost on the TV show *Who Is the Prettiest of Them All*. Even though, I must add, the judges told her she was too "normal" when she was voted off. Ever since, though, she's become insufferable.

She made me promise not to tell, but she actually got a little *Who Is the Prettiest of Them All* mirror tattooed on her ankle. It looks like a weird, lopsided oval with a fancy edge, but who am I to judge? I wimped out of getting the shooting star on my foot. I mean, I let the tattoo guy touch my skin with that thing and then I freaked out and possibly admitted to being underage and the guy got supremely angry and threw us out of his shop, but not before Jules' ugly mirror was done.

But I digress.

I'm going to call her. I hardly ever do anymore and it's not good for our friendship.

Jules: Hello?

Me: It's me, listen, I need your advice.

Jules: Is that you, Maggie?

Me: Uh, Jules, it's me.

Jules: Drew?

Me: For god's sake, it's me.

Jules: [sounding deflated] Haley, *what*?

Me: What WHAT?

Jules: You wouldn't believe how much liposuction hurts. I'm on three different painkillers. Do you think if I get addicted to them I could go into rehab with famous people?

Me: No.

Jules: You never know.

Me: I suppose not.

Jules: Anyway, I can't talk right now. My thighs hurt.

Me: You don't need your thighs to have a conversation.

Jules: I have to go.

Me: Fine.

Note to Self: Find new friends, stat.

10:34 a.m.

Spent all of money saved from tips on new pens and paper. Spent rest of the available time before work arranging pens and paper artfully on table in The Van, only to have the whole thing fall off as soon as The Van was moved during driving practice, not that this was at all anywhere near the highlight of driving practice.

It's hard to know where to begin.

Probably somewhere around the point where Dad nodded off in the passenger seat and began snoring loudly enough to wake The Cat, who was apparently asleep in the back. Much panic ensued as The Cat, obviously cleverer than he looks, mistook Dad's unusual breathing for the mating call of a hot Siamese and leaped on Dad's head, causing him to lunge forward, hitting his forehead on the dashboard and grabbing the wheel out of my hands and causing me to drive the van through someone's open front gate and into their decorative pond.

The surprising thing was that I wasn't hurt. I mean, please. I'm ALWAYS the one who gets hurt.

Unfortunately, Dad's head needed three stitches and I got a nasty warning from a policeman who was in no way cute or flirt-worthy and instead went on and on about what would have happened if there had been kids playing in the decorative pond at the time.

I tried to point out that the decorative pond was almost completely empty due to the ridiculous heat and empty reservoir and that the house was also empty, so if kids had been playing in the decorative pond, they would have been trespassing.

And he said, "Keep talking and I'll give you a ticket for having bald tires."

"But it's summer," I said. "It's not like I need the traction on snow and ice."

"Actually," he said, "I'm going to give you a ticket for excessive engine exhaust."

"What?" I said. "What are you talking about?"

"You're damaging the environment," he smirked. He had that look of someone who had been some kind of All Star baseball player as a kid who had gone on to become a jerk as an adult. "You're hurting the air my kids breathe."

"Good thing they weren't playing in the decorative pond," I said.

My dad groaned. He was holding a wad of paper (my new paper!) to his bleeding head. "My head hurts," he said.

"You should get that looked at, sir," said the policeman. "After I've written up this ticket for your daughter."

"Pig," said my dad, which I'm sure you'll agree was the wrong thing to say.

"Actually," said the cop, "I think I'll issue a citation that forces you to get your emissions tested before you can drive again."

"There's no such thing!" I said.

"Yes, there is," he said.

"This is ridiculous," said my dad. "It's like Kent State."

"How is it like Kent State, sir?" said the cop, writing madly on his little ticket book.

I could see things were going badly. So I did the only thing I could do. I burst into tears.

I know it's a lame thing, but I had to. I had no choice.

"You're making my kid cry!" Dad said.

"I'm just doing my job, sir," said the policeman, leaning on the front of The Van, which was a huge mistake because The Van was only just balanced on the edge of the decorative pond, causing her to fall forward the rest of the way with a sickening crunch as the front bumper crumpled against the decorative concrete frog.

Luckily the tow truck and ambulance both showed up at the same time, and Dad was whisked away for stitches and The Van was hoisted out.

Sadly, the frog sustained some damage.

The cop let us go. Which leads me to believe that either a) he wasn't that bad after all or b) he was really unsure as to what to do about that creepy stone frog.

The tow truck driver turned out to be a friend of Dad's. It always surprises me when Dad's friends show up, as he rarely leaves the house. How does he meet people?

Anyway, he drove us home.

To make a long story short, the guy said he'd fix The Van for me. Which is great, but I'm not sure I like the way he grinned at my chest while he said it. Dad's friends, I should add, are invariably creepy or stoned.

Sigh.

This kind of driving lesson could be part of the reason why I never pass the test. And why I never will get this book written, for that matter.

Tuesday, August 26
Ideas for Introduction to TCGGTPP

1. Write chatty-type letter of introduction that will make reader want to BE me and want to KNOW me.
2. Follow example from the beginning of *A Heartbreaking Work of Staggering Genius*, or whatever it was called, where the introduction was about twenty pages long and included an illustration of a stapler, because that was funny, only don't use a stapler (or any other office supply) because everyone will think you copied the idea from someone else.
3. Read more travel books from the library to get better ideas.

4. Dedicate introduction to supportive boyfriend (HBG) who insisted I go on road trip even though we'd only just met and mmm ...

5. No, no, never mind that. Dedicate book to Brad, who is actual boyfriend (AB) (which could also stand for Absentee Boyfriend), and not stupid schoolgirl crush.

Wednesday, August 27
7:30 a.m.
Dear Junior:

For some reason, I can't stop waking up at 7:30 a.m. on school days, even though I don't go to school anymore and never work until the afternoon. Which is ironic, really, because while I went to school, I couldn't wake up at 7:30 to save my life. Well, I could. And I did. But I didn't *like* it.

I should mention that I am taking driver's test again today. Wish me luck. I know everything about driving now. There is no possible way that I can fail this test. I've practised parking (with Melody, who seems to know how to do it marginally better than Dad does) on a hill with a curb, without a curb, between cars, behind cars, everywhere.

I CAN DO THIS.

I hope.

Love,
Soon-to-be-Driving Girl

12:44 p.m.
Oh my god, I passed.

12:55 p.m.

Am planning ways to tell Dad and Melody about road-trip idea and book.

1:47 p.m.

Have better idea! Will not tell them, will just go.

2:00 p.m.

But then they will report me as runaway.

2:14 p.m.

Will tell them something else.

3:03 p.m.

Will tell them the truth. Am sure they won't mind as Dad spent most of his hippie teenage years travelling around in a VW van. Celebrated the decision to tell them by driving down to the fish and chips place downtown. Sadly, on the way home, accidentally drove too close to the sidewalk and peeled off both tires on that side and had to wait in traffic for creepy tow-truck driver to come and tow van to service station for tire repair.

Walked home in lieu of getting ride with creepy tow-truck driver, who has taken to calling me "Sweet Thing." There is nothing right about that. Wonder if I can press charges against him for being creepy and gross.

5:00 p.m.

Will postpone telling them until some future date.

5:10 p.m.
Will tell them am driving across North America, touring different university campuses. Brilliant. Will definitely do this.

6:45 p.m.
They will see through this horrible lie as obviously am not doing any such thing.

6:47 p.m.
Will just start writing and plan will come together.

> **TCGGTPP**
> *Chapter One*
>
> ...
>
> ...
>
> ...

OK. It's wrong to think I can just dive in like that. Must start with an introduction that is funny and pulls the reader in, without completely copying one out of another book. Er, will consult other book for inspiration.

> **TCGGTPP**
> *Introduction*
>
> ...
>
> ...
>
> ...

Maybe there's something good on TV.

Maybe I should read some other books for research.

No, no, no, that's silly. Will go for a run and come up with something very clever and talented while running, thus accomplishing two things at once (writing book and getting into better shape).

7:38 p.m.

Unbelievably, have tripped while running (OK, walking) and somehow have sprained my wrist. I don't know how it happened! I was just running (walking) along the school field and WHAMMO. How there can be tree roots when the closest tree is five blocks away, I'll never understand.

Came home via walk-in clinic (where they know my name now) and now have wrist wrapped in splint and can't be expected to write book.

Friday, August 29
Dear Junior,

At least work is getting easier now that my wrist sprain is healing (and/or I'm just getting used to the pain) and I don't need to wear it in a sling anymore. I can also type again, although I'm typing with one hand and it's very slow. Thank goodness for spell checker.

Jules and Kiki are leaving on Monday. Both of them. Leaving.

I'm going to throw them a surprise party tomorrow night and getting this ready may have slightly stalled my plans to work on the book. Not to worry. I'll get to it eventually.

The party will be great! When I think back to all the

great parties that Jules, Kiki and I have been to ... OK, most of them weren't so great, but the IDEA of them was great.

None of them were great.

Would it be wrong to have a party and not invite anyone else? Now that I think of it, when we go to parties together we usually end up talking to other people and not each other and we should be bonding and whatnot as we will NEVER SEE EACH OTHER AGAIN.

Love,

Party-of-One Girl

> P.S. — Brad hasn't called for over a week. Am beginning to panic, but not really. (Am secretly relieved. Don't tell anyone.)
>
> P.P.S. — I will call him.
>
> P.P.P.S. — I think.

12:15 p.m.

OK, on to serious business. Or the serious business of book writing. You know, I've been thinking of something that would be really great. And that is, having my book launch party at the bookstore in the mall owned by HBG. I think I would probably wear a really plain black dress, like a shift. Is that what they are called?

Something that you might have seen in a really old movie, and not an '80s movie, I mean like something from the '40s. Like Kim Novak in *The Birds*, only obviously without the attacking birds all over me.

Ideally, I'd have her hair, also.

In summary, I'd want to look pretty and elegant and yet also slightly eccentric in a clever writer sort of way. I'm not sure what would make me look eccentric. Maybe a tattoo? But everyone has tattoos these days and maybe HBG would think that a tattoo was tacky, not that it would matter what he thought. Besides which, I know how much they hurt.

A lot.

More than you'd think.

I could just get my eyebrow pierced. But I hear that hurts, too. Why does everything cool and/or edgy have to be so painful?

Maybe shave my head?

But then I wouldn't have the pretty hair.

Besides, no one likes a bald girl, unless they're pretty weird themselves or unless the bald girl is preternaturally pretty to begin with. Am sure HBG wouldn't want a bald girlfriend.

Not that I'm shopping for a boyfriend.

Why am I talking about this? MUST GET TO WORK.

TCGGTPP

Introduction

This is a book. It's a story and it's also true, or most of it is, and some of it I made up. I won't tell you which is which, except I will if you ask because I don't want to be accused of writing a fictional memoir or basically of being a liar.

Come to think of it, to avoid complication, I'll make it all true.

Although maybe if I lie a bunch of times, I'll get on Oprah and Larry King.

Anyway, I'm hoping that it's funny and you read it and laugh out loud and think, "I wish I had done what she did." I hope you think it's an adventure.

Here is a stapler:

No, I can't use that because someone else did.

Here is a photo of my favourite pen:

Is that too copycat-ish? How many people out there have read A Heartbreaking Work of Staggering Genius *anyway? Oh, 800,000, according to ask.com (great website, btw).*

Well, I guess I shouldn't do that, then.

Forget all that. I'm starting over.

TCGGTPP

Introduction

Dear Reader:

Thank you so so so much for buying my book. I wrote it instead of going to college or moving to New York to become a model (not that these were actual options for me, but I digress). I totally appreciate that you bought

my book, or even that you borrowed it from someone.
Really, I'm just glad you're reading it. Except you, Dad.
And you, Melody. Don't read it. I'm serious.
Oh god, my dad will read this book.
I can't put that in the introduction.
Never mind.

TCGGTPP
Introduction
Once upon a time there was a girl named Haley (that's
me). Instead of doing something productive, she decided
to write this book. I hope you like it.

OK, It's not MUCH of an introduction, but at least it's
true. I'm very distracted by the idea of my DAD reading
this book. I mean, say I meet someone great on the road
and, I don't know, I write about something personal, like
boy-girl stuff. He'll kill me! Or will he? Is he the kind of
dad who WOULD kill me? He won't kill me. Worse, he
won't even care! He'll give me a high-five! Or worse, he
won't say anything!

What if I don't meet anyone on the road anyway? What
if I just end up driving down and back and nothing
happens and I talk to no one and there is nothing amusing/
interesting/insightful to report?

Once the book is available in bookstores nationwide,
clearly, everyone I know is going to read it. What will
EVERYONE think?

What if no one reads it?

What if I never get past the first sentence?

What if I'm a complete failure and spend the rest of my life working at Hefty's?

Note to Self: Find a different job.

Stop stalling.

Get on with it.

Write the book.

Stop obsessing.

Really must do something about hair before party.

Saturday, August 30
3:01 p.m.

"... so we're going to have to let you go," says Dick Richardson (or Dick Dick, as we like to call him). Dick is my manager at Hefty's. I probably don't have to describe him as I'm sure you can imagine what a forty-five-year-old man who manages a place called "Hefty's" looks like. He's not exactly all that. There is no need to bore you with a detailed list of the four different types of food I can see lodged in his upper (crooked and pointy) teeth or his ridiculous comb-over that manages to sprinkle dandruff all over his left shoulder.

"What?" I say. There is a stain on his shirt the exact size and shape of a rutabaga.

"It's just that we've had c-c-c-complaints," he says. He seems very nervous. Nervous people make me nervous, as I've mentioned before.

"About what?" I say nervously. It's possible that when he first started talking to me, I was very busy refilling the ketchup bottles (boring) and missed the general gist of what he was saying, which usually ranges from topics as gripping as cars to the even more fascinating topic of internet poker.

"Your hair, Haley," he says. I can tell he's getting impatient because he's tapping his pencil against his nose. I tried it once and it hurt. I can't imagine why he does something that physically hurts himself. Tapping, I can understand. But not on your own nose.

"I know," I say. I swallow hard. I will not cry, I repeat to myself, staring across the food court at Banana Republic. They are having a really good sale on summer stuff, but I hate buying summer stuff at the end of the summer because I won't wear it until next year, unless I wear it in the winter when it would be cold and out of season.

"Haley?" he says. He looks like he's going to cry too.

"What?" I say. I mean, what else can I say? I tried to get my hair altered slightly for the party-of-three event (why, I have no idea) and it turned a gentle shade of green that I like to call "sage." (I was experimenting with the idea of Tippi Hedren blonde). But the thing is, the guy at Magicuts said that if I did any more to it, it would all break and fall out, so I'm making the best of it.

They can't fire me for having bad luck with my HAIR, can they?

Oh.

Apparently they can.

So it's not like my life could get any worse. I'm now unemployed and have The Most Hideous Hair in the Universe.™

Oh, wait, it can get worse.

"Good lord, what happened to your head?" said HBG, leaning in closely to inspect my hair as he passed by on his way to his usual table.

"Uh," I said.

"It looks frightful," he said. "I don't understand young people these days."

Which leads me to believe the following:

1. My hair looks awful.
2. HBG does not even consider me flirt-worthy as he thinks I'm a "young person" and he clearly thinks of himself as a "non-young person."
3. He doesn't even like me enough to be fake nice.
4. He sounds charming even when he's being rude.

4:50 p.m.
"This is the worst day of my life," I tell The Cat, as I drag multicoloured streamers around the inside of The Van. (I've taken him outside for his own protection, but more on that later.) "For real."

The dumb part is that even as I'm saying it, I know it isn't true. It was a pretty bad day. For one thing, I finally caved and called Brad when I got home and got his answering machine.

And he didn't call back.

Not that he has to call back right away, but he used to, when he used to like me. I can tell that he doesn't like me as much as he used to, and it makes me want to make him like me again. Does that make sense? It was like it was safe when he liked me, for me to not like him that much. But now that he's losing interest, I feel panicky.

Maybe someone told him how awful my hair was, although I don't know who would have as no one I know would have talked to him before me, unless JT did, but JT has not yet seen my horrible hair.

And I don't care if he does.

I feel like I have to sit down with my head between my knees and breathe in deeply. Which I tried doing while getting my hair coloured at the salon (and I use that word loosely) on the corner. Instead, all that happened was I burned the inside of my nostrils from the overwhelming smell of bleach. And I got some on my favourite jeans and wrecked them.

Which sucked.

And then to get fired, to top it all off. Well, damn.

Although, if I'm going to be perfectly honest here, I'm kind of happy to not have to work at Hefty's. I was *almost* happy to be fired if only so that I don't have to watch the line cooks scraping the cockroaches off the grill before they cook on it.

On the other hand, I don't want to be a person (à la my dad) who cannot hold down a job for more than six minutes.

And I need the money.

Just thinking about it makes my heart race and I start seeing stars.

"Calm down," I say to myself out loud. Then I slap myself (gently) in the face. Sometimes that helps.

Positive Things to Put Horrible Day into Perspective:
1. I will likely get large advance for book.
2. Have filled out application for Visa card, so am not totally broke.
3. Oooh. Am excited about having a credit card.

Things to Buy on New Visa Card When It Arrives:
1. New pens for writing book.
2. New paper for writing book.
3. Sign up for writing class at college. Or maybe correspondence class of some description, about writing, of course. Correspondence is better. Or maybe will not take writing class as already know how to write. Perfect.
4. Sign up for auto mechanics class at college. Took one in high school but remember nothing about it. However, did already attend so maybe will know what to do in an emergency, should one arise, so really don't need to take one, after all. Am saving money already!
5. New clothes for road trip.
6. New luggage for road trip.
7. Full cleaning of The Van before leaving for road trip as it smells a bit like feet and old hair.

Have I mentioned how much I love my van (or The Van, as I call it)? Well, I do. It's so perfectly cute and utterly, well, *green*. It's like a tiny little home of my own. Albeit a home of my own that's parked on the lawn of my dad's home. MMMMelody's home.

The home I grew up in, which will be the home my brother (sister) grows up in, which will soon no longer be my home as I will probably move out and grow up, although not necessarily in that order.

I look searchingly at the house. It's a funny-looking house. Already it looks smaller to me than it used to. I think that is a sign that I'm almost ready to fly from the nest, as my dad calls it.

But then it will be my brother's (sister's) nest. And not my nest anymore.

I know it's wrong, but I can't help but feel like I'm being replaced.

It's crazy.

I wish ...

Well, never mind that.

This van — The Van — is all mine. That's where I am right now, writing. (And preparing for Jules and Kiki's going-away party-of-three.)

It's my office, remember? When I'm writing, which is ALL the time that I'm home, except when there is something on TV or I'm too injured or I can't be bothered.

Also, The Van provides a good escape from Melody (soon to be Mrs. Dad), who is going through a strange nesting part of her pregnancy and is obsessively cleaning and recleaning the house when she's not planning for The Wedding (but ugh, that's another LOOOONG story). (Frankly, it's something I try not to devote too much time to thinking about or participating in. It just seems so entirely ... ugh.)

I swear, she vacuums every day. I hope she doesn't inadvertently kill the pets with all the fumes she creates with all the "organic" cleaners she's using. I'm sorry but "organic" does not necessarily mean that you can mix them all together and pour them on the floor and not expect all the skin on your feet to come off if you accidentally step in the puddle.

I miss school.

I actually almost miss Hefty's already and I've only been away from there for a few hours.

You know? I mean, I miss *people*. When you're at school, you see people all the time. Granted, they are usually people like Bruce Bartelson (former class president) or Izzy Archibaud (class pep squad), i.e. people you don't want to see, and, in fact, would run away from if you saw approaching on the street.

When you're done with school and your friends have left, when do you ever see anyone? Especially when your two best-ish friends are leaving in twenty-four hours and you'll likely never see them again?

Note to Self: Stop procrastinating.

9:45 p.m. a.k.a. The Party That Wasn't

"This bus smells funny," said Jules. A piece of streamer drifted down and she tore it off the wall, leaving a patch of white on the yellowish background. "Why is there all this birthday party stuff stuck all over?"

"Um," I said. Suddenly I felt embarrassed. So naturally, I lied. "It's for Melody's surprise baby shower? That I'm having for her?"

"In here?" she said skeptically. "It can't be good for a pregnant person to be in here. I'm sure the air is toxic."

"It is not," I said, but even as I said it, I started to feel light-headed. What if the air *was* toxic?

Can air BE toxic for no reason?

She ran her finger along the wall and a cloud of yellow dust fell down.

"Gross," she said, inspecting it. "This van is filthy and gross. Is that a nicotine stain? That covers the entire interior? That's SO gross."

Sometimes, I hate Jules. I do.

I pressed play on the CD player and music blasted out.

"Shit," she said, falling over and catching herself on the table, knocking it off its base, and landing on the ground. "Double shit," she said.

She got up gracefully. How that is possible, I have no idea. But that was Jules. She did everything right. She inspected the knee of her perfect designer jeans (Citizens of Humanity). "I'm getting filthy," she said. "Can we go outside?" She blew a smoke ring at me.

I shot her a look designed to say, "Why are you so evil?" and said, "No, we're having a party!"

"What's YOUR problem?" she snarled.

"I planned this to be a party," I said. "And don't be a bitch about The Van. It's mine." For some reason, I felt like crying. Nothing was working out. Kiki was late and Jules was in a Jules-mood, i.e. was being mean to me and making me feel awful.

"Yeah," said Jules. "Who else would want it?"

Tears stung my eyes. I blinked vigorously and chanted "Supportive Friend" in my head. I do that sometimes to remind me to be a supportive friend to Jules, even though she's a total bitch, and getting to be more so every day.

Melody says that Jules is mean to me because she's jealous.

Yeah, I'm so sure. Beautiful, perfect Jules who is on her way to New York is jealous of dumpy, balding me because I own a filthy van? Looking at it through Jules' bitchy eyes made me realize how shabby it was.

"It stinks," she reiterated, lighting another cigarette from the first one. I was going to say something but I didn't. She was right. The Van couldn't smell much worse.

There was a super awkward silence, inasmuch as there can be a silence with a Green Day CD blasting in the background. "I am one of those melodramatic fools," they sang. Jules raised her eyebrows at me.

Please.

I'm not melodramatic.

Am I?

I inspected my fingernails and started to chew on a hangnail. I know it's a gross habit, but I do it when I'm nervous. I have no idea why I was nervous, but I was. It just all felt so strained. If we were dating, I'd assume that she was about to break up with me. Not that we would be dating, but you know what I mean.

Maybe this is what growing up is all about. Maybe it's about outgrowing your friends, or having them outgrow you. Then you outgrow your family and then I guess you move somewhere else and start over.

Can friends break up with friends? I chewed another fingernail. We'd been friends since we were three years old or something. Ages. Forever. We stared at each other.

At least, I think she was looking at me. I couldn't really see her eyes through all the smoke.

It didn't stay awkward for long, though, because Something Awful happened. In my experience, when any sort of mammal comes flying through the air and attacks anyone's head, awkwardness is replaced with, well, shock and horror.

So when, out of nowhere, The Cat jumped in through the open door and clawed Jules in the face, that was it for awkwardness.

Which, in a way, was a relief. Though not really.

Even though I hate Jules, she *is* my best-ish friend. I stood there with my mouth open. I don't know why I didn't do something. But what could I have done? The Cat seemed really possessed. He scared me.

I mean, it was liking watching a movie. I felt like it wasn't happening. It was surreal. I saw my hand reach out, but The Cat, spitting and making a terrifying sound, much like Linda Blair in *The Exorcist*, had already done five laps of the inside of The Van, tearing off nearly every streamer on his way, and leaped out the driver's side window.

"Argh!" Jules screamed. "Your fucking CAT has ruined my life!"

And she raced out, hitting her forehead and slamming the door behind her so hard that it shook the picture of Ben Affleck (it's a joke, OK?) right off the wall.

"Jules!" I said, but it was too late. She was gone. I could hear the screech of tires as she left. The door kind of hung there for a second, then crashed to the ground.

I just stood there.

Let's face it, historically, it's been *me* who is accident-prone, although there was that horrible incident where Jules fell off the roof and broke her arm. How did The Cat know that I was idly thinking (not really seriously) that Jules would be lost if anything ever happened to her face? That she'd be a loser just like me? That she was wrong to look down on me the way she looked like she was doing?

Bad karma will come my way for even fleetingly thinking that it served her right, which of course it didn't.

"Bad Cat," I said out loud, so that the Fates (or whatever) would know that I wasn't really thinking it was justified that Jules got scratched. "Sorry, karma."

What if it's really serious?

If it's not serious, it is sort of funny.

Not actually FUNNY, but you know what I mean.

Just at that moment, my cellphone rang and startled me, causing me to smash my funny bone against the counter really hard. So hard that I saw stars, which may or may not have indicated a detaching retina.

Damn.

I guess the Fates haven't turned, after all.

"Haley," said Kiki, breathlessly. "I'm so sorry, but I can't make it tonight."

"Oh," I said.

"It's just that Stephano is surprising me with a really nice dinner, I'm so sorry. I'm really sorry. I just ..."

"It's OK," I said, letting her off the hook. I mean, that's what best-ish friends are for, right? "Go, don't worry about it."

I hung up and sat down. I thought about phoning Jules to see if she was OK and then I didn't. I don't know why I didn't, I just couldn't bring myself to do it. I sat there for a long time. I mean, I suppose if my life was a movie, this scene would be pretty boring, just some girl with unidentifiably coloured hair sitting in a VW van staring at nothing for ages and ages, but that's what I did. I can't make it sound any more interesting than that, can I?

I guess I thought about some stuff, but I didn't write it down. Sometimes it's better if you just keep it in your head, swirling around.

Sometimes it's better to say nothing at all.

SEPTEMBER

"Yeah, so the thing is, we need you? Because, like, everyone is s-s-s-sick?"

I paused before answering, not just because I was still asleep. I have a very hard time talking when I first wake up. I opened my mouth and made a croaking sound and started to choke, possibly on my own saliva, which would be a horrible and embarrassing way to die. I had to put the phone down.

I wanted a job still, but going back to Hefty's sounded like the most horrible fate in the world. On the other hand, it would be for such a short time and would give me a chance to see HBG again, not that this was a good reason for working at a horrible job for a lousy wage.

Not that I wanted to see someone who thought of me as a young person with bad hair.

"Um," I said. Which I guess must have meant "yes" because next thing I knew, I was getting dressed in my Hefty's uniform again. There should be a law against polyester. Seriously.

On the way to work (driving The Van) I stopped at Starbucks, NOT to hopefully accidentally on purpose bump into HBG, but rather to get a cup of coffee. I've decided that coffee is good for the metabolism, or I read it somewhere. And god knows my metabolism could use some help. All my pants were getting tight, and not in a good way. There is nothing more disgusting than that flap of belly that hangs out over the top of your waistband when your jeans shrink (or when you grow). I swear, I could feel my fat folds chafing together and it was like nails on a chalkboard. I think it was *Glamour* magazine. Or *Shape*. That mentioned about the caffeine-metabolism connection.

In any event, my metabolism needs all the help it can get. It's not my fault that while I was ordering my extra hot latte, HBG walked in.

He smelled really good.

Best Way to Tell Things about Boys:
1. They smell good.
2. Their hands.
3. Their shoes.
4. Their eyes.
5. Cuteness.

Anyway, he asked me out!!!!!!!!!!

!!!

!

Sort of.

I mean, I think he did.

Actually, he said, "Hey, haven't seen you around Hefty's lately. Gibberish gibberish gibberish." (Think Brad Pitt in *Snatch*).

"Huh?" I said, prettily.

He winked. "Don't take my coffee!" he said.

"Oh," I said. I think I blushed so hard that my head nearly flew right off from the extra blood pressure.

"Take care!" he said.

"You're welcome," I said, cleverly.

I wish I knew what the gibberish part of what he said was. Probably he was asking me out! Or not. Of course he wasn't. I'm so stupid. What am I thinking? He was probably offering up another witty critique of my hairstyle.

I accidentally threw my coffee in the garbage on the way out, too. I meant to add some sugar and I put it down on that counter they always have in Starbucks with the hole in it. And it fell right in. Then I had to pretend I did it on purpose, which is pretty much the same as taking four dollars that I can't spare and ripping it up and putting it in the trash. I can only hope that HBG was far enough out the door that he didn't see.

GAH. Am such an idiot. I don't know why I ever even leave the house.

Note to Self: To avoid further humiliation, think about becoming reclusive and mysterious in the style of J.D.

Salinger, only without the whole nut-eating weirdo stuff.

Friday, September 5
HBG Incidents:

1. Saw him enter Hefty's. Immediately dropped tray full of Cokes on the ground, breaking six glasses and spilling Coke all over elderly regular customer named Cedric. Cedric called me a "nincompoop" and took back his tip. HBG looked as though he might possibly be laughing at me. Either that or he had something itching his nose.
2. Walked by the bookstore and was craning neck to see if he was there when he suddenly popped up in the window, startling me and causing me to step backwards into the path of oversized baby stroller, nearly killing self and oversized baby.
3. Saw him at Starbucks and kept eyes cleverly averted. No upsetting incident occurred. Except for the fact that HBG ignored self and did not smile, say hello, or make any coffee-related small talk.

10:30 p.m.
"So," said Melody, leaning over the counter scarily. Her belly dangled underneath her much like a kangaroo's pouch, if a kangaroo was carrying around a large, round semi-trailer.

"So," I said. I made myself busy with a cup of tea. I don't actually like tea, but I like making tea. There is something very satisfying about turning all those dead, shrivelled leaves into a pretty, hot drink. Too bad it doesn't taste better. "Want some tea?" I said.

"Sure!" she said. "That's SO nice of you!"

"Uh," I said. "Whatever."

"How's Brad?" she said.

I shrugged. "Oh, he's busy," I said. Suddenly, my heart skipped a beat. I hit myself in the chest a few times and coughed to try to get it started again.

"Are you OK?" she said, patting me on the back.

I shook her hand off. "Fine! Fine," I said, brightly. "I'm fine." I mean, it's a little difficult to explain that you think you might be in atrial fibrillation requiring paddles, right? I coughed a couple more times to make sure my heart had fallen back into its regular pattern again.

The thing was, I had no idea when the last time was that I'd talked to Brad. Meaningfully, anyway.

"I have to go!" I said, and thrust my cup of tea into her hands, sloshing it all over the counter in a puddle that The Bird promptly landed in, squawking like a house on fire.

"That's SO sweet of you," she called after me. Really, she tried so hard to be nice, it was almost heartbreaking. "Thanks SO much! For the tea and for the chat!"

Or would be heartbreaking if it weren't so annoying. Also, she still oversmelled like patchouli. No wonder she's thrown up for the entire duration of her pregnancy.

10:36 p.m.

Conversation with Brad:

Me: Brad! So, how have you been? I've been thinking about you a lot.

Brad: [sounding suspicious] What have you been thinking about?

Me: Oh! You know, just about you! And so on! What have you been doing?

Brad: Um. Playing hockey.

Me: Great! How's that going?

Brad: Listen, Haley, I'm glad that you're interested, but this conversation seems a little weird.

Me: Weird? Weird how? What do you mean? I just wondered how you were doing and all that. I mean, you haven't called, which is fine, you don't have to call me every day or whatever. It's fine! I'm good!

Brad: Are you drunk?

Me: No!

Brad: OK, well. Er, so hockey is going really well. I'm starting in the game next week against the Wheeling Nailers.

Me: The Wheeling Nailers? What's that?

Brad: It's a hockey team, you idiot.

Me: I know! I just meant, "Wow, what an interesting name. What does that mean?"

Brad: I don't know. Look, are you OK? What's on your mind?

Me: Nothing! I'm fine! I'm good!

Brad: Because this conversation is weird enough that it almost feels like you're breaking up with me or something.

Me: No! Absolutely not. In fact, I was thinking ...

Brad: What?

Me: I love you!

Brad: You do?

Me: Yes?

Brad: Wow. That's really ... great. I'm surprised. I thought you said that you weren't sure about stuff when I left.

Me: I'm never sure of stuff! But that doesn't mean that I don't love you!

Brad: Haley, that's really sweet. Maybe I'll come home and visit you soon. I think we have a game against your team one of these days.

Me: Great! I can't wait to see you.

Brad: [warily] Good. I can't wait to see you, either.

Me: Good night.

Brad: Good night.

I love you????? I LOVE YOU????

What's wrong with me?

I'll tell you what's wrong with me. I'm a BLURTER, that's what's wrong with me. I don't love Brad.

Or do I?

Maybe I do.

Maybe I'm just confused.

My feelings for HBG are just a crush. People get crushes all the time. It's totally normal and does not mean that I don't love Brad.

Totally.

It's all good. I can love Brad and have a crush on unattainable HBG at the same time. It's fine. There's no problem here.

Phew.

Well, that's a relief.
Or is it?

11:58 p.m.
Can't sleep. Am panicking. What was I thinking?

Saturday, September 6
1:17 a.m.
Still panicking.

3:33 a.m.
Sure it's not that bad. I do love him. Besides, what's the big deal? Am sure I've said it before. Now we both feel better and more on track. Am behaving like a proper girlfriend and not a slag with a crush on an older guy who owns a bookstore or a crush on boyfriend's cousin with the nice eyes, not that I even see or think about JT ever anymore.

Huge relief.

4:57 a.m.
Have strangely racing heart. Perhaps not related to panic at all, but to earlier fibrillation episode. Wonder if I, in fact, have that random heart ailment that strikes athletes down in their prime, like that skater whose name I've forgotten or that kid playing basketball or FloJo.

Probably will not live to see morning, so the whole "I love you" episode was for the best as will at least have date for own funeral.

5:33 a.m.

I don't want to die! Have cheated on my promise to stay away from medical websites to discover this:

(*from* Science Magazine *at www.sciencemag.org*)

> It has been known for quite a while that genetics plays a role in conditions ranging from congenital heart malformations to fatal disturbances in heart rhythms, but none of the genes at fault had been identified until 8 years ago, when researchers found the first mutation, in myosin, a key protein in heart muscle. Since then, discoveries of heart-handicapping mutations, including one reported on page 108, have been pouring out of numerous labs at an ever increasing rate, yielding more than 100 mutations in more than a dozen genes.

Wonder how one finds out if one has gene mutations? Is there a blood test?

Obviously, I'm at high risk as my dad was so baked when I was conceived it would be a miracle if I wasn't entirely the result of a genetic mutation.

Evidence of Genetic Mutations That I Might Have:

1. Am sure that one leg is slightly shorter than the other, resulting in perceived "clumsiness."
2. Bizarre level of blushing indicates unusually large blood vessels.
3. Eyes are murky non-colour and retinas are loose.
4. Freckles form distinct patterns (perhaps more suggestive

of weird astrological connections? but still worth mentioning).

5. Hair falls out.
6. Tend to get random, unusual sickness, suggesting weak gene pool.
7. Heart palpitations.
8. Difficulty breathing.

Argh.

Wish I could sleep.

9:30 a.m.
Slept through alarm and was half-hour late for work.

Saturday, September 13
Written Warnings I Have Received at Work:

1. Hair is unprofessional.
2. Lateness is unacceptable.
3. Breaking dishes comes out of paycheque (!).
4. Am not taking good enough care of table bases.

Apparently, scrubbing the BASES of the TABLES is part of my job, waiting tables at Hefty's House of Horrors. Which, naturally, is what I was doing the next time I saw HBG.

And he was with a WOMAN.

Am trying to convince self that this WOMAN was his mother, his sister, his auntie or just a lady he was making conversation with. Which was hard to do as I happened to be under the table, scrubbing the base (the grossest things imaginable are down there, don't even ask) when I saw his hand drift over onto her leg.

It's possible that my heart is broken.

And also my head, because I got up really suddenly, smashed my head on the table, and tipped it over, knocking off all the dishes and also making a spectacle of myself, and cutting my head open.

Cost of dishes: $25 (am sure this price was inflated)
Cost of stitches: $150 (will be reimbursed by medical plan)
Cost to pride: EVERYTHING

2:14 p.m.

"It's dried BLOOD!" I yelled. Which, granted, wasn't very nice, but I was in The Worst Possible Mood.

"I can help you with it!" said Melody. She kept patting me on the back, which was beyond infuriating. Was she practising to burp The Baby?

"STOP it," I said. "Just leave me alone."

I pushed by her and stomped heartily up the stairs. The Cat followed me, but took one look at my face and ran back down again. The Cat is smarter than he looks, albeit occasionally overcome with Evil.

But aren't we all?

I was looking for my dad, but he wasn't home. I'm not sure when it happened, but he used to be home all the time. Now he's out and about. What does he do? Who does he know? I have this weird thing where I feel like I have to know where he is so that I know he's not getting in trouble. Believe me, there is a basis for this — he used to sell marijuana. I know this doesn't make him a drug lord or anything, but I like to keep an eye on him. For one thing — and don't get me started on this topic — he doesn't think that herbs should be illegal. His argument totally falls apart when it comes to other "herbal" drugs, like, I don't know, heroin.

But someone once told me that I had to learn to trust him and that I couldn't parent my parents.

And that's obviously true. I mean, give me a break. My mom is a nun.

For a minute, I felt nostalgic for the days when Dad was home and did nothing but laze around all day, watching Tivo'd episodes of his favourite talk shows and smoking marijuana. Granted, it made him slow and stupid, but at least he was HERE.

I flopped down on my bed, which hurt my head horribly. It was likely that I had a concussion. I got up and looked in the mirror to see if my pupils were the same size as each other. For the record, that's a good way to tell if you are bleeding inside the brain. And I didn't just look it up, don't worry. I'm not doing that anymore. It's just something that I happen to know. The gash along the very top of my forehead (or what was now my forehead and used to be under my hair) was about five centimetres long. The stitches made me look like Frankenstein, and the doctor had had to shave my hair along the cut line, making it look like I had a receding hairline.

"ARGH!" I screamed. For some reason, The Bird interpreted this as a reason to fly directly at my cut head and stick his gnarly little feet into my wound. I batted him off

— which was gross because he kind of stuck there for a minute — and he fell to the floor.

"Shit," I said. I picked him up. He seemed a bit shaken.

"Sorry, Bird," I whispered. He gave me a dazed bird look and flew away, flapping his gnarly wings into my mouth, where I surely inhaled a million disgusting bird mites. At least he was OK. Killing The Bird accidentally would be more than I could take right now. I lay back down on the bed. My sheets were all lumpy and gross and there were clothes heaped up all over the floor. My headache pounded. I couldn't stop the film reel in my brain of HBG looking over in alarm as I burst out from under the table with blood streaming down my face.

I think he might have screamed.

And who could blame him? It was like a scene from *Scream*. Except worse.

Then the story gets even more bizarre. Who popped into the picture and offered to take me to the clinic and held a wet cloth to my head?

IZZY ARCHIBAUD. In my defence, I was dying, so I didn't say no. Why is she always around? Why is she so nice to me? What does she want?

Note to Self: Just STOP it.

Conversation with Brad:
Me: You wouldn't BELIEVE my horrible day.
Brad: Yeah? What happened, baby?
Me: Baby????

Brad: What?

Me: Forget it.

Brad: Forget what?

Me: I hit my head!

Brad: Oh no, not again.

Me: Yes! I have the worst headache! And my bangs were shaved off! I might as well shave my head.

Brad: Uh huh, you should.

Me: Are you even listening to me?

Brad: Can I call you back? The guys are here and we're playing Xbox.

Me: GoodBYE.

Conversation with Izzy

Me: Hello?

Izzy: It's me!

Me: Me, who?

Izzy: Izzy!

Me: Oh.

Izzy: I'm so, like, totally worried about your head!

Me: It's not a big deal. Uh, thanks for the ride and stuff.

Izzy: No problem! It was fine! I wanted to do it! Boy, that was weird when you fainted in the clinic waiting room! That must have been embarrassing!

Me: Yeah.

Izzy: I'm so totally totally glad that we're friends now, Hale.

Me: Uh.

Izzy: I'll let you go! Call me if you need anything!

Me: Um.

If I need anything? Like what? A cheer? Nonsensical chatter? A salad?

Honestly, of all the people to have rescue me, why did it have to be Izzy? Why couldn't it have been HBG? As it was, he saw all the horror and was involved in none of the rescue.

GAH.

MUST stop thinking about this.

11:37 p.m.

Worst Rash Decision of All Time:

1. Shaving my head in effort to even out shaved bang line.

Can never leave the house again.

Why is it that some people look good bald and some people (apparently) have LUMPY SKULLS? Oh my god! I have a lumpy skull! What was I thinking? Am I crazy? I look like I'm having chemo. I'm an insult to cancer patients everywhere, not to mention the people with alopecia.

I look TERRIBLE.

. Why did I do this?

It all seems surreal.

My ears are ringing. I definitely have a concussion.

This is probably a good time to leave on my road trip. Alone. And to not return until my hair grows back.

I went downstairs to get some Tylenol and my dad and Melody were snuggling on the couch. I swear, they didn't even look up when I walked by them BALD to get some water from the kitchen sink. I'm BALD! And, apparently, INVISIBLE.

My life could not possibly get any worse.

And my head is cold. It's very surprising how much you can feel the air circulating around a shaved head.

Oh well, maybe when I go to sleep, my brain will hemorrhage and I'll never wake up. That would probably be a good thing.

Sunday, September 14
12:47 a.m.

Great. Now I can't sleep as am afraid of dying.

Possibly, I should write my book, but I can't for the life of me even begin to be funny when I'm BALD.

The gravity of this cannot be overestimated.

8:45 a.m.

Call from Kiki:

Kiki: Haley! I miss you so much. I feel like I've been a terrible friend to you.

Me: Hi, Kiki. I miss you, too. No one goes running with me anymore.

Kiki: Really? That's so weird. Did I tell you that I'm going to run the Boston Marathon this year? I'm so excited. It's my dream, you know.

Me: Uh, that's great. So how's school?

Kiki: It's SO great. I love it here. It's so pretty and all my classes are interesting. I can't believe how different it is from there.

Me: I'm sure.

Kiki: So how are you? Tell me everything.

Me: I'm bald.

Kiki: I couldn't hear you! Maybe this is a bad line?

Me: I shaved my head!

Kiki: Oh my god, you didn't. Are you crying?

Me: Not anymore. Now I'm just itchy.

Kiki: Oh my god, Haley, what is wrong with you?

Me: Nothing!

Kiki: I'm worried about you. You know what? You should come and visit. You can sleep on the floor in my room!

Me: Sure, that sounds great!

Kiki: Really?

Me: I can't.

Kiki: Why not?

Me: I have to go! Bye!

I mean, seriously. How could I visit beautiful Kiki at Harvard? Her smart new well-dressed and worldly friends would think she'd taken in a street urchin for Charity Week. I dragged myself out of bed (it's sleep-in day! I'm not lazy!) and looked in the mirror. My scalp was covered with what looked a lot like leg stubble.

Fan-tastic.

Also, I had a zit on my chin the size of a dime. I dabbed some drying stuff on it, and then some toothpaste for good measure. I was just putting on my Crest White Strips (extra strength) when the phone rang again.

Phone Call with Jules:

Jules: Hi.

Me: Hi, Jules.

Jules: So, do you miss me or what?

Me: [sarcastically] I can hardly sleep at night.

Jules: Seriously, I DO miss you, you know. No one here is quite like you. [snickers]

Me: Jules, I'm not in the mood to be made fun of.

Jules: I'm not making fun! [bursts into tears] All the other models are such snobby bitches!

Me: Oh.

Jules: They won't talk to me! It's probably because I'm prettier than them, but still ...

Me: Uh huh.

Jules: They're totally jealous that I was on *Who Is the Prettiest of Them All*. Don't you think?

Me: No doubt.

Jules: What's wrong? You sound all mopey.

Me: Not that much. I have stitches in my head. My life is a shambles. I'm bald.

Jules: God! Ha ha! You're so funny!

Me: I wasn't kidding.

Jules: Imagine if you really *were* bald. You'd make such a weird-looking bald person. I'd probably look good bald because I have a nicely shaped head and good bone structure.

Me: I *am* bald.

Jules: You're so funny!

Me: Ha. Ha.

Jules: You know what? You should come out here and visit. The girls would really think you were funny.

Me: I'm not really a travelling act.

Jules: Don't be a bitch, Haley, you know you want to visit.

Me: No, I don't.

I hung up. Well, I didn't so much hang up as leave the phone on the bed, where The Bird was perched, pecking at the sheets. It looked like he was really listening to her. I wondered how long it would take her to notice that I wasn't responding.

Finally, I just filled the tub and went and lay in it, with water all the way up to my nose. If/when I leave for my road trip, I'm going to miss baths. Baths are the best. I sighed and tried to close my eyes and meditate. I've never been good at meditating. It makes me too aware of how fast my heart is beating (too fast) and how I breathe. Then I start thinking about breathing, and thinking that if I stop thinking about it, will I remember to do it? Did anyone ever die by simply just forgetting to inhale?

I was just getting comfortable (if by "comfortable," I mean "hysterically close to hyperventilating") when my cellphone started to ring. I reached out and picked it up, nearly dropping it in the water but luckily catching it just in time at the expense of my elbow (now bruised).

Conversation with Izzy:

Me: Hello?

Izzy: It's me again! It's Izzy!

Me: [sarcastically] Oh, goodie!

Izzy: It's great to talk to you, too! Listen, do you want to go to a movie tonight?

Me: No.

Izzy: Great! I'll meet you there at 7:15! I'm totally psyched!

I went to flip the phone shut and, this time, dropped it in the water. It made a sad, electronic, blub blub sound and slid under my back. I grabbed it, but of course it was already wrecked.

How was it that I'd lost control of my life? And my phone?

"Argh!" I yelled.

"What's wrong?" said Melody, popping her head around the door.

I hate hate HATE it when people just randomly come into the bathroom when I'm bathing.

"GET OUT!" I howled.

"Sorry!" she chirped. "Hey, did you know the phone was off the hook?"

I could hear her in my room, hanging it up. Followed by the sounds of my bed being made. Great. I closed my eyes and slid under the surface.

It hurt my stitches (which aren't supposed to get wet) like crazy, but what did it matter? Likely they would get infected and I would die from complications of blood poisoning.

And who would care?

To take score, I'd guess "nobody."

Amongst the people who wouldn't care, I'd list:

1. Jules (former best friend).
2. Kiki (former best friend).
3. Izzy (fake trying-to-be-friendly-for-suspicious-reasons non-friend).
4. HBG.
5. Brad (supposed boyfriend who never calls).
6. Melody (not even my stepmother yet and already wrecking my life).
7. Dad (blinded by his love for Melody and The Baby).
8. The Cat (too independent to care).
9. The Bird (too unintelligent to care).
10. JT (not that he should care, I'm just saying).
11. The Baby (not born yet, so unlikely to miss someone he never met).

The only place I could still safely scream without interruption was underwater anyway.

11:31 p.m.

Reasons to Not Go to Movies with Izzy:

1. She talks through the whole thing.
2. She has terrible taste in movies.
3. She smacks her lips when she eats popcorn.
4. She laughs in all the wrong places.
5. She hogs the armrest.
6. She smells like too much perfume.
7. She's too overly nice to be for real.

Saturday, September 20

Dear Junior:

Huge news!

Brad is coming home today. Why he didn't call and tell me sooner, I have no idea. He's not calling me as much as he used to, and when he does, there are usually people in the background and he's in the middle of something. I've never understood why people make calls when they are in the middle of doing something else. It makes no sense. Call when you aren't busy!

But never mind. That's OK. I am sure he's *always* busy. Probably doing more productive things than analyzing the stain on his bedroom ceiling (now looks like the Soviet Union before it got renamed) (now it looks like whatever it's named now, which I can't seem to remember) and procrastinating.

In any event, to prepare for his return, I shaved my legs and bought a wig.

OK, I know wigs are lame, but I can't let him see me as Stubble Head Girl. He'll be grossed out and will dump me immediately. The stubble is now about a millimetre long and very very very frightening looking. Also, it's sharp.

And itchy.

Especially when I think about it.

On the plus side, my favourite jeans are fitting again (working with food somehow has ruined my appetite and helped me lose weight) and my teeth are really white. I know this because I was at work yesterday and HBG came in and said, "Wow, you have the brightest, whitest teeth I've ever seen." At least, that's what I think he said. His accent is very strong and he had a mouthful of chicken sandwich.

So I said, "All the better to chew things with!" Which, at the time, seemed witty. But he gave me a weird look and said, "Please bring me a Pepsi with no ice!" In a way that I interpreted to mean, "Stop talking to me, Crazy Girl, and serve me! Your teeth are alarming." So, whatever. I never really liked him anyway and it doesn't matter because Brad (My Brad!) is coming home this afternoon.

Must start getting back into "girlfriend" frame of mind. To be honest, Brad's been gone for more of this relationship than he's been home for and I've kind of gotten used to the whole AB (Absentee Boyfriend) thing.

I'm taking Izzy with me to see his game. This doesn't mean that we're friends, it just means that she badgered me until I said yes. I don't know why she's so determined to be my friend when I so clearly don't LIKE her, but she sticks to me like glue. I'm too weak to fend her off. What can I say? She reminds me of one of those strange green prickly balls that stick to your clothes after you get lost in the woods and have to break a path through the thick undergrowth. Then, when you get home, you have a million burrs to pick off your sweatpants.

Izzy is a human burr.

But I'm lame enough that I'm sort of friendly (i.e. I don't actively tell her to butt out of my life) because I want at least one person to like me enough to come to my funeral when I die of something unusual, such as Mad Cow Disease or chronic insomnia.

Anyway, I'm excited to see Brad.

I'm going to pick him up at the airport in The Van! I'm sure he'll be really excited to see me driving.

Love,

Haley, Brad's Girlfriend

3:16 p.m.

Crisis!

Had to parallel park at airport and accidentally got one of those baggage buggy things stuck under the front of The Van. It's not really my fault. My dad's best advice about parallel parking, when I was learning to drive, was to avoid it when possible. Then he often did it for me, giving me the illusion that I knew how to do it.

Which apparently, I don't.

Note to Self: Put a chapter into book about parallel parking tips and tricks. Find out what they are first, and use them in your life to avoid future buggy/parking accidents.

So I was just trying to pull the buggy out when some uniformed traffic enforcer came and told me I couldn't park there. But I couldn't move without dragging the buggy across the pavement, which I tried to explain to him, but he gave me a ticket anyway. I should also mention that it was very stormy. It was like a freak end-of-summer hurricane, if you want to know the truth, although we don't live in a place where we ever have hurricanes. If we did have them, this would have been one. It was windy and the rain was being pounded into my eyeballs, dislodging my contacts and no doubt irritating my already delicate retinas.

The ticket guy's name was Hank. Hank had lots of hilarious stories about parking misadventures in his youth (I think — it was hard to hear him over the wind), which I listened to because he helped me unwedge the baggage thing. Sadly, he accidentally pulled off my front bumper at the same time, which I believe was very shoddily put in place to begin with by Creepy Tow-truck Guy, who, luckily, I've avoided seeing lately and don't want to see again.

I tossed the bumper into the back of The Van, where it somehow ripped a hole in the bench upholstery.

Finally, late, I went into the area to find Brad. Unfortunately, I was a bit unkempt and I guess my wig had slipped.

"Haley! Haley! OH MY GOD!" Izzy shrieked. She grabbed my hand and practically hurled me into the bathroom, causing me to go over on my ankle and pull the baby-change table off the wall. I flexed it experimentally (my ankle) and tried to reattach the baby thing. It didn't seem broken. My ankle, that is. The foldout change table had definitely seen better days.

"OUCH," I said loudly.

"Thank god I caught you!" she said. "Look!" She forced me to look in the mirror. Which was terrifying. There was a little bloom of zits on my chin, my mascara was everywhere from the rain, apparently I'd scratched my cheek with black Van-related oil (?) on my hand, and my hair ...

Yikes.

I mean, my wig ...

Well, I guess it was a good thing she freaked out because I don't know how Brad would have reacted to seeing me in a wig that was half hanging off the back. I looked like a demented escapee from a '50s horror movie.

Important Question: Why was Izzy at the airport anyway?

In any event, Brad seemed happy to see me (probably because my wig was straight). At least, he hugged me really hard and kissed my cheek.

"Where have you been?" he said. "You look great. I thought you weren't going to come."

"Of course I came," I said huffily. "I drove myself, too." I shook my car keys at him.

He looked worried.

"Uh," he said. His eyes drifted up over my head and then widened in what looked like terror. "Uh!" he said again.

"Why did you kiss my cheek?" I said. "I mean, aren't you my boyfriend?" I draped my arms flirtily (I thought) around his neck (which felt weird and wrong, but seemed like the right thing to do). He disentangled himself.

"I have to ride into town on the bus!" he said. "With the team!"

"Really?" I said. "Because I thought that ..." My voice trailed off because I noticed what he was looking at.

Izzy.

"I'll call you as soon as I get home!" he yelled and practically sprinted away.

Weird.

"Hey," said Izzy. "I wanted to say hi to Brad!"

"Huh?" I said.

I looked at the place where he'd disappeared. There was just a crowd of people, hugging and stuff. Everyone looked so happy. I felt inordinately sad.

"What are you doing here anyway?" I said snappily.

"I came to support you," said Izzy. "Isn't that what friends totally do?"

I shrugged and screamed a little inside my head.

I am sure he was happy to see me, though.

Maybe.

Why wasn't he happy to see me?

5:12 p.m.

"What's the matter with my girl?" my dad said, coming up behind me and nearly scaring me to death.

"Why don't you ask her?" I answered cleverly. "I think she's watching TV in the other room."

"Not THAT girl," he said. "You."

"Nothing," I said. "I'm fine. I'm good. I'm late, though."

"We never spend time together anymore," he said sadly. "Give me a hug."

I did. I mean, he's right, we don't. But that's because he spends all his time with Melon-y. I mean, Melody. (She currently strongly resembles a melon and I've taken to calling her Melon-y in my head.)

Not that I'm bitter. I miss my dad, though.

I gave him another hug for good measure and inadvertently clunked his chin with my forehead. I don't know which of us it hurt more. I'm a walking disaster. My forehead is definitely not healed. It's very itchy, I must add.

"No problem," I said. I had to run upstairs to check for bleeding. My head wound has only just healed up. (*Note:* I got my stitches out yesterday and nothing in this WORLD is as gross as the feeling of a stitch being pulled out of your skin.)

It looked OK. I added some more makeup to be safe, which made it itchier, but beauty is more important than comfort. I think. Except when it comes to shoes, maybe.

The last thing that Brad needs is a girlfriend who looks like Bride of Frankenstein in front of all his new teammates. Right? Right.

11:11 p.m.

Oh man.

So this is what happened.

I was only marginally late to pick up Izzy, but for some reason this made her furious and she didn't talk to me until we got to the rink, when suddenly she became my best friend again. She's seriously unbalanced. I wonder if she's on some sort of medication. She's like the human equivalent of The Bird. Which may be an insult to The Bird.

In any event, the game was really crowded. It was disconcerting because I was used to Brad playing for highly unattended events. Unattended, that is, by anyone outside of the players' parents and the occasional random creepy adult who seemed unattached to anyone and likely to show up in a news headline at some later date.

This was different, though. The stands were packed. I guess the WCHL somehow drew a crowd of actual adults who were not related to the players. It was kind of exciting. I may have told one or two people sitting near us that Brad was my boyfriend. I don't know what came over me.

"My boyfriend, Brad, loves playing in town!" I said to the hairy old guy next to me. "He especially loves the ice here!"

I had no idea if any of this was true, by the way. I just couldn't shut up.

"Huh," he said.

"Yup," I said. "My boyfriend really loves this city."

Finally, Izzy elbowed me in the ribs and hissed, "Stop embarrassing yourself!" Which I thought was rude, but should be grateful that she stopped me. I might have been a bit OTP (over the top). But I was proud! I think it would have made Brad happy to know that I was telling everyone.

It was a great game. Great! Really! Unfortunately, I accidentally bought a really big pop and drank it and I had to pee so badly that I couldn't sit through the entire last period. I tried to wait for the end, but I couldn't. He'd stopped about a billion goals, so even though his team was losing to the local team, it was still a good game. I mean, if he hadn't stopped a billion of them, it would be 10,000,000,008 to 4 instead of just 8 to 4. I felt bad for him, because I think he wanted to impress me. Which made me love him just a little more.

As I was saying, I had to pee. Izzy said she'd come with me, and she found me this little washroom that was away from the rest. Apparently, she used to work here. Who knew? So I went in there, but then I couldn't get out. I don't want to point fingers or anything, but pretty obviously she locked me in. At first, I thought she was kidding around, so I kind of knocked on the door and said, "Ha ha, OK, let me out." Then I didn't hear her on the other side. And I started to panic. Of course, because I was panicking, I hyperventilated and had to put my head between my knees. I was really dizzy. I'm not sure how long it was, maybe about twenty minutes (which felt like about twenty hours) when some janitor opened the door and jumped about a mile when he saw me. I swear, his eyes bugged right out of his head.

"Argh!" he screamed.

"Argh!" I screamed. I was so relieved, I could have hugged him. But I was a mess. There was no mirror in that washroom, so I couldn't see how much of a mess exactly, but I know that I was pretty sweaty and shaky.

I pushed through the crowd to see if I could find Brad. I knew that after the game, which apparently ended in a score of 8–7 (I must have missed a lot in the bathroom), he'd have to do interviews or whatever. Not like in the NHL, but I think the local TV cameras were there. I couldn't see him, so I assumed he was in the dressing room.

Safe assumption, right?

WRONG.

I couldn't find Izzy, either.

After walking around for about ten minutes, I finally spotted Brad.

AND Izzy.

Is Izzy after my boyfriend again?

That can't be real. I'm sure I'm imagining it. She couldn't possibly be that duplicitous. It would require too much thinking and she's not that smart. Besides, she's my friend. Right? RIGHT?

Question to Self: What kind of friend locks you in the bathroom?

"Haley!" said Brad. "THERE you are." He tried to hug me and I hugged him back, but he was still wearing all his pads and it was kind of like hugging a giant sweaty refrigerator box. Then I noticed the bandages.

"What happened to your face?" I said.

"You didn't see?" he said.

"She was in the washroom," said Izzy.

"What HAPPENED?" I said again.

"You were in the washroom?" he said. "In the last two minutes of the last period in a nearly tied game?"

"I had to pee," I explained. "And the door locked."

"The door locked," he said slowly. "You haven't seen me for ages and during my big moment, you're locked in the washroom."

"Izzy locked it!" I said, glowering at her.

"I don't understand," she said. "What do you mean?"

"What do you mean what do I mean?" I said. "You locked it!"

"Why on earth would I lock it?" she said.

"That's what I'm asking you!" I said. "Why WOULD you lock it?"

"That's a good question," she said. "And I'm sure you can totally see that there isn't an answer to it."

"What?" I said. "How can there be no answer?"

"Ahem," said Brad. "Isn't this about ME and my GAME?"

"What happened to your face?" I said again. I was starting to feel really irritated, or like I was speaking a different language that no one else understood.

"There was a fight," said Izzy. "Brad was a total hero. He was so great. He ripped off his mask and got right in there."

"Yeah," said Brad. "But got a big penalty and probably won't be allowed to play tomorrow."

"It was SO worth it," Izzy simpered.

"Izzy," I said. "What are you DOING?"

"What do you mean?" she said. "I'm just making your boyfriend feel good about his game."

"That's MY job!" I shouted. There were tears in my eyes. I felt like everyone was against me. It was just totally NOT working out how I'd imagined it. "Go AWAY, Izzy!"

"Sorry, Haley," she said. "Wow, you seem, like, really mad."

"I AM REALLY MAD!" I yelled.

"Sheesh," said Brad. "Look, I've got to go get changed."

"You know what, Haley?" said Izzy. "I'll find my own way home." She turned around and ran into the crowd.

I was just standing there, like an idiot. My head was itching like crazy under my wig. Growing out your hair is not easy, believe me. It felt like ants swarming all over my skin. I pulled the wig off. What did it matter? Brad was mad at me, for whatever reason, and Izzy had taken off, not that I cared.

Ugh.

Summary of Night's Events:
1. Possibly broke up with boyfriend inadvertently.
2. Possibly was locked into bathroom by supposed friend.
3. Possibly overreacted to all of it and made a mess of things.
4. Possibly am allergic to wig material.
5. Possibly will never leave the house again.

Monday, September 22
TCGGTPP
Introduction

It was a lame and stupid night. The roar of the crowd was deafening, but I could hardly hear it from where I was locked in the janitor's bathroom. This was the straw that made me drive away. I had to go to San Diego, if for no other reason than to get back together with my reasonably cute, reasonably nice, reasonably tall, reasonably talented boyfriend whom I loved. A reasonable amount.

It's a love story.

I sat back and looked at what I'd written. I liked the first bit, but the love story bit was a bit lame. OK, a lot lame. Actually, come to think of it, the rest sucked too.

I wrote my name on my wrist with a Sharpie. They make retractable Sharpies now. I don't know why this makes them better, but it actually does.

Do I really just love Brad because he's ... well, he's OK?

That's incredibly horrible.

Suddenly, I just needed to hear his voice.

Me: It's me!

Brad: Oh, Haley, what now?

Me: Nothing! I mean, I'm sorry I didn't get to see you more. What happened to you on Saturday night? And, well, Sunday morning? Not that I was expecting anything [I waited by the phone all day on Sunday] because I'm totally not the kind of girlfriend who waits by the phone. In fact, I was busy all day. Busy, busy, busy ...

Brad: I'm sorry I didn't call. Look, I was mad, OK? It hurt my feelings that you were off being all HALEY about everything when I thought you were watching what I was doing.

Me: I WAS watching.

Brad: Uh, NO. Actually, you were locked in a bathroom.

Me: It wasn't my fault!

Brad: It never is, is it?

Me: What are you saying? Are you breaking up with me?

Brad: What do you think?

Me: Why doesn't anyone ever directly answer my questions?

Brad: Who else doesn't answer your questions?

Me: Argh.

Brad: Oh, Haley.

Me: Is that an, "Oh, Haley, of course you're still my girl" or an "Oh, Haley, goodbye"? [I started crying at this

point. I'm not proud, but it's true. Suddenly losing
Brad felt like the worst thing in the universe.]

Brad: Don't cry!

Me: I can't help it.

Brad: I just need some time to think.

Me: Argh!

Brad: I'll call you later ... in the month.

Me: Later in the MONTH?

Brad: Well, I need some time to think!

Me: That's too long!

Brad: Maybe I don't need that long, then!

Me: Fine!

Brad: Goodbye!

Argh!

  Argh!

  A million times Argh!

  I hung up the phone by throwing it against the wall. It
didn't break, which is good, because it was expensive to
get a new one after I dropped the other one in the bathtub. I couldn't believe how upset I was. Brad broke up
with me! The weird thing is that we saw each other so
rarely, it really didn't matter that much. But it DID. It did
matter.

  It DOES matter.

Note to Self: You are too *neurotic* to be likeable and will die
single and alone, like Bridget Jones, only when she
said it, it was funny because it was clear that she wasn't

actually really going to die alone, whereas you probably
will. Neurotic is not likeable at *all*. Stop being yourself.
Be more like Izzy. People like Izzy, notwithstanding the
fact that she locks people in washrooms and has a very
grating tone of voice.

4:15 p.m.

"Oh, honey," said Melody, patting my hand. "It's so upsetting to be dumped by your first little boyfriend."

"He's not little," I said. "He's big. Really big."

"OK," she said, looking confused. It wasn't hard to con-
fuse Melody lately. She was all discombobulated by her
giant belly and puffy face.

"I'm not upset," I added, even though I was crying, so
possibly it was hard to pull off such a lie. "I'm fine. I'm
just going to meet Izzy at the mall."

"Ohhhh!" she said. "Can you give me a ride?"

"Uh," I said. "Sure."

"I'm going to buy some baby furniture," she said. "Do
you think you could wait for me and we could bring it
home in The Van?"

"No," I said. "I mean, sure."

And that was the plan, and I had no intention of running over her foot. How was I supposed to know her foot
was there anyway? She screamed like I was killing her,
which I guess I was. It probably hurts to have your foot
backed over by a van. But I did tell her I was backing it
out. Why was she standing there?

5:10 p.m.

"Why did you do it?" my dad said, wrapping Melody's foot in a billion bandages.

"She didn't mean to!" said Melody at the exact time I said, "I didn't mean to!"

She laughed. I smiled tentatively. Laughing was good, right? She must be OK. The last thing I want to do is be responsible for her having The Baby early due to shock or due to the pain in her foot. Melody is a naturopath, so she can heal herself. At least, she believes that and I'll go along with it because I feel horrible for running over her foot.

I don't like her that much, but I honestly didn't mean to hurt her.

6:09 p.m.

"Look," Izzy said. "You're, like, totally late, and I'm not even mad at you. That's how good a friend I am! I don't know why you think I'm not your friend!"

"YOU LOCKED ME IN THE BATHROOM!" I yelled for the billionth time. "And I'm sorry I'm late, I ran over Melody's foot accidentally."

I slumped down in the booth. We were at Joe Slim's, which was the competitor to Hefty's. I just couldn't face Hefty's on my day off. From where I was sitting, I could see it, though, and that was bad enough. My boss was leaning over the soda machine, sweating. Probably his sweat was dripping into all the drinks and infecting people with ... well, with whatever he has that's resulted in him being a restaurant manager well past middle age.

I groaned. "My life is pointless," I said.

"Don't be like melodramatic," she said. "It's totally not pointless."

"It is so," I said. "I can't even be a long-distance girlfriend."

"You can make up with him," she said. "I'm sure of it! He's totally smitten with you. He doesn't have eyes for anyone else."

"Hmmph," I said.

"What?" she said.

"Well," I said. "I have this idea." And then I told her about The Book. I have no idea why I told her. NO IDEA.

Obviously, I've lost my mind.

I'm insane.

Crazy.

The weird thing is that I guess I wanted to make her my friend even though she kept doing unfriendlike things.

"That title is sooooo great," she said.

I like her more all the time.

NB: Be nicer to Izzy. Izzy is a good friend.

Wednesday, September 24

Dear Junior:

The unimaginable has happened. I can't even begin to describe it. For one thing, I decided to be a better friend to Izzy. She was being supportive, in spite of the fact that she's totally annoying. She was doing her best. I don't even know what I was thinking! All I know is that one minute, there I was, with Izzy, in the mall. We were talking about my book, and she dragged me into the bookstore to buy a travel guide because she was all hopped up on the idea of driving to San Diego with me and that would be my book, a kind of two girls on the road book. But it was the bookstore. THE BOOKSTORE.

HBG was there, of course, because he's ALWAYS there, and he remembered my name, out of the blue and said, "How's your head, Haley?" Or something like that. And I introduced Izzy. Because I'm POLITE. And they were chatting about my road trip (well, our road trip, I guess) and he was suggesting books, and blah blah blah. I don't know what happened, he was all, "Haley, I didn't know you were a writer" (or something), "Izzy, will you join me for coffee?" And next thing I know, they were both gone, pushing me out and locking the door behind them.

Both of them.

Gone.

How did that happen?

HATE Izzy.

I mean, Brad is my boyfriend (or one day will be my boyfriend again), but she just swiped HBG out from under my nose without the smallest bit of effort. Why is it so effortless for her? Why is it so effortful for me? WHY? WHY?

GAH.

Love,

Haley, Girl Loser

Sunday, September 28

11:45 a.m.

"I'm so sorry, Haley," said Melody for the millionth time. She was crying like crazy, but since she got pregnant she's been crying a lot. Crying and eating, but that's another story. She reached out for me with her bloated arm.

"Dad!" I yelled.

"Haley," he said. "Calm down, she didn't mean to."

"That's hardly the point," I said. I was holding The Bird in my hand. Well, what used to be The Bird.

Not to put too fine a point on it or anything, but Melody is a murderer.

Melody KILLED The Bird.

MY BIRD. Whom I once risked social humiliation in my pyjamas to rescue from his attempted escape. Whom I taught how to talk. Who annoyed me on a daily basis.

She killed him with the vacuum cleaner. Part of the reason why Dad and I hardly ever vacuumed was because The Cat was scared of it and The Bird was always on the floor. How could she not have seen The Bird?

HE'S VERY BRIGHTLY COLOURED.

"He was an old bird," said Dad. "He had a good bird life. He was loved, and that's what's important, right?"

"It was cut short too soon!" I screamed. "He was a young bird!"

"I'm sorry!" said Melody again.

"You should be!" I said, and she cried harder.

"Haley," said Dad, "don't be like that."

"She killed my bird!" I said.

"Technically, he was my bird," my dad reminded me.

"Whatever," I said. "I'm going for a run."

I put The Bird down on the table, which seemed wrong. But I didn't want to throw him away. I picked him back up and held him for a minute. He felt very light. They were both watching me like I was a deranged person who needed, well, watching.

"What?" I said. I put The Bird into the freezer and then glared at them. Neither of them said anything, but Melody started crying harder. She'd been freezing organic baby food in there like crazy, which was stupid because by the time The Baby was old enough to eat it, it would be all freezer-burned already. But what did I know?

Now it would have feathers in it.

I slammed out of the house and started jogging down the street. I wasn't exactly wearing the right clothes for it, but what did it matter? The thudding of my feet on the pavement actually made me feel a bit better. It was one of those fall days that are cold and crisp and completely blue and the trees were still red and orange and yellow. It was pretty beautiful. I felt calmer.

It took about ten minutes for "calm" to turn into "nauseated." I flopped down on a bench and counted my pulse for a while. Then, when I was too freezing to continue, I walked home. No one was there when I got there, which was probably a good thing. I had no idea how to say that I was sorry to someone who had just killed my bird. But I felt bad. Instead of moping around, I got ready for work.

OK, that wasn't really a choice, I was already late. I showered quickly and jammed a wig on (I chose the black one with bangs that looked like Uma Thurman in *Pulp Fiction*) (sort of, and also it itched less than the other ones) and stuffed myself into my uniform. There is something so inherently gross about polyester. It never feels like it actually fits properly. Also, I was already sweaty, so it was going to be a smelly shift.

7:30 p.m.

"Well, I'm sorry about your bird," said HBG.

"Don't worry," I said. "I'll be OK."

"I certainly hope so," he said. "I'd hate to imagine that you'd collapse into a fit of despair, never again to re-emerge and dump a drink on me."

"I'm sorry!" I said. "I didn't mean to! But it was just water."

"Right," he said. "Very good defence. You should be a lawyer."

"I didn't get into college," I said. "Besides, I'm a writer."

"I know," he said. "And you're going off on a little mad adventure to write about."

"Yes, I am," I said. I felt a little defensive. There was something in the angle of his mouth that made it seem as though he was laughing at me, just a bit. "How's Izzy?" I asked.

"I thought she was your friend," he said. "I'd imagine you'd know more than me."

I blushed. "Never mind," I said.

"You're not jealous, are you?" he said.

"No!" I said. My face began to throb, I was blushing so much. I hadn't blushed this much since, well, since JT.

I wiped my cloth over the table and said, "Well, I've got work to do!"

He looked around and actually did laugh. "There's no one here!" he said.

"Yes, there is!" I said triumphantly as a guy strolled in, hands in pockets.

"Oh god," I said. "JT!"

"Haley," he said, nodding. His eyes were drooping adorably. Not that I think JT is adorable anymore, because I don't. I really don't. He's not in the least bit adorable. He's JT and he's an idiot. He also always seems to pop up in my life whenever I think of him, a bit like a superhero, only like a superhero who is not heroic and who is also a complete loser.

"What do you want?" I said. "I mean, what can I get for you?"

"I'll have a Coke," he said.

Frankly, I was happy to have something to do. HBG was making me nervous. Not that JT wasn't, but at least I was used to being nervous about JT.

I crunched on some ice while I poured his soda and nearly choked to death on it. I gasped a bit, and my boss slapped me on the back so hard that I nearly fell into JT's lap. Where did he even come from? I didn't hear him come in.

I spat the ice into the sink, along with something white.

"Haley!" he said. "Thanks for helping out!"

"What do you mean?" I said, frantically digging around in my mouth with my tongue to see if the white thing was one of my teeth. Did I just lose a tooth?

"I was being sarcastic!" he said. "You have customers!"

"I'm getting him his drink!" I said. My tongue settled on a sharp hole right in the front of my mouth. "My tooth!"

"What?" he said. "Stop worrying about your teeth. Get out there and serve the customers."

I slid JT's Coke down the counter and kept my mouth firmly closed. It was my front tooth.

"So, Haley," said JT. "How's Brad?"

I shrugged and tried to look casual.

"Haley," said HBG, "I'll just settle up and leave you now."

I nodded and went and got his bill.

Really, not talking wasn't that hard.

Even not talking to my top two favourite crushes, well, a former crush and my current crush, at the same time.

"Bye!" said HBG.

"Bye!" I said.

"Hey," said JT. "Are you, like, missing a tooth?"

Argh.

Summary of Bad Things:

1. Bald, stubbly head.
2. Bad skin.
3. Missing bottom half of top front right tooth.
4. Bird dead.

Summary of Good Things:

1. Can't have bad hair day as have no hair.
2. One less tooth to whiten.
3. At least both JT and HBG seem to know my name.

OCTOBER

As part of Melody's pregnancy eating plan, she insists on eating grapefruit with every meal. At least grapefruit is better than egg, but it's still not breakfast. It's a bitter, nasty fruit that hurts my tooth root.

My tooth, by the way, is getting fixed at the same time as my wisdom teeth are being removed. Apparently, if I don't have my wisdom teeth removed ASAP, their roots will wind around my facial nerve and leave me drooling and hopeless for the rest of time. On the other hand, the risk of the surgery itself is that I'll be left drooling and hopeless also. Or worse, I could get a bone infection and die, not that I'm overthinking this or anything.

I took another bite of grapefruit and winced.

"I'm so glad you're embracing grapefruit," she said. "It's so good for you. It's one of nature's superfoods, you know. Like blueberries! And eggs!"

"Right," I said. "Super."

"It's so great for your memory," she added.

"Huh," I said. "I think it would probably be better for me to be a little more forgetful."

I looked at the clock. It was about one minute later than the last time I looked.

"So, Haley," said Dad. "We're talking about names for the new baby. You want to help us choose?"

"Sure," I said. "If by 'sure,' I mean, 'no.'"

He looked at me with the look that said, Don't be a jerk.

"Sorry," I sighed. "Yes, names. I mean, no. Isn't that personal? You guys should make that decision on your own. It's nothing to do with me." I caught Dad's eye again. "It IS to do with me, because it's my brother, I mean," I added. "I just like the name Noah, that's all."

"Noah!" said Melody. She closed her eyes. Was she meditating? Her eyes snapped open. "No," she said. "That's no good. I was thinking of 'Red.'"

"You were thinking red?" I said. "The name Noah made you think of red? Is that an expression? Like seeing black?"

"No, as a name," she said. "I was thinking of it as a name."

"Oh," I said. "Wow."

"I love it," said Dad. His eyes lit up. Let's keep in mind that he thought "Haley Andromeda Harmony" was a good name too.

"Super," I said. "Well, I'm off."

"Where are you going?" said Melody. "I hoped you'd want to stay home today because we're having a blessing for the baby!"

"No, thanks," I said. "What's a blessing?"

"It's when people come over and wish things for the baby, like blessings," she said. "It's spiritual."

"Ugh," I said. "I mean, neat. But I have to go. I have to … see Jules."

Which wasn't totally a lie. Jules called yesterday and said she might be in town today. Which meant that she was absolutely in town because she had a plane ticket and was flying in today. I wasn't sure what time, but at that moment, even camping out on Jules' front lawn to wait for her sounded like a more attractive idea than eating citrus fruit with my crazy family.

"Green is good too," she said thoughtfully.

I slammed the door behind me. I wasn't mad, per se. I was just feeling edgy.

And my tooth hurt. A lot. My tongue kept going to the place where the tooth used to be. I was wearing a scarf on my head. I went and sat in The Van for a while and practised breathing. The other day I was tidying up the living room and found one of Melody's books about anxiety. Not that I'm anxious or anything, but it had some good exercises in it.

I was just inhaling and counting to four when I heard Jules arriving. Jules has a certain way of stomping and breathing. I could tell she was smoking.

I pushed The Van door open, narrowly missing her face, and jumped out and hugged her. She hugged me back, which is a good sign that she really did miss me and wasn't as tough as she was pretending to be, but whatever.

She pulled back.

"Jesus," she said. "You look terrible. Were you in a fight?"

"Ice," I said. "It just broke."

"It was all that stupid whitening stuff you use all the time," she said. "It's weakened your enamel."

I breathed in through my mouth and concentrated on breathing out through my nose.

"Do you have a cold?" she said. "Because I totally don't want to get sick. I have a go-see next week for a really cool show."

"Nice," I said. "I'm breathing calmly. Want to come in?"

"No, thanks," she said. She waved her cigarette at me. "Let's walk," she said.

"Really?" I said. "I thought you hated walking."

"I do," she said. She laughed. "I guess I'm just used to it because obviously in The City we walk everywhere."

I rolled my eyes. "In The City," I mimicked.

"Haley," she said, "don't be like that."

"I'm not being like anything," I said. "It's good to see you too."

"Come on," she said.

So we walked. It was raining and cold. But she didn't seem to notice. She was kind of race-walking too. Maybe she wasn't lying about all the walking she did in The City, after all. She was in pretty good shape. I couldn't talk a lot as well as breathe.

Huh. I would have thought I was in better shape than her, but I guess not. She's a smoker! Maybe I have something wrong with me cardiovascularly. Maybe my latent heart problem is acting up.

Maybe I have a clot in my lungs.

I concentrated on breathing. Sweat trickled down my spine.

She kept up a long babbling self-involved monologue, which I tried to concentrate on, but it was difficult because I was distracted with images of my own demise. She launched, without pausing, into a second very long story about some people I'd never heard of. I hate when people do that. How are you supposed to care about people you don't know and who said what to whom and why? And what they were wearing? But it was good to see Jules. It was like old times.

"... and she was wearing white pants, which were completely last season and she looked almost like she might be fat!" She laughed hysterically.

"Do you ever talk to Kiki?" I asked, when I could get a word in edgewise.

We were passing the old school. "It looks so small and weird," she said. "It's totally different."

"Well, it IS totally different," I pointed out. "They spent the whole summer painting it purple."

"Maybe that's it," she said, cocking her head, as though somehow that would make it appear more normal. "Maybe I'm just used to bigger buildings."

"No doubt," I said. "But as I was saying ... do you ever talk to Kiki?"

"Of course," she said. "I talk to her at least once a week, when I'm in town."

"Which town?" I said. "This one?"

"No," she said. "New York, silly. Sometimes I go to the Hamptons on the weekends."

"Ooooh la la," I said. "Fancy."

"Anyway," she said. "Kiki is cool. She's at school and stuff. Don't you talk to her anymore? She said you were all weird and self-involved last time you phoned her and didn't ask about her."

"I asked about her!" I said, trying to remember when I last talked to her. The thing with Kiki was that she was so hard to get hold of that when I finally did, I had to ask a bunch of advice. Kiki was great at advice, and it's not like she ever needed it in return. She was smarter than me in every single aspect of life.

"Whatever," said Jules, shrugging. She pushed her hair off her shoulder. Her hair was now dark brown.

"Your hair is nice," I said.

"Yeah," she said. "It is, isn't it? Brown is totally the new blonde."

"Huh," I said. I adjusted my headscarf. "Sure."

She glanced at me. "Well, it doesn't matter here," she said. "This isn't exactly the style capital of the world."

Ugh.

Just remembered why Jules drives me CRAZY.

Things That Bug Me about Jules:
1. Her hair DOES look good.
2. She always looks good.
3. She makes me feel like a loser.
4. She makes me feel like the whole TOWN is a loser.
5. HBG smiled at her.
6. She's sometimes right.

Sunday, October 5

Dear Junior:

You aren't going to believe this one! Jules has decided to become a Scientologist, à la Tom Cruise. I've tried to tell her that Scientology isn't all movie stars and weird diets, but she won't listen. I was just deciding that she wasn't that bad, after all.

Now I think she's nuts.

Think about it. It's a religion started by a man who wrote science fiction for a living. He's a writer! He wrote *Battlefield Earth*! I mean, it's crazy. It's a cult! Anyway, apparently she has to go to L.A. to get jumped into the gang or whatever, but she can't tell me more about it because all of it is a secret.

Junior, I don't know if I can keep being friends with Jules. She's too insane. She's too much. Next to her, Izzy seems almost normal, and that's unbelievable. She's been bugging me a lot lately too. I almost feel like they are both competing to be my friend. Which is weird, because neither of them seems to like me that much.

I miss Kiki. The more I think about it, the more I feel like I let Kiki down. She was my favourite best-ish friend and maybe I didn't ask after her enough. I've left her five messages this week and she hasn't called me back.

Ugh. Maybe I'm just a bad friend.

Am too depressed to write more.

Love,

Lonely Girl

ll:ll p.m.

Dear Jr:

Went to freeeeezing cold beach for party-like drink-event with JT and Izzy. Don't ask. Big mistakelkjfj. Oops. Sorry bout that.

Now have tattoo on arm that says "Brad." Oooooh, Brad. Love Brad. JT made me see that Brad is the right boy for me. Izzy was friends with the tattoot, I mean tattoo guy. She's so nice to me. She really helped him draw this on my arm and it's so cool and it's ...

Hey, wait a minute. This says Bard. Bard?

Jkjfjkdl.

lkj

Haley

Wednesday, October 15

Money saved for trip: $1675.00

Hair regrowth: 1 centimetre

Cost to have tattoo removed from bicep (if I decide to do it): $1000

Cost to have hair extensions: $1000

Summary: Life is full of difficult choices. MUST go on trip to get material to write book and must stop procrastinating departure date and must just DO it already.

MUST.

Then will quickly become rich and can have tattoo removed (or at least corrected) and get glamorous hair extensions. And possibly extensive plastic surgery to make self pretty instead of plain, lumpy and bald.

Tuesday, October 21

3:34 p.m.

"Jules, please come with me," I begged. I know begging isn't pretty, but I was desperate. "I'm begging you!"

"Don't BEG," she said. "I'll come. But you wouldn't come with me when I needed you to hold my hand for liposuction."

"But that's different," I said. "I was politically opposed to liposuction."

"Hmm," she said. "Maybe I'm politically opposed to wisdom tooth removal."

"Don't be ridiculous," I said. "There's nothing political about impacted wisdom teeth."

"Why don't you get your new best friend, Izzy, to go with you?"

I could be wrong, but I swear she sounded almost jealous.

"She's busy," I said. Then I quickly added, "She's not my new best friend anyway. I'm not even speaking to her. She spelled my tattoo wrong."

"You have a tattoo?" Jules laughed. "I'll come with you if you let me see it."

"No!" I said.

"Haley," she said. "Please."

"Fine," I sighed. I thought about what she'd said. Izzy was NOT my new best friend. Was she? The sad thing is that she probably was. And she was dying to come with me, but she was bugging me and I didn't want her to see me all freaked out. I was trying to be normal in front of people who didn't know me well enough to know that I was faking the normal bit.

Jules, after all, had seen me in much worse situations.

"Deal," she said. "I'll meet you there."

Which is how she came to be dragging me down the street an hour later when I bolted from the office. Did you know they don't put you to sleep for wisdom teeth? They just use local freezing! I had a panic attack! It could have happened to anyone!

6:06 p.m.

OK, as it turns out, they do put you to sleep. It's called a "twilight sleep," which isn't the same as a real anesthetic, but who cares? The procedure was a piece of cake. The after-effects (i.e. throwing up on Jules in the car) will take longer to recover from. And the blood. Ugh. No one tells you about the blood. It's too horrible to even write down. Needless to say, you swallow a lot of blood.

Ugh.

On the plus side, at least they capped my front tooth while they were at it. If my mouth weren't so ridiculously swollen (or "cute" as Melody called it — she actually said that my face looked better a little "fuller," which was about the most insulting thing anyone has ever said to me), I'd go stare at my new tooth in the window.

Luckily, have lots of painkiller drugs and will take some and go to sleep. When I wake up, am sure swelling will be gone.

Wednesday, October 22
Swelling is worse. Swelling is so bad, can't even type.

Thursday, October 23
Swelling worse still. Apparently am allergic to painkillers. Antihistamine makes me sooooo sleepy that I …

Hey, aren't I supposed to be on a road trip by now? Help!

I am forgetting to do the things that I …

These drugs are really …

So tired, really. More later if I …

OK, bye.

Friday, October 24
Bard, I mean Brad, is in town! My Brad!

Am debating the merits of trying to get him back by stalking him at his parents' house. Maybe I could woo him with flowers. Brad is totally the kind of guy who would love it if I gave him flowers. I think.

Actually, I'm not that sure what kind of guy he is.

But he's my boyfriend! (OK, my ex-boyfriend.) Shouldn't I know that about him? No matter. Stalking is probably a bad idea. But I did call his house and leave a message with his mom and he hasn't called me back.

She probably didn't tell him. I knew she never liked me.

I heard this from JT, who actually phoned to tell me. JT! Phoning ME! Not that I care. I no longer have a crush on him. In fact, I can't stand him. I wish I could remember hazy details of my night out with JT and Izzy. According to her, we're all really RILLY good friends now. If that's the case, then I feel like I've fallen into a coma and woken up in the Twilight Zone. How could I be really good friends with JT?

Besides, he's an idiot.

Furthermore, I think there may be something wrong with my liver. I only had a couple of drinks. How could I have been so drunk? I'm so humiliated. Why do I keep doing things like that? What if he tells Brad?

Hmmm.

Note to Self: Never drink again.

It probably doesn't matter that much because on close inspection in the mirror, I've realized that I can't let Brad see me. I'm too swollen! There's no way he'd want to get back together with me with my face like this. I'm hideous. I'm the Creature from the Black Lagoon.

I'm hiding.

Besides, what will Brad say when he sees my tattoo? Bard? He'll know I'm a lost cause. I'm hopeless.

Oh, Bard. I mean, Brad.

Damn.

Monday, October 27

Dear Junior:

Brad was in town and he didn't even *try* to see me. OK, he tried, in that he finally called me back. But I didn't answer the phone. He didn't try very hard, though. He went out with Izzy and JT and they've both told me not to worry.

What does that mean? How can I not worry? Brad is the most important part of my life.

Well, Brad AND getting my book written.

Brad might come slightly behind the book on my list of priorities, come to think of it. But that's because the book could change my life.

On the other hand, Brad may be The One.

Can't wait to get to San Diego to figure it out.

Love,

Swollen, Unrecognizable Girl

Quirky Girls or Whatever [insert finalized title here]
Random Notes

Before you leave for a road trip, make sure you have all medical eventualities planned for. For example, if you've still got your wisdom teeth, have them removed. The same probably is true for your appendix. Why do we have those anyway? Have it removed for good measure. You don't want to be dealing with these things while on the road.

Ooh, that reminds me. Must find out about medical coverage for road trip.

Thursday, October 30

Dear Junior:

I know I was going to stop writing journal entries, but I can't help it. I need to write things down so that I don't forget them. Also, it helps me to not get too freaked out in my own head about things that I've done.

For example, today as I was swabbing tables (Why do

people insist on pouring pop all over the table at restaurants? Are these people equally as sloppy at home?) I happened to accidentally swab a puddle of Orange Crush onto the lap of HBG. I don't know what's wrong with me, but I've lost all ability to speak to him at all.

"Grabifmlsoc," I said.

"That's all right," he said. "I don't mind. Bit of orange looks nice on a white shirt."

"Grxxx!" I said.

"I'm a big Shakespeare fan too," he said, which made no sense to me. And he was staring at my tattoo when he said it, which made me flustered. How could I explain "Bard"?

"Uh!" I said. And ran away. Well, I didn't run, but close enough.

Am such an idiot. Getting Brad back is the best idea I've got because at least he doesn't make me blush and stammer. Not very much anyway. If I had an actual boyfriend who made me palpitate with nerves, I'd be a wreck all the time. It's better to have nervous-making boys as crushes and have nice, solid, steady, boring boyfriend who doesn't make me physically incapacitated with fear.

Yes.

I really should be working on the book, but now that we have an actual departure date (November 1!), I feel like I should wait until something actually happens. I keep doing this thing in my head whereby I pretend that, say, we've already taken the ferry to the mainland and something has happened, say the ferry gets grounded somehow or the captain takes a wrong turn or I meet a cute boy in the cafeteria or someone falls overboard. Not that I'd wish this on them, but it would all make for a good book. Once I was on the ferry and I looked out the window and a body went rocketing by me. I nearly had a heart attack, then I realized it was just a drill. Why they didn't make an announcement saying, "We're having a drill that involves throwing lifelike dummies off the side!" I have no idea. It would have been a reasonable thing to do. Anyway, if that happens this time, I can use it in the book.

Maybe I'll push Izzy off. No, no, I'm just kidding. Don't worry. I wouldn't do that. I am sort of mostly glad she's coming. Travelling alone would be daunting and besides, if nothing else, she'll say and do a lot of humorous things that I can use in the book.

Everything is material! I read that somewhere.

Have bought you, Junior, some extra batteries and a charger so I can charge you up using the cigarette lighter in The Van. Not sure how that works, but as long as I can always type, I should be OK.

Am so excited.

Oh, on an unrelated note, Izzy talked me into going to a Halloween party tomorrow night. Have I mentioned how much I hate Halloween parties?

Ugh.

Love,

HAH

Halloween

DISASTER.

I'm never going to a Halloween party again. For one thing, it's HALLOWEEN. You'd think that people dressed in costumes would not be mistaken for hookers and arrested for talking to an undercover police officer. ALL I SAID WAS, "Want to come to a party?" And that's because Izzy dared me to do it. I should probably backtrack and explain that Izzy was encouraging me to meet new people to get my mind off Brad, and she was right. Other than HBG, and JT, I hadn't spoken to another boy in months. How was I supposed to know that my Material Girl costume (Madonna, circa 1988) made me look like a prostitute? I thought it made me look fun and funky.

Now I may have to just crawl out of my own skin from the humiliation of it all. I did, however, learn some new words in JAIL. Where I was until Melody wobbled in the door to rescue me.

She really IS getting very large.

But that was nice of her, all the same.

Am starting to like Melody better and better. She didn't even tell on me. Not that Dad would have cared, but I appreciate that she was trying to protect me.

On the other hand, am worried about how little she knows Dad if she thinks something like this would bother him. Oh well, this isn't my problem.

My Problems:

1. Have quit my job! Which is only a problem because I won't see HBG until I get back from road trip. Granted, this will probably be a good thing because it will give him time to forget about what an idiot I am and besides, when I get back, my hair will be longer and I will look glamorous and thin (plan to eat nothing but salads and

fruit while on the road) and will have good skin. From the healthy California sun. And will have lots of witty, writerly anecdotes to impress him with.

2. Accidentally have not told Melody and Dad about road trip. Inadvertently mentioned to them that Izzy and I got a job up north (!) at a ski resort. I have no idea where this lie sprang from, I swear I didn't plan it, it just happened. May be some latent form of Tourette's syndrome, but instead of a tic I spontaneously tell outrageous lies for no apparent reason. Luckily they are both flaky enough that neither asked any intense questions. Which is good, because I couldn't have answered them. up north WHERE?

3. I realize that I haven't explained the fact that Izzy is coming with me. Much like the whole "up north" story, I have no idea how this happened. Obviously, I agreed to it under incredible duress. Or else I am clinically insane. Who can say?

   Let's not forget the whole locked-in-the-bathroom incident. She'll probably kill me and leave my body by the side of the highway. I must be crazy. But am afraid to go alone. Don't tell anyone.

4. Am scared to go on road trip — this is possibly one of those things that sounds like a much better idea in theory than in practice.

5. Am worried that long-distance trip to get Brad back will backfire horribly and I'll be humiliated and alone forever.

6. Melody and Dad bought me skis and lots of warm clothing (where did they get all this money????) for my

job up north, which makes me even more embarrassed for lying about it and now will be driving to San Diego with about a million dollars of ski equipment taking up all the room in The Van, but can hardly complain as it was a very thoughtful gift.

I am so excited (if by "excited," I mean "terrified") about tomorrow, I don't know how I'll be able to sleep.

10:45 p.m.
Still too excited to sleep.

11:50 p.m.
No sleep.

1:40 a.m.
Leaving in seven hours! Still too excited.

2:13 a.m.
Nope, still not sleeping.

4:44 a.m.
And again ... not asleep.

NOVEMBER

Tuesday, November 18

OK, we would have left on November 1 (which would have made more sense) but just as we were pulling out of the driveway, The Van started making a terrible sound (think "chukka chukka chukka," but not in the usual friendly Volkswagen way, more in an alarming, lurching, smelly way), and smoke came out. I've been too depressed to talk about it until now, but it's OK to do it at the moment because we are actually on the road. I'm waiting outside Izzy's house for her to get into The Van.

So what happened was that there was a noise, and then ...

"Fire!" Izzy screamed and pounded at the door, which immediately fell off, dragged a few feet along the driveway, sparking like crazy, and then the window gave way and broke into about a billion pieces.

I think you can agree that this wasn't the most auspicious beginning.

Naturally, I started laughing and laughed so hard that I nearly peed my pants. OK, I *did* pee my pants but don't tell anyone because it's just embarrassing. Maybe I have a bladder infection or something. I mean, I'm sure it's not normal to be laughing-until-peeing until you're about fifty-five and have had six babies.

"Haley!" Izzy screamed and grabbed me and threw me onto the lawn. Which was even more ridiculous because The Van wasn't on fire, it was just some steam coming from under the hood. Honestly.

We lay on the grass and laughed for a while (I think I was hysterical from lack of sleep) and The Van made these funny little sounds, like a wind-up toy that was just winding down and then eventually stopped altogether. Luckily, I took auto mechanics in high school. I should be able to fix it.

Right?

RIGHT?

Oh, here comes Izzy.

Her mom sticks her head in the window. "Have fun at camp, girls!" she says.

"Thanks," I say.

"I think it's so great that you're going to work with underprivileged children for a month!" she says. "I wish I was as generous as you girls with your time. It's so super!" (I could see easily where Izzy got her perkiness from. Her mom — BUFFY, and I'm not kidding, that's her actual name — was practically bouncing off the pavement as she spoke.)

"Right!" I say. I have no idea what she's talking about,

but it doesn't much matter. Izzy apparently is as adept at random lies as I am.

Izzy is stuffing her crap into the back, and I can't help but notice that she has about eight more bags than she did last time we almost left.

"Bye!" I say, and we pull out of the driveway.

"What did you tell her?" I ask Izzy as we make our way toward the highway.

"Oh!" says Izzy. "I wanted her to think we were doing something so great! So I made up some stuff about poor kids."

"Izzy," I say slowly, "I thought we agreed to have the same story. What if our parents talk to each other?"

"Huh?" she says. Then, "Hey, isn't that the bookstore guy you have such a crush on?"

"Where?" I say, and I swear, I was LOOKING at the road. I was. I just turned my head the tiniest bit.

I have no idea where that shopping cart came from.

So, anyway, we drove into a shopping cart, which caused the tires to get stuck, which caused us to careen into a dumpster and caused The Van to grind to a smoky, creaking halt.

Saturday, November 29

Hello? Is this on? This is Izzy. I'm helping Haley to write her Top Secret Book, which isn't a secret because she's told everyone. Problem is, she's driving, and ... oops, hang on.

She just bumped into the neighbour's recycling bucket at the end of her street. It's no problem, though, because it didn't leave very much of a mark. Not like last time! That totally took about ten days to fix. Oops.

It was loud, that's all. It startled me. Haley's a really good driver, and I say this because I don't know how to drive. Although we lied to her dad and said that I could drive and I showed him a driver's licence to prove it, only it was my sister's licence. I have a feeling that we're going to get in a lot of trouble for this, but the thing is that I was tired of waiting to leave on our trip to find Brad and to reconcile them (or whatever!) (wink!). You know, like Fate is a funny thing.

Haley, I AM writing travel stuff.

Sort of.

Hey, give that back!

11:45 a.m.

Dear Junior:

OK, not to worry. We're on the ferry. Sorry I let Izzy get hold of you. She says she's going to write the proper travel stuff and then I can fill in the good parts as we go along. She got really good grades in English (well, in everything) and so I believe her. I read somewhere that when you write a book with another person, one of you just pretty much stands around looking out the window and the other one does the work. I haven't decided yet if I'd rather write or look out the window. I mean, you'd think it would be obvious that I'd rather look out the window, but before I was just scared of starting. Now we're actually on the ROAD and we're doing it, I kind of want to make it all my project again. But also, I'm doing all the driving.

Frankly, I'm just hoping Izzy doesn't drive me completely around the bend. I'm getting used to her, just like you get used to ice skates. You know how when you first put them on and you think you never will get used to the throbbing pain in your ankles, but then, when you take them off, your feet feel weird? It's like that with Izzy. Kind of. I mean, she just went down to the cafeteria and I was sitting here waiting for her to get back and it felt weird not having her yakking away in my ear about whatever she goes on and on and on and on and on about ...

Kind of like how Jules used to be, you know?

Oh, we're pulling in to the dock! I'm a bit disappointed that nothing happened on the boat. An elderly man asked me where the washroom was, but other than that, I don't think anyone even spoke to me. I guess I should take some notes on the weather or whatever because it might be important.

Or maybe I'll get Izzy to do those boring parts.

Love,

Haley, Girl Reporter

Notes on the Weather, by Izzy:

The weather is totally nice. The sky is blue, but it's like really cold. I don't know how cold. Pretty cold. Cold enough to see your breath in little clouds. Oh, and there's some ice on the roads as well, but not like shiny ice. Black ice. Wait, it's actually sort of cloudy. So it's

not that nice. It's really cold. The heater in The Van is
working really well, though, and we're both sweating.
It's actually really hot. But not outside, just inside.

"Haley, turn it off," groaned Izzy. "I can't type, I'm sweating on the keyboard."

"Gross," I said, and tried to turn the heat off, which was hard because when I took my hands off the wheel, The Van wobbled back and forth a bit. It was only a bit disconcerting, if by "disconcerting," I mean "terrifying."

"ARRRGHH!" Izzy screamed, nearly scaring me to death.

"Don't DO that," I said. "You nearly scared me to death."

My stomach growled. I wasn't sure if it was because I was a) nervous or b) hungry or c) being consumed by an abdominal tumour that I didn't know I had because I'm not allowed to think/talk about physical ailments anymore. (Not that Kiki and Jules are around to keep tabs on me, or that they've even CALLED me lately to see how I am.) I pressed my hand there to see if I could feel a lump, which I couldn't.

"I'm hungry," said Izzy. "I'm going to try to eat nothing but 1000 calories a day exactly and then this will be totally like a diet and a road trip at the same time. Do you mind if I write in my blog while we're on the road? How much battery power does your computer have? I just love it when it's cold outside. DO you take a multivitamin? Because I brought some for you, too, in case you didn't, and I don't think you do because if you did your skin wouldn't be so like yellowish."

"Uh," I said, which is the only way of responding to so many questions at once. I squinted at the road and turned the radio up slightly.

"OK," she said. "So is this the most exciting trip you've ever been on in your life? I can't believe we're doing this. I'm so glad we're friends now because I always liked you. Do you think I should get my hair cut short?"

"No?" I said. I wasn't sure exactly which question I was answering. While she droned on, I kept writing and rewriting (in my head) the opening passage of the book. Starting it with the ferry trip would be such a good idea because, obviously, it's like pushing out to sea and it's symbolic and everything. But nothing really funny happened on the ferry trip itself. Nothing.

I guess I could make something up, like that time I was on the ferry with the dummy-rescue thing I told you about. I could use that. Would that count as "times and dates have been altered" or whatever books always say in the front of them? It wouldn't exactly be a lie, because I did see it happening, just not on this trip.

I'm a bit worried that nothing funny will happen on this trip at all, other than the obvious — I kill Izzy or she kills me or I die from the sheer annoyingness of her. Once, a long time ago, when we were in high school (feels like a lifetime ago), I had to share a tent with Izzy on an outdoor adventure weekend for the student council (don't ask) and it was the longest two days of my life.

"IZZY," I said out loud, really loud, just to make her shut up. She looked kind of hurt but she stopped talking. Which was good, it's what I wanted. I felt only a bit mean.

OK, a lot mean.

"Sorry," I said.

She shrugged and looked out the window. "I'm used to it," she said. "Hey, we should talk about the book."

"Unh," I said. I kind of wanted to think about the book without talking about it. "Why don't you write your blog now and we'll upload it whenever. Like when we get home."

"Oh!" she said. "Good idea."

Then she typed away for ages. I'm dying to know what she wrote, but I won't look.

I won't.

Oh, crap, she's put a password on it so I can't read it. Bitch.

I kind of wish I'd known she had a blog before now so I could have read it before we left for this trip. What if she's saying mean things about me? I mean, I'm sure she's not, she's pretty friendly. If she was a dog, she'd be a golden retriever and I don't think they ever hurt anyone. I figure she couldn't possibly be as annoying as she presents herself to be. Deep down inside, she's probably OK. Maybe something awful happened to her once and she'll confide in me on this trip and I'll understand why she's so IZZY all the time and I'll forgive her for bringing up stupid things constantly.

"Have you totally shown Brad a picture of your tattoo?" she said. "You've got to know that JT's told him by now. He totally thought that was the funniest thing in the world, you know. I mean, no offence."

I gritted my teeth. "Thanks," I said.

"Sure!" she said. "Totally."

Sometimes I think that if you took the word "totally" out of her vocabulary altogether, she'd either deflate like a burst balloon or she'd entirely run out of things to say.

"So what do you write about in your blog?" I said. "I hate blogs."

"That's rude,' she said. "I'm not going to tell you now."

"I didn't mean yours!" I said quickly. "I mean, I hate writing them because I don't want other people reading my private thoughts."

"It has a password," she said snottily. "It's totally private." She looked significantly at my hair. I have this horrible feeling she's saying stuff that's mean about it on her blog, because she kept looking over at me while she was typing as if to suggest my hair was bad.

But so what?

Obviously I know that my hair sucks.

But how can I ask her if I can read it? She'd have told me about it if she wanted to. It's not like I'd want HER reading MY diary (which is NOT a blog, but just a private diary).

How arrogant do you have to be to post your diary on the internet? Who reads them anyway? Shouldn't a diary (excuse me, BLOG[5]) be private? Who does she give her password to? Does she have some kind of fan club?

---

[5]   I hate the word "blog." All made-up internet-related words irritate me no end. Don't even get me started about IM jargon — like LOL. Argh! LOL is the worst. Worse than "blog." WAY worse.

Words That I Hate:

1. Blog.
2. Synergy.
3. Flesh (it just sounds gross).
4. Foamy.
5. Any internet jargon (like cya and yt) — ugh.
6. Malignant.
7. Horseradish.
8. Pimento.
9. Aspartame.

Same Day
Notes for Book
By Haley and Izzy, World Travellers
You type something. I don't know what to say.

OK, ummm ... . How about ... Crossing the border between Canada and the U.S. can take up to a billion hours. Be prepared! Bring cards.
That's a good idea.

I know, I wish we'd done it.

Hey, want to see if there's a vending machine around here?

I don't think we should get out of the van. Besides, I can't eat any more junk food today, it's bad for my skin. I've already had a Diet Coke.

I think we should turn the engine off, though, we're totally wasting gas.

OK.

It's cold in here, we should totally turn the engine back on.

Totally.

We should write about the Peace Arch.

Totally.

Why are we typing this? Why am I overusing "totally"? That's your word.

Totally.

"This book writing is totally harder than I thought," Izzy said. "You're lucky I'm going to help you!"

"Uh," I said, immediately wishing I could retract any conversation we'd had in which it may have seemed like I wanted her to help.

I most certainly did NOT want her to help.

Unless she was a really good writer.

No, not even then.

We'd been stuck in the border lineup for hours between British Columbia and Washington State. To cross, you have to go through this gate-type thing and be interviewed by an intimidating Customs Agent, who will make you feel like you've done something terrible, even if you haven't. I was dreading the interview, but I was also dreading being trapped in the lineup forever and/or The Van overheating and breaking down due to the hours of idling.

Apparently some renegade thugs had made a run for the border (really, this does happen outside of movies) and it had caused traffic to just completely stop moving. Or so some guy told us through our open window. He was really a little too excited about it. I'd have been more excited to GET GOING.

...., Izzy said, in a total cut-you-dead way. The guy looked flustered and carried on. I wish I was pretty enough to convey, through one grunting sound, all that she conveyed. She flipped down the mirror and started inspecting her eyebrows. "God, I wish I'd brought eyebrow tweezers," she said.

"I hate tweezing," I said.

"Mmmm," she said. "I can tell. Your eyebrows are really natural. They look ... great." She shivered and stuffed her knees up under her sweater. "This is weird, don't you think?"

"What?" I said, trying to see my eyebrows in the mirror. The mirrors in The Van were really old and hazy. Or else my contacts were dirty. I used to pluck all the time, I just decided I didn't like the pain.

Besides, I don't think they look bad.

"You and me going on a trip together," she said.

It took me a minute to remember what she was talking about. "Not really," I said. "Look, we were both bored and needed an adventure. It's not a big deal. It doesn't mean that we're, like, best friends or something,"

"I know," she said, rolling her eyes. "I wasn't suggesting that we were."

Which led to an uncomfortable silence. The truth was that I'll never forgive her for trying to steal Brad or for locking me in the bathroom at the hockey game or spelling my tattoo wrong (and talking me into it to begin with). If you think about it, it's sort of her fault that we broke up.

In a way, it's slightly possible that I'm using her because I'm afraid of going to California by myself to win him back. I'm not afraid of winning him back. I'm just afraid of being on the road alone.

I needed moral support. Obviously, she was a weird choice, but it's not like people were lining up to come with me. It's just not a good idea to go alone. I mean, what if I got killed by a serial killer at a truck stop? These things happen, you know.

"My best friend went away to college," she said. "This van smells weird." She rolled down the window and we both nearly instantly froze to death.

"Argh," I said. "Roll it back up!" Which took about ten minutes of wrestling. I'll admit that some parts of The Van aren't exactly in tiptop shape.

"Yeah," I said. "Mine, too. My best friends, I mean. Like what you were saying before. They've gone to, well, college and New York."

"I know," she said. "Duh. I probably know more about you than you know about me. Hey, do you have any other music?"

"I know plenty about you," I said, which wasn't true. But whatever. I knew she was basically annoying and pretty and shallow.

"Don't!" But before I could stop her, she'd jammed a cassette into the tape deck.

"Argh!" I screamed. Because there was a reason why the tape deck was empty — and that's because tapes get jammed in there and can't ever come out.

"What's your problem?" she said.

"Now it's stuck forever," I said.

"Whatever," she said. "I love Duran Duran. It will be like the theme music to our road trip."

"How could you love Duran Duran?" I said. "My DAD loves Duran Duran."

"They're retro," she said. "They're cool."

"Oh," I said. Every once in a while, I get the feeling that the whole world knows what's cool except for me. Like I missed school the day that the "cool handbook" was handed out. Only a handbook about cool would be uncool by default.

"Do people even SAY cool anymore?" I said out loud. Great, now I sound like Jules.

Izzy looked at me. I swear, her eyes filled with tears. "Totally," she said. Which I now realize is pretty much Izzy's response to everything in the world. I sort of felt like apologizing, but not really. She so far has insulted my taste in music, my eyebrows and the smell of my van. What do I have to be sorry about? Being snarky? As if there was an alternative. I glared out the window and debated the merits of making Izzy get out and find her own way home while I carried on alone.

But then I thought about how I'd probably not be able to handle being alone.

In fact, just thinking about it made me start to hyperventilate.

"Quit breathing like that," she said. "I'm going to write in my blog."

"Whatever," I sighed. Her little blonde ringlets were

making me mad. It didn't make any sense, but for a minute, just seeing her sitting there, hunched over MY computer writing in MY van, I hated her for not being Kiki. Or Jules.

Or even The Cat for that matter.

It was going to be a long trip.

We took a picture of the Peace Arch instead of writing about it. I mean, what is there to say? It's an Arch. It was built for Peace. Gateway to the U.S., and all that, via the booming metropolis of Blaine, Washington.

On the plus side, whenever I take a picture, I'm taking notes, so it's sort of like the book is writing itself!

Picture: Peace Arch Park — Blaine, WA & Surrey, B.C. It's an Arch. For Peace. There's an admission fee. We didn't go in because who wants to lose their place in line? It's, er, big.

Totally Izzy!
Date: November 28
Mood: Bored
Weather: Cold
Haley: Annoying

Hey, all y'all out there in blog land. Sorry I haven't updated for ages, but like I was saying before, I'm currently on a road trip with Haley "The Hippie" Harmony. If y'all read back to last year, you'll remember how I had to go camping with her and she was such a whiner. It was SO fun too. She really brings me down! I can see why she wasn't a cheerleader. This girl is just not cheery. Or a leader, for that matter.

Who would have thought she and I would have ended up here? It's complicated, but I promise, it won't be boring at the end of it all. She's nice enough and everything, but like we talked about before (see: Love and Other Good Stuff), she can't stand in the way of me and Brad. Oh, Brad. The real funny part is that she practically forced Brad to break up with her by being so weird and now she's going down there to totally get him back. What she doesn't know is that she's going to have competition. And she's not looking all that good, frankly. She shaved her head (?), don't ask (I know I don't want to) and she's all big eyes and weird clothes. I'm like the bad guy in this story, I guess, but I'm not a bad person.

I'm totally doing it for the right reasons. Think about it: remember how I told you that my mom totally let the boy she loved get away and ended up marrying my dad because she was getting old and stuff? And they pretty much hate each other and fight all the time? Imagine if she'd gone after the boy she loved instead. That's what I'm doing. Hey, I want my kids to be happy!

And, look, I'm not ALL bad. (Post your comments and I'll totally read them, but not if they tell me not to go through with this!!!!) I mean, I'm travelling with her in this stinky van and everything and being a good friend by listening to her talk. (Did you know her mom is a nun? Total weirdness.) And it's been good for a few giggles — although I don't need to tell you that I can find the funny in anything! I was, after all, in the

Optimists Club! I'm just very upbeat, I can't help it.
Don't hate me.

You can hate her, though. Haley. She's really totally high-strung, this girl. She reminds me of one of those horses that's so wound up he's shaking and foaming. Not that she's foaming! Ha ha! But she does shake sometimes.

Why? Because she's scared of everything. She's always talking about different things that can kill you, like botulism or a stranger at a rest stop. Totally paranoid. And her brows are MAJORLY unruly. I probably shouldn't be typing this on her laptop, but it's not like she'll be bright enough to figure out the password (HaleySucks) and I don't want to forget anything 'cause it's all good stuff for y'all to read. Like, it gives you a good idea of who all the characters are in my story.

I think I'm really maybe an awesome writer! And also I was reading somewhere that if an author is good-looking their book sells better, and I think we all know that I'm totally cuter than Haley. Not to be mean or anything!

You know, I read a lot of blogs, and like totally lots of people have been getting book deals because their blogs are so funny. So I am writing a book about this trip after all, just not the book that Haley thinks we're writing (some kind of humour/travel book, like there's a market for that?). It will be a better book. And I'll call it "Love and How to Chase It: The Non-Stalkers' Guide to Catching the Boy." Or something like that. You know, it's all still in the planning stages. And I've got lots of time to plan, you know, to write it all out in my brain.

So while Haley talks (or ignores me), I've invented this fun game of seeing how many times I can spell Brad's name using passing licence plates! You know, it's like karma! And believe you me, there are going to be lots of passing licence plates! Because this stinky old heap doesn't move very quickly.

Peace out, kiddies.

The Last Word

New Stuff: *puffy vest from the Gap, totally necessary because it's freezing out here.*

Calories consumed today: *680, so far, which means I've still got 320 left for dinner! Yahoo!*

Number of guys who have flirted with me: *7 (if you count all four of the guys in the car a lane over, who may or may not be laughing at this stupid ugly van, but are totally into me because they keep looking and smiling). Oh, and one more thing. Y'all can stop writing to me and telling me that I sound stupid and Southern because I say "y'all." I'm not Southern. I'm Canadian. OK? I just like the way it sounds, like Reese Wither-spoon (and a lot of people tell me I look like her). Maybe you'd rather I said "eh" all the time, but guess what? Canadians don't do that. And if you must know, I never say "y'all" when I'm talking, just when I'm typing. It's like I have an accent when I type! I like to think that I'm, like, channelling my inner Reese. So y'all take THAT.*

Three hours later.

"Where you going?" The customs official stuck his head through the window. His nose wrinkled. "What's that smell? You girls smoking pot in there?" He couldn't have sounded any more gruff or serious if he tried. Even his hair looked angry. It was bristly and spiky. Not that mine wasn't, but you know what I mean.

"NO," I said loudly. "I'm opposed to the use of marijuana as a recreational drug."

"I'm sure," he said dryly. He looked over at Izzy. "Hey," he said.

"Hey," she twinkled back. What is WITH her? Does she have to flirt with everyone? I mean, really.

I cleared my throat.

"We should take a look in your van, girls," said the guy, going back to his bored face again.

My hands started shaking a bit. I have no idea why I feel guilty for things I haven't done. I haven't done anything! My dad might have smuggled marijuana over the border back in the day, but I AM NOT MY DAD.

Izzy giggled. "That guy is totally cute!" she said.

"Whatever," I mumbled, following the cones to the pull-off area.

We got out of the car and immediately about four guys in uniform descended on The Van and started pulling everything apart. Which was pretty upsetting because it had taken me a long time to pack everything just so. Also, it was freezing.

"Any reason why you're taking skis to San Diego?" he said.

"No," I said.

"Yes," Izzy said.

"I mean, yes," I said. "They're a gift. For, er, a friend."

"Uh huh," he said, inspecting them carefully as though they might be a block of cocaine in disguise.

"Hey!" said Izzy. "We could totally put this in the book."

"Yeah," I said sourly. My heart was beating really hard and I could feel myself starting to hyperventilate. I mean, what if they found something? There was nothing to find, but maybe Dad left something in there. He DID drive The Van to work last week. I swear, I nearly was having a stroke when they came back and said, "You're good to go, have a good trip."

We were just kind of standing there, not knowing where to go or anything. That was it? They didn't even put the stuff back properly. But I wasn't going to let it ruin the mood of the trip.

"Great," I said. "We're through!"

"Huh," said Izzy. She looked really bummed out.

"What's wrong?" I said.

"I don't know," she shrugged. "I thought that guy might want my number."

"IZZY," I said. "Seriously, why would you care? He lives in a different city."

She gave me a weird look. "I don't know," she shrugged and giggled. "It's no big dealio. Let's hit the road!"

So we did.

Honestly, sometimes I think she's so weird. I just don't get her at all.

Picture: The World's Largest Egg, Winlock, WA
That's a big egg. It's all decked out with the American flag. Apparently, it's some sort of tribute to 9-11. Not sure how a giant egg connects to terrorism, but whatever. Really big egg. Really cold outside so couldn't investigate for too long.

Picture: Mount St. Helens, WA
Big volcano. Did not get out of Van. Too cold.

Sunday, November 30
Noon-ish
Dear Junior:

Well, we had our first night in The Van. To be honest, I thought this whole trip was going to take longer. For example, Washington State. I figured we'd stay a couple of nights there, at least. Or even a week? Well, ha. It turns out you can drive all the way through the state in only a few hours. And the I-5? Most boring highway known to man. (With some good tourist attractions, if you consider looking at an eleven-foot egg to be "good.") (Which it *is*, come to think of it, because it fits into the Quirky part of the Quirky guide.)

I just can't help but think we missed a lot of good stuff. For example, the world's longest driving beach (you can drive on it!), which was on the other highway. And when we were at the Egg, we ran into "Richie" (who had a very weird, hot pink complexion), who told us about some kind of UFO landing strip that we'd missed.

Oh well.

OK, so it wasn't totally boring, what with all the honking and stuff because The Van doesn't move as fast as other cars. Anyway, we pulled into the first spot that looked OK past Mount St. Helens, a billion miles off the highway, which we thought was a good idea because sleeping in a city seemed scary. We got onto all these side roads and I think we ended up north of the mountain again. Who knew? It was dark and it's not like we could ask anyone. So eventually we stopped. NOT in a rest stop.

I had this idea that NOT sleeping in a rest stop would be a good way to avoid being murdered. I don't know why I'm obsessed with the concept of being killed in a rest stop, but I saw an episode of Oprah once where I saw this guy interviewed who wrote a book about people being afraid and stuff, and the point of it was that sometimes you are afraid for a reason. Like sometimes, it's your INTUITION and not just PARANOIA.

Izzy says I'm terrifyingly paranoid and that I probably DO have a brain tumour. I must say she isn't as perky after a whole day or two of sitting in a smelly van, NOT that my van smells, but you know what I mean. She got pretty cranky when she found out that we were sleeping in here. Honestly, she couldn't have been paying attention to ANYTHING when we were planning the trip. She's kind of a ditz. She wanted to pay to sleep in a Motel 6, but it was about $60 and I thought that was a waste of money. We don't HAVE that much money between us, frankly, not enough for that. I thought it was cool to sleep in The Van.

OK, it was freezing.

Really, really cold.

There was frost on the inside of the windows, that's how cold it was. Hopefully, we won't get hypothermia or anything. If by "we," I mean "I." If Izzy gets hypothermia, I'd have good reason to somehow send her home. Though how she'd get there, I have no idea. Maybe I could just drop her on the doorstep of a hospital, like how people leave babies at churches in baskets.

Only she's not a baby.

We slept in sleeping bags and layers and layers of clothes. It's not like you can get frostbite in Washington in November. It was close to freezing or colder. I kept thinking about people that I'd seen on the Discovery Channel sleeping in tents in blizzards on Mount Everest in 30-below-freezing weather and I figured if they could survive that, we could survive this.

I didn't get much sleep, I must admit.

Not that this had everything to do with the cold, and not a little something to do with Izzy, who snores more loudly than my dad and The Cat combined.

I've been thinking about it (and believe me, there is lots of time for zoned-out thinking while driving down The Most Boring Highway in the World™) and I think Izzy doesn't like me any more than I like her. But I can't figure out why she came if she doesn't. Life is so weird. We always end up doing stuff with people we don't like and then we look over at them and we think, Why are you in my life?

I have to get over the idea that none of my friends like me, I guess. Maybe she does. Maybe this is how people who like me behave: hypercritically and rudely. Come to think of it, everyone treats me that way except my dad.

I always thought Jules didn't really like me (she doesn't). I used to think that Kiki was different, but she always sounds irritated with me too.

I'm actually dying to call Kiki on my cellphone because last time I talked to her she sounded homesick. Don't get me wrong, she was still overachieving like nobody's business, but she said, "Hey, I wish I was there so we could go for a run," which sounds a lot like she misses home. I can just tell. She's not my best-ish friend for nothing. Anyway, I'm sad that she's coming home for Christmas and I'll miss her because I'll still be on the road with Dizzy Izzy.

I should be writing my book.

One more thing: I haven't called Brad to tell him that we're coming. I think I should, don't you? Or not? I wonder if he wants to see me? I'm weirdly nervous about it and I keep thinking about him. Letting him break up with me was the dumbest thing ever. I miss him. I remember once when we went bungee jumping and it was so much fun. Well, except for the terrifying height and the bitter cold.

Actually, it wasn't that fun, but that's not the point, is it?

Anyway, as I was saying, we had our first night in The Van. We parked in this old gas station. It was clearly deserted, so it hardly mattered. It kind of sucked to squat and pee outside, though. I may or may not have fallen over and scratched my skin badly on a broken bottle, which hopefully won't give me tetanus.

It was the quietest place I've ever been, I think. It kind of weirded me out to be in such a small town so close to what amounts to the busiest highway I've ever seen. The sign said it had a population of 185. We figured they wouldn't mind us using the parking lot at an old gas station. How were we to know that it was scheduled for demolition that morning?

I can tell you, there are few worse ways to wake up in the morning from The Worst Sleep Ever™ than having five or six ugly construction guys knocking on your windows and shouting about hippies. I mean, at first I was terrified, but then I was just mad. They didn't have to be so rude.

OK, I admit I was scared to death. I thought they were serial killers for sure. It took me about fifty miles for my hands to stop shaking. Unfortunately, it was fifty miles in the wrong direction because I was so flustered I accidentally went "north" instead of "south." It was an easy mistake to make! It could have happened to anyone.

Besides, it's not like we're in a hurry. What's the rush? We need to go more slowly so that more happens for the book.

Love,

Road-Girl

"I want to drive for a while," said Izzy, pushing the laptop off her lap. "At least I know the difference between north and SOUTH." She wasn't even writing anything, she was practising drawing using the mouse.

"You don't have a licence," I said. "No way."

Truthfully, I wanted her to drive too. My eyes were starting to cross from the boring highway and lack of sleep.

I yawned.

"I know!" she said. "I'm totally tired too! I don't think I slept at all last night!"

"Huh," I said scathingly. I didn't even have the energy to point out that she'd actually snored all night at about the same volume as a housecat in a leg-hold trap.

"I was awake for soooo long!" she said. "It was so cold! I can't imagine how you slept! I didn't sleep at all!"

I could feel my blood pressure going up. I swear, I could feel a tiny popping in my brain, that's how bad it was. It was all I could do to not yell, "DO YOU SNORE WHEN YOU ARE AWAKE THEN? BECAUSE ONE OF US WAS DOING AN AWFUL LOT OF THAT!" But I didn't because I'm trying to get along.

"I can drive," she said. "Who would know?"

"The state troopers when they pull us over?" I said, flicking on the windshield wipers. It was starting to rain. The combination of rain and the road was making me nearly comatose. I yawned and nearly had a heart attack when the phone suddenly rang.

Of course, it wasn't anyone interesting (e.g. Brad, Kiki, even Jules), it was Melody. She's taken to phoning about every six hours.

"Hey!" she said. "It's me!"

"Hi, Melody," I said, rolling my eyes at Izzy.

"Hi, Haley! Just checking on you!"

"Well," I said. "We're driving, that's about it! Thanks for calling, though. Bye!"

I don't know why she irks me so much, she just does. I took a deep breath and held it.

"Wow," said Izzy. "You're totally uptight. She's just being nice."

"I know," I admitted. "She just doesn't have to be nice every six hours, you know?"

"My mom hasn't called at all," she pointed out. She bit her lip. Was she going to cry?

"Uh," I said. "Well, mine hasn't, either. Melody is NOT my mom."

"Whatever," she said. "I just think you have a nice relationship. She's cool."

I bit my tongue because, well, what was she basing that on? That one night when Izzy came for dinner and Melody had to leave in the middle and go lie down because the baby was kicking her ribs and she kept crying because it hurt so much?

"My mom's a *nun*," I said. I don't know why I brought it up, just to make conversation about something I didn't really want to talk about, I guess. In other words, I wished I hadn't.

"Get over it," snapped Izzy. "I mean, sorry. I'm just totally sensitive because my mom and I just totally don't get along, you know?"

"Sure," I said. "Why not?" I didn't really want to know, but when you're in a van with someone, you have to ask their life story. Either that or listen to Duran Duran for the fiftieth time in a state and a bit.

Izzy shrugged. "I don't know," she said. "She totally wants me to go to Hollywood to become a famous actress because I totally look like Cameron Diaz[6] or like a skinny Reese[7]? But blah blah blah blah blah," she continued.

Honestly, I stopped listening after the Cameron Diaz part. Is Izzy just JULES in different clothing? Why am I surrounded by these perfectly beautiful women?

Why doesn't ANYONE look ordinary except for me?

After a while, she stopped talking and I turned Duran Duran back up again. I know I'm not a very good friend to tune her out, but I was concentrating on the road, OK?

Totally Izzy!
Hey, again! It's me. This isn't an official entry, it's like a P.S. to the last one. I have a funny thing to tell you! It's just that — and maybe you don't know this — Canada uses the metric system. Well, Haley (who isn't that bright, as y'all know) apparently forgot there was a difference. What a fluff-brain she is! What's really hilarious is that even though this deathtrap stink-bus doesn't move very fast, it moves so slowly it actually earned a ticket for GOING TOO SLOW! From a totally NOT CUTE policeman, who may actually have been a really manly woman. I couldn't tell! I could tell that he/she wasn't into flirting, though.

Totally.

---

6 She does NOT look like Cameron Diaz.
7 She most certainly doesn't look like Reese Witherspoon, either. Oh, OK, maybe a little. DAMN.

So Haley apparently didn't get the memo about the fact that the U.S. uses MILES and not KILOMETRES. Which is funny, if you think about it. I mean, duh, everyone knows that, don't they? Wasn't it obvious that everyone was passing us?

Ha ha ha!

This trip is going to be so freaking funny.

Picture: Bridge between Vancouver, WA and Portland, OR Please note Izzy's facial expression in the picture. Look, none of it was my fault. We found our way back onto the I-5 again, but it wasn't easy. And we stopped for gas in this little town and she offered to pump it, which was good, she should do something. It's not my fault that the pump didn't have an automatic shutoff and her clothes got soaked with gasoline spray. I made her throw them out. Hence the angry look.

Granted, that's not really a tourist attraction, but still, it counts.

6:15 p.m.

Izzy was slumped over the keyboard. I sat across from her at the first Denny's we came to and stirred my coffee frostily, or as frostily as I could muster.

"I didn't mean to delete it," she said for the billionth time.

"Fine," I said. "I accept your apology." To make a long story short, she accidentally (if by "accidentally," I mean "totally intentionally because it's impossible to do accidentally") deleted my trip-book file. So we have to start again with NOTHING.

The fact that I hadn't actually written anything good yet is BESIDE THE POINT. I have some pictures! Not very many because I didn't want to fill up the whole camera, but we still have some, and that's a start.

Also, she doesn't know that. She feels terrible (she SHOULD) because she thought I had done an outline and whatnot. So I'm mad at her like I would be if she had deleted a thousand pages of writing, which might not be fair as I hadn't written anything, but the truth is that Izzy's mere presence is so infuriating I can hardly breathe.

It can't be good for my health to be around her. I'll probably have a stroke or small cardiac infarction (heart attack) before this trip is over.

"Look," she said. "Let's try something different. OK? We'll write it like we're having a conversation! Look, I'll start." She grabbed the laptop and knocked over my coffee, which poured into my lap. I screamed and jumped up from the table, clawing at my pants.

OK, so I took OFF my pants. But I was being scalded! Scalds are the worst of all the burns. Luckily the restaurant was empty, except for the waitress, who was missing all her front teeth. She looked very sad, if you ask me. I mean, wouldn't you get some kind of fake teeth — even if they were cheap and plastic — instead of having that kind of hole in your mouth? She threw me a towel and I covered myself up with it.

Izzy was laughing so hard she snorted. This wasn't her prettiest feature. Then she choked on whatever mucous she was snorting.

Lovely.

"I'm going to choke to death!" she screamed. "Stop it! You're so funny!"

Now I for one find it annoying when someone repeatedly says, "You're so funny" when I'm not being funny. I was being BURNED and SCALDED. I ran into the washroom (which was gross, by the way) (see attached Picture) and checked my legs. They were a little red (see Picture) but not as bad as I'd thought. I tried to rinse my pants out in the sink and put them back on. I hate wearing wet clothing. Immediately my skin started itching. Which made me irritated. By the time I got back to the table, Izzy was typing her head off.

The Book
Introduction, by Izzy

The road unfurls beneath our wheels as the radio cranks out the music and we lean back and watch the states peel by the window. It's November and raining, and we're free to follow our dreams down the highway. Who needs college?

I mean, "unfurls"? Seriously? I hit delete, but on purpose. "ARE YOU SURE YOU WANT TO DELETE?" it asked.

Huh.

I clicked "yes."

Now Izzy isn't speaking to me.

Good, silence is golden.

Picture: My burned legs
No further explanation required.

7:30 p.m.

Paid for a motel room so we could get some proper sleep. Am too tired to think properly and nearly fell asleep behind the wheel, which was too scary to contemplate. At this point, I'd be happy to sell blood to pay for the extra cost of a proper bed.

Had fantastic dream wherein HBG took me to dinner at a fancy restaurant and I did not spill any food on my front, which, in real life, I probably would. If it happened. Which it wouldn't.

Note to Self: Stop dreaming about HBG and start dreaming about Bard, I mean Brad, your boyfriend, I mean exboyfriend, who you are going to woo back.

DECEMBER

Monday, December 1
3:15 p.m.

> **Picture**: The World's Smallest Park, Portland, OR
> OK, it's really like a plant pot with a tree and some tiny sculptures in it. I can't believe we drove around in circles for forty minutes to find this.

5:35 p.m.

> **Picture**: Paul Bunyan Statue, Portland, OR
> It's a big statue, but for some reason, it's not where the book says it is. Instead, it's inside this grungy weird building and the reason I look scared in the picture is because I am.

7:17 p.m.

I don't think Izzy spoke to me all day. She can be a total bitch when she wants to be, which is all the time. Perky, but still a bitch.

Even her hair and makeup look bitchy when she's mad. I should add that the amount of time she takes to apply makeup in the morning is about the same amount of time it probably took Sir Isaac Newton to discover gravity.

She started talking to me after about nine hours of blessed silence, during which (in between looking for quirky tourist attractions) I spent some time planning out my wedding to HBG, but not in a literal way, only in a brief, fleeting way.

OK, I spent a long time on it, deliberating between getting married on a beach in Hawaii or in Vegas in a slapdash romantic manner. Not that this would ever happen, as I am too young and he is Not Interested.

What is wrong with me? I must stop thinking about him.

So, anyway, in retrospect, I didn't mind the silence, to tell you the truth. It was soothing.

We gave up on finding the Church of Elvis, which was mentioned in our guidebook and sounded cool in a retro way, but apparently didn't actually exist. And by "we," I mean "me" because Izzy wasn't looking for it at all. She was painting her toenails and singing along with Duran Duran.

Between this music and Izzy's voice, I swear ... well, remember that guy who sued Mary Hart on *Entertainment Tonight* because her voice gave him seizures? I'm just saying it could happen.

Izzy looked up from her pedicure (the fumes were making me dizzy) in time to spot Lloyd Center and to squeal about shopping. I like shopping as much as the next person, but Lloyd Center is not exactly "quirky" or unusual or charming so doesn't really fit in with the theme of our book — MY book — or our trip for that matter.

I agreed to stop. Mostly because I had to pee, and if you don't pee when you need to, you could end up rupturing your bladder, which is a scenario I didn't want to entertain. Also, I was hungry.

I hate malls. Malls are just a reminder of my horrible life back home and the fact that I don't have any money to spend there.

Lloyd Center is a big mall, to me anyway. I'm used to something much smaller. It actually even has an ice rink in it. I know we're from a kind of small city, but I've never seen a mall with an ice rink. I know they exist. I wasn't raised in a bubble. I've just never actually seen one.

I can't say I'm crazy about the idea of everyone who is shopping being able to watch me skate, however.

"Cool," said Izzy. "Let's skate." Which I took to mean, "I'm really sorry I deleted your stuff and I'm not mad at you about wasting half the day looking for some random tourist attraction that doesn't exist, let's skate."

I wanted to skate. I like skating.

Sort of.

I like the *idea* of skating, in any event. I don't actually *like* to be cold. Or bruised. Or humiliated.

But ice reminded me of hockey, which reminded me of Brad, which made me feel closer to him. Brad! The boy-who-isn't-my-boyfriend-but-will-be-again.

I wonder if HBG is a skater. Probably not. I can't imagine Hugh Grant skating, so therefore I can't imagine HBG skating. There is actually a remote possibility that I've forgotten what HBG looks like and have just recast him as a young Hugh Grant (think *Three Weddings and a Funeral* Hugh and not *Bridget Jones* Hugh) instead of his actual self.

Not that it matters, because it's just a stupid crush, much like the stupid crush I had on JT that wasted my entire life so far. Well, not "wasted," but certainly "distracted" me from the life I probably was meant to lead, which was no doubt more glamorous and entertaining than driving down through the western states with Izzy Archibaud.

So we rented skates.

HUGE MISTAKE. Not the renting, in general, but the whole concept of skating.

Why, oh why, did we not just go to the Gap and go shopping? (Not that we need to go to the Gap as the Gap is exactly the same everywhere and we have one at home.)

No, we *had* to skate. I blame Izzy, who I'm starting to hate with a ferocity that rivals that of an angry small dog being held in Paris Hilton's purse. She, naturally, knows how to skate and proceeded to twirly-twirl around the ice with her hair bouncing like a shampoo commercial.

My hair was too short to bounce anyway, but even if it had been longer, it would not have been bouncing. Except off the ice, that is. With my head. Which is probably concussed.

Immediately (before I could even fall for the first time), Izzy found some boys to flirt with. They were cute, in that they were male and human. They were not HBG cute.

They weren't JT cute. They weren't even Brad cute. Not that I cared. I'm not able to flirt when I'm trying to stay upright on skates, and besides I have a boyfriend (or I'm about to get one back, but same difference, right?). One thing I will say is that I love the sound of skate blades on ice. Amongst the sounds I don't love are the sound of my head hitting the boards and the sound of my knees smashing on the ice.

And the sound of myself crying. I'm eighteen years old (almost!). Argh. I can't believe I cried. I'm beyond humiliated. I'm *devastatingly* mortified. I'm grotesquely suicidal with abject humility. I'm ...

I guess I should tell the story of what happened. There's not that much to tell. We stepped out on the ice and Izzy proceeded to do her imitation of Lynn-Holly Johnson in *Ice Castles*.

"Look at me!" she squealed. I'm not even kidding. She was making a total spectacle of herself.

I, on the other hand, was clinging to the boards. I only just remembered how awful and slippery ice was when I stepped on it. In an effort to not be a loser, I tried to push off a little bit. That was when one of the idiot males that Izzy was flirting with decided to turn and skate backward.

Because as we all know, everyone is desperately impressed by backward skating. OR NOT.

He flung himself backward so hard that I swear I was lifted off the ice and chucked unceremoniously head first into the boards, whereupon a fat kid — maybe seven years old — immediately fell onto me and twisted my knee and smashed it against the ice. I nearly passed out from the pain. I was lying there, seeing grey and weird lights (possible retina detachment) thinking, "Oh no! I hope I don't die here because then my dad will know that I'm not actually 'up north' and I'll have to explain everything," when out of the blue some guy in a suit — I'm not even kidding, it was a blue suit with pinstripes and a yellowish tie — came skating up to me and put his card into my hand. Which I could barely move from the frostbite I was getting from lying on the ice. (Why wasn't anyone helping me up, anyway?)

On his card, it said he was a lawyer. I just stared at him blankly.

"In case you want to sue!" he said helpfully.

"Are you kidding?" I said.

"You could be really hurt," he said, crouching down. "We at Hassle, Freak and Mortimer specialize in on-ice injuries!"

"Are you serious?" I said.

"Yes!" he said. He looked so proud of himself that I was almost distracted from the horrible bone-crunching agony in my knee and head.

"Can you help me up?" I said.

"No!" he said. "I've called 911. An ambulance is coming. You can't be moved, in case your neck is broken."

"My neck isn't broken," I said, trying to sit up. "Maybe my tailbone." Pain was shooting from my coccyx down my legs. And I was freezing. In fact, I was starting to shiver. This was really unbelievable. What would Bard, I mean Brad, say when he heard this story?

"Haley!" said Izzy, finally skating up to me. "Isn't this the best time ever?" Her cheeks were actually sparkling, I swear.

"Are you kidding?" I said.

"I think she's in shock," said the lawyer. "I've called an ambulance."

"Is she, like, totally crying?" said Izzy, bending over and looking so deeply into my eyes, it looked like she was going to kiss me or something.

"Get away!" I said. "Or help me up!"

"Don't move her," said the lawyer.

"They say not to move you," said Izzy loudly, like I was deaf and not just wounded.

It was only then that I noticed a crowd around the viewing area. There were about a hundred and fifty people watching me. Could it get any worse?

Yes.

Of course it could.

It could absolutely get much worse than you could even imagine. Because that's when the ambulances showed up. Well, they didn't actually show up, because that would be ridiculous. But paramedics with stretchers suddenly appeared. Only some of them must not have got the memo about how ice tends to be slippery, so they just kind of shot out onto the rink on their asses and the first stretcher nearly ran me over. The second group cleverly did not bring their stretcher onto the actual ice, but around the outside of the boards.

Not that I needed a stretcher or anything. I mean, please. I just hurt my knee. OK, and my head. I had that horrible ringing feeling in my skull, which I'm sadly altogether too familiar with.

I may have cried.

Not because of the pain so much as the Rampant Bad Luck™ that I seem to be plagued with. Seriously, I've never even heard of anyone having the same degree of RBL as I have had. And I'm not even eighteen yet, for heaven's sake. What if this goes on for the rest of my life? By the time I'm fifty, I'll be in a full-body cast as a sheer protective measure against further breakage.

I wiggled my knee, which hurt enough that I nearly fainted. The ambulance guys were sliding around me, trying to figure out how they could lift me up without slipping and falling, which was when I inadvertently kicked Izzy with my skate.

I did NOT mean to do it, I swear. And it made the tiniest of all cuts on the side of her hand. You'd think she was hemorrhaging away her lifeblood after having her arm eaten off by a tiger shark the way she carried on. Naturally, because she has long-ish blonde curly hair and perfect teeth, she got all the attention and I was left to languish on the ice, shivering.

Life isn't fair. I'm working on a new theory about how pretty people get all the breaks, and attention from ambulance attendants.

In any event, finally, after they'd put a Band-Aid on her little cut and helped her off the ice, they hurled me unceremoniously onto the stretcher and took off my skates, which caused unknown further damage to my knee. They weren't very gentle. I'm sure if I'd had better hair, it would have been an altogether different story. Also, my eyes were puffy from crying and my lips were BLUE FROM COLD. They started to wheel me out when they were approached by the other team of ambulance guys and their stretcher. I swear, a fourteen-minute debate ensued about who had the right to take me to the hospital. This seemed to wind down when they both decided to bill me and both of them took my Canadian health insurance information. And my credit card number.

Eventually, after what felt like forever, I got to the hospital (surprisingly empty — I swear hospitals at home always have ten-hour waits in the emergency room) where some guy named Ashley (seriously, a guy named Ashley, not very manly) very quickly wound my leg up in a bandage and some kind of cardboard splint, gave me some crutches (if by "gave," I mean "charged me $200 for") and declared it a minor sprain, and dismissed me. For some reason, I couldn't mention my tailbone, which hurt more than my knee by a long shot. It just felt wrong. Besides, what could they do if it was broken? It's not like you could put it in a cast.

And if the crutches were $200, I hated to think how much an X-ray would be.

Also, it was embarrassing. Who breaks their backside? Other than me. And the pain was confusing. It hurt so much that I couldn't think straight, or maybe that was the concussion.

At least it was warm in the hospital. They had those hot sheets. I love those. Particularly after I've been lying down on the ice for an hour.

Oh, and then the guy I thought was a doctor (but who was actually a nurse) asked the ambulance guys to go get him some spicy chicken wings.

"I can't believe you *cried*," said Izzy, as she helped (read: shoved) me into The Van.

"It hurt!" I said. "I think I broke my coccyx!"

"Your coccyx?" she said. "What IS that? How do you even know that word? Besides, the guy said you, like, sprained your knee."

"Why are you MAD at me?" I said. "I didn't do it on purpose! It's my tailbone. My knee is fine." Which, embarrassingly, was true. I mean, it was all wrapped up in a billion elastic bandages ($75 worth) but it really didn't hurt that much at all.

"You broke your ASS?" she yelled.

"No!" I said. "I think it's just cracked. I didn't want to pay for the X-ray. It was probably $350!"

"Why don't you have insurance?" she said.

"I don't know," I said. "I do! But they said it was Canadian so I had to pay up front and then bill it to my insurance company when I got home! I got confused. I have no idea."

"You didn't plan this very well!" she said.

"I didn't plan it at all!" I yelled. "No one said anything about skating! I just wanted to see the World's Largest WHATEVER might be in this city! I didn't want to skate!"

My tailbone was killing me. There was absolutely no comfortable way to sit and drive. I was going to have to let her do it, but I couldn't. I unwrapped my knee because it was the only thing I could do in order to work the pedals. What kind of idiot would go on a road trip with someone who doesn't have a licence?

Me, that's who.

"Let's just go home!" I said. "I'll drive."

"BUT I WANT TO SEE BRAD!" she yelled.

Then there was a weird silence. I mean, naturally there was a weird silence.

"WHAT?" I said, just as loud.

"I mean, you," she said, blushing.

"What?" I said. I put my head down on the steering wheel, which started the horn honking. Which made me jump, which made me hit my forehead on the dash.

I felt like crying again.

"I mean, YOU want to see Bard! I mean, Brad." She stared straight ahead. My head hurt and I felt dizzy.

"You drive," I said, finally. "How much worse can this get?"

Secretly, I was thinking that maybe if she got caught driving, she'd get arrested or thrown in jail or both and I could escape.

We swapped seats (moving was almost too painful to bear) and she started The Van, which immediately stalled.

"What are you doing?" I said.

"I'm trying to start the car!" she said, turning the key again. It made that sound that cars make when you try to start them and they've already been started.

"Don't wreck my van!" I yelled. I was a tiny bit worried about throwing a clot from my injury. What if I died from having a broken butt bone that I didn't tell anyone about?

I took the stupidly expensive elastic bandage and made a little cushion for my butt, which was marginally better, but not really.

"We could stop and get you one of those inner tube cushions," she said helpfully as she jerked The Van back onto the road. "You know, like they give people with hemorrhoids? My mom totally has one, she says it rocks."

"Uh," I said.

"For real, Haley," she said. "You should try, look, I'll just pull into this all-night drugstore and grab one for you!"

"OK," I said. Frankly, I was too tired to debate the point. Also, they'd given me some sort of painkiller for my pain, which was starting to help in that I was feeling completely disoriented.

It felt like Izzy was gone for an hour, but maybe it was two minutes. I've really no idea. She came tearing out of the store like her hair was on fire (sadly, it wasn't) with the inner tube thing clutched in her hands, and leaped into the driver's seat. She then peeled out of the parking lot and Junior fell off my lap.

(Sorry, Junior!)

"Settle down," I said.

"Haley," she said, "I think it's better if we don't talk now."

So we didn't. I blew up the inner tube thing, which made me lightheaded. Blowing up balloons also has this effect on me. Anyway, she was right. It did totally help.

Tuesday, December 2

7:00 a.m.

Can't believe I slept so well! Must have been the drugs. Izzy is still snoring. I wonder if she has sleep apnea. Probably she does.

Oh well.

Won't tell her about it. I'm sure eventually she will figure it out for herself.

7:12 a.m.

Am slightly bored. Would go for a walk but tailbone is still in too much pain. Have bruise the size and shape of India on my butt. It looks a bit like a very bad tattoo.

Would never put a tattoo on my lower back. Hate lower back tattoos.

Actually, hate tattoos in general now that my arm is forever ruined by Bard.

Oh well, maybe Brad will think it's funny.

Unlikely, though. Will probably just take it as further evidence of my lack of good girlfriendness.

Sigh.

7:20 a.m.

Still bored.

Wish I could break into Izzy's locked files. Wonder what she is writing about on here.

Maybe should do some work instead of just wasting time.

Wish Izzy would stop snoring. Wonder if it would be wrong to gently place a pillow over her head.

Hmmmm.

The Book
by Haley

The state of Washington goes by very quickly. Make sure you exit off the highway once in a while so you can actually see something (other than rest-stop bathrooms) (and Denny's) instead of just rocketing through the entire state in one fell swoop without really noticing, and being distracted by the tape in the deck which is stuck and playing the same set of songs over and over until you feel like you might go nuts from it and you've missed the whole state and have nothing to write about in your travel book. It's possible that the quirkiest sites exist off highways other than the I-5.

Also, never EVER go ice-skating in the middle of a road trip. It's dangerous and stupid.

The Pacific Northwest is cold in November.

This is a horrible book. I can't write. Someone please shoot me.

Noon-ish

Conversation with Kiki:

Me: You'll never believe where I am!

Kiki: Where are you?

Me: Standing in a parking lot at McDonald's in Portland, freezing to death.

Kiki: Why are you calling me?

Me: I'm waiting for Izzy to come out of the bathroom. She's been in there for about twenty minutes.

Kiki: I'm thinking of dropping out of pre-med and going into journalism. I want to be a writer.

Me: What? You can't be a writer. I'm the writer.

Kiki: What? What does that have to do with anything? We can both write. Stephano says.

Me: Oh no.

Kiki: What?

Me: The Van has a flat tire!

Kiki: So, change it.

Me: I don't know how!

Kiki: Of course you do. How hard can it be?

Me: I have to go.

Kiki is going to be a writer? Hate Kiki. I'm sure she'll be a better writer than me and will publish dozens of successful, amusing yet insightful travel books. And she WOULD know how to change a tire.

Twenty minutes later

Have managed to find jack under the carpet in back of Van. WHERE is Izzy? Can no longer see her through restaurant window sipping her coffee pensively (if by "pensively," I mean "irritatingly slowly while flirting with some boys at next table"). Can't go in and find her having embarrassed self in front of boys already by getting hiccups from too much caffeine.

Have weird feeling that, much like in *The Vanishing* (starring Kiefer Sutherland), she's been kidnapped by a psychopath and buried alive.

Or she's in the bathroom fixing her hair.

Somehow, don't care.

Twenty minutes later again

Have managed to get jack under Van and lifted it up, no thanks to the boys who just left the restaurant and offered to help as I was obviously "too stupid to do it myself."

What makes people so rude? Don't they know I have a sprained knee (sort of) (not that it actually hurts) and a broken butt?

I'm a feminist! I can change a tire! Men are like fish without bicycles or whatever!

Izzy should be doing this. I hope she has been kidnapped and buried.

Only not really.

Five minutes later

Found Izzy in bathroom. She refuses to come out until the tire is changed. Nice.

Fifteen minutes later

Nice trucker in parking lot (resembling trucker who kidnapped Kurt Russell's wife in that other kidnapping/road-trip movie) changed tire for me. I was only slightly afraid. But when The Van fell off the jack and nearly crushed me to death, it seemed the safer of the two options.

Will tell Izzy I did it myself.

Am weirdly proud of self for changing tire alone (albeit with the help of a pudgy man named Ron). I am woman! Hear me roar!

Twenty minutes later

Unfortunately, freak weather system (read: blizzard) has swept terrifyingly quickly (or not that quickly, but we've only just found out about it as have no radio and can't get weather forecasts from tape deck playing "Rio" over and over again) down the I-5. Have been forced to hole up in overpriced scary motel as is too cold in Van and we would likely have died of exposure.

Izzy still not speaking to me.

Frankly, can't remember why not. Izzy is reminding me too much of Jules.

Miss Jules.

I dialed Jules' number from the hotel phone. Please note, at the time, I had NO idea that it cost $5/minute. How could I know that? There was no sign posted. I'm not sure why I suddenly needed to talk to Jules. I actually wanted to talk to my dad, but was too afraid that Melody would answer. She's called four times today to say that she's been put on bedrest and it's giving her lots of time to call me with useful tips from Dr. Phil and Oprah. She totally monopolizes the phone and all I get to say to Dad is basically, "Hi! Bye!"

I miss my dad.

Anyway, Jules' answering machine came on. It played a song ("Bootylicious") and I was just leaving her a message when she picked up. She sounded all out of breath.

"What's wrong?" I said. "What were you doing?"

"Nothing!" she said. "I've got company! Why are you calling me?"

"I don't know," I said. "I'm on this road trip with Izzy. It's pretty ... um. Well, anyway. Maybe it wasn't a good idea."

"Probably not," said Jules.

"Don't be like that," I said. "Actually, it's kind of fun. A medium amount of fun anyway."

Now, I have no idea why I said that. This road trip is anything but fun, as evidenced by the cuts on my hands (the bolts on the tires were stripped and it was so cold and rainy that somehow I managed to skin all my knuckles and now will probably get tetanus and die), my throbbing coccyx, and the fact that Izzy is sulking on the other bed. If by "sulking," I mean "snoring."

AGAIN.

"I'm jealous," said Jules, in a tone that implied that she wasn't jealous. "I wish I had so much free time that I could just drive around pointlessly. But I'm SO super busy. You have no idea!"

"Yeah," I said. "I guess I don't. Tell me what's new. How's Scientology? Have you been hooked up with any stars yet?"

"Scientology?" she said blankly. "What are you talking about?"

"You know," I said. "You said you were going to be a Scientologist."

"God, Haley," she said. "I was probably kidding."

"It didn't sound like you were kidding," I said, confused. I didn't know whether to be relieved, or mad that she was such a flake.

"Whatever," she said. "Why are you calling? To bug me about religion?"

"No," I said. "I just wondered if ... I don't know. Just what you're up to."

"Well—," she started. "Oh, I should go!"

"Why?" I said. "Don't you want to tell me about all the glamorous stuff you're doing?" For some reason, don't ask me why, I kind of wanted to hear it. Sometimes listening to Jules talk is like watching an episode of a TV show you're not sure you like but can't stop looking at. Like *The O.C.*, only I like *The O.C.* Which has nothing to do with why I'm going to California. I mean, please. It's not like I believe, deep down inside, that if Adam Brody set eyes on me, he might fall instantly in love and recognize that I am really his soulmate.

I'd even abandon my stupid and embarrassing crush on HBG if that were to happen. Not that I have a crush, because I don't.

Adam Brody looks a bit like a dark-haired version of JT. Which means that he's probably an idiot.

"Blah blah blah," Jules said.

"What?" I said. "Sorry, I was distracted by ... um, a mouse."

"There's a mouse in your hotel?"

"No, not a mouse," I said. There was a silence. "Um," I said.

"Anyway, Todd is sleeping in the other room!" she hissed in a stage whisper.

"Who's Todd?" I asked.

"My boyfriend," she hissed again, then giggled. I rolled my eyes.

"OK," I said. "I'll let you go." For a minute I was kind of bummed out. As much as she bugs me, I do miss her.

"No!" she said. "I totally want to tell you about this party I went to the other day. You would have loved it. It was so cool. There were all these models there? Blah blah blah blah."

I must admit I was very sleepy. I'd taken the last painkiller from the hospital and it worked really suddenly. Sometimes that happens to me. I think I metabolize drugs differently than most people. (Hopefully, this is not an indication of some kind of dreaded liver disease.)

I wanted Jules to go on and on because it distracted me from the horrible fact that not only have I not successfully started The Book, but I'm trapped with some kind of Evil Malicious Izzy in a Motel 6 on the I-5. This is not what I planned!

"Blah blah blah," said Jules. It was sort of soothing, in a kind of boring way. (Models don't thrill me, they intimidate me and irritate me, so whatever.) I stopped listening around the time she started telling me that some hotel was paying her to walk around the lobby and look pretty so that people would think it was a cool model hangout.

I mean, seriously, that's a JOB? Hefty's was a job. Writing this BOOK is a job. Walking around a hotel lobby looking pretty? NOT A JOB!

NOT FAIR!

Izzy snored vigorously. I looked outside the window at the snow swirling down and the ice forming on the glass.

Jules rambled. Finally I fell asleep. I guess Jules eventually hung up because when I woke up with the sound of glass breaking, the phone was dead.

"IZZY!" I shouted. "Wake up! It's an earthquake! Get under the bed! Get into the doorway! Get into the bathtub!"

Izzy leaped out of bed like she'd been spiked by a hedgehog. (She had a crusty string of drool on her chin. Gross.) "What! What?" she yelled. "WHAT?"

I pointed at the window, which was pretty unnecessary as the howling wind blowing in should have been enough of an indication as to what happened. A huge tree branch stuck through it.

"It's not an earthquake!" she yelled. "It's a TREE!"

I giggled. I couldn't help it. I mean, really, it was the last thing I expected would happen. For some reason, I'd been thinking CALIFORNIA and BEACHES and SURFING. And here it was in December, somewhere in Oregon, freezing cold, and a tree was sticking into our window.

She smiled.

Then before I knew it, we were both laughing so hard we fell over. We laughed for ages, if by "ages," I mean "a few minutes." Then it was too cold to keep laughing.

"What do we do?" she said. "This is like the weirdest thing ever!"

"I don't know," I said. "I guess we change rooms?" I picked up the phone to call the desk but it was dead. So we had to bundle up (in all our clothes as we brought mostly summer stuff — for California) and run across the parking lot to the office to tell them what happened.

Which was fine, but the office was closed.

And unfortunately (or naturally, as the case may be, with my luck), the room locked behind us.

"Argh!" cried Izzy. I swear, there were tears in her eyes. "What are we going to DO?"

"I don't know," I said. It was really cold. And dark. The only thing that could make this worse would be something like, say, a pack of wild dogs.

"What is THAT?" cried Izzy. She was kind of clinging to me, which I didn't mind that much as I was getting a bit terrified. It was all too much like a scene from *The Blair Witch Project*, except without the videocamera and the woods and so on.

I heard something too.

"Um," I said. "It sounds like a dog?"

It was snowing really hard, so it was hard to see, but I could totally hear barking. "Argh!" she screamed. "I hate dogs!"

"I love dogs," I said. Which was true, but generally I loved dogs more when they were in someone's living room or on someone's leash. Or on TV.

The sound came closer.

"Shit!" Izzy screamed.

"Shut up!" I yelled. "The dogs will hear you!"

"What dogs?" she said.

"I don't know!" I yelled.

"I want to go home!" she yelled. She was really crying at this point. I kind of felt like crying myself, but for some reason I wasn't. I guess because she was, and it was bugging me. Besides, I changed a tire by myself! I was sure we could handle this.

"The Van!" I yelled.

"It's locked!" she said.

"I know," I said. "But I know how to get in." Which was true, because it actually never locked properly and I never got it fixed. We ran over to The Van. If by "ran," I mean "slipped all over the ice." I managed to work the door open and we fell inside. It wasn't much warmer in there than outside, but at least we were protected from the snow. And of course, we had the shiny silver blankets. Just a note about those shiny silver blankets — I know they are for "survival" and everything, but it was much like wrapping yourself in tinfoil. We did the best we could, though, with those and our sleeping bags. I guess, in spite of everything — the storm, the ghost dogs, the crisis and Izzy snoring — I must have fallen asleep, because when I woke up it was super quiet and all I could see through the windows was white.

OK, it was quiet except for the sound of Izzy snoring.

For a second I felt panicky, and then I felt relieved. I mean, something finally happened to us! Something for the book!

Unfortunately, the computer was in our hotel room.

"IZZY!" I yelled. Granted, I didn't need to yell because she was right beside me, but still. She shot out of bed and banged her head on the ceiling, which was oddly satisfying.

"What? What?" she said.

"It's morning," I said.

"Oh," she said. Then, "I guess we're talking to each other again."

"I guess," I said, and that was that.

> **Picture**: Tree sticking out of motel room, Beaverton, OR
> Seriously, we could have been killed. The tree, for the record, was some kind of fir — a grand fir, I think.

> **Picture**: Inside of new motel room, Beaverton, OR
> Pretty self-explanatory. Did you ever wonder how many people have slept on the same pillow as you at a motel? Gross.

Wednesday, December 10 (I think)

Dear Junior:

The blizzard is still raging. This reminds me of that old episodes of *Little House on the Prairie* where Laura had to walk through the field in a blizzard (or was it Mary?) and got lost right next to the barn and nearly perished.

There's five feet of snow outside the window and it's still falling. We are officially almost out of money and I have no more room on my Visa card. I think. To be honest, I'm too scared to look. Maybe the motel guy will give us a discount because we're trapped or because he thinks Izzy is cute.

Sometimes her gross flirtiness is useful.

On the plus side, the cellphone battery has finally died so Melody can stop calling me to give me home-decorating tips she's gleaned from watching twelve hours a day of the Home and Garden channel. On the plus side, I don't have to lie about the weather as I'm sure this kind of weather is exactly what is happening "up North" anyway.

Probably, the whole storm is bad karma from my lie about where I was.

On the minus side, if I have to spend one more minute with Izzy, I think my head may explode.

Things That Izzy and I Have Fought about:

1. The Book (we've both deleted each other's entries).
2. The cost of the motel.
3. Brad (why she cares, I have NO IDEA).
4. The motel soap.
5. TV (she likes watching stupid cop dramas and I like reality TV).
6. Eyebrows (mine).
7. Hair (also mine — who died and made her my critic?).
8. Money (we have none).
9. The number of calories in a club sandwich.
10. Whose turn it is to run across the parking lot to buy more sandwiches.
11. Whether we should keep going or go home.
12. Whether hockey is more interesting than baseball.
13. Whether or not God exists.
14. Whether or not we should have known to bring snow tires and chains.
15. Coke vs. Pepsi — which is REALLY better?
16. What to do if we're stuck here until Christmas.

As you can see, we pretty much disagree on everything. Which is why I'm at the coffee shop and Izzy is back in the room.

What was I thinking?

Love,

Little House on the Prairie Blizzard Girl

"How's work going?" Dad asks gently. Or at least, I interpret his tone as "gentle." It probably wasn't, because he doesn't know I'm upset. He can't know I'm upset because then I'd have to tell him why.

"I don't know," I said, twisting the payphone cord around in my hand before remembering how grossly germy payphones are. Did you know there are more germs on payphones than on public toilet seats? I saw it on TV. "I mean, work's great. I'm, uh, learning how to ski and stuff."

"I thought you hated snow?" he said.

"Oh, I DO," I said emphatically. "But skiing is fun! It's ... fun! Except, of course, I hurt my, um, back in a skating accident."

"Skating?" he said.

"Ha ha, did I say skating? I mean, skiing!" I said.

"Wow," he said. "Why didn't you tell Melody? She said she called you yesterday and the day before. When did it happen?"

"Oh, last week," I said. "I didn't tell her because ... I don't know. I guess I felt dumb."

There was a pause. "Well, we miss you," he said, finally.

That rankled a bit. Can't he just say, "I miss you"? Why does Melody even have to be in the subtext of our conversations?

"Yeah," I said. "Me too."

"Maybe I should come and visit you up there," he said.

"Up where?" I said. For a second, I forgot that he didn't even know where I was. He thought I was "up North." I could be dead and he wouldn't know it! In Oregon! "Right," I said quickly.

"There's something wrong with the call display," he said. "It said you were calling from Oregon."

"Weird," I said. "Must be a glitch. How's Melody?" I didn't ask for any reason except to change the subject, which worked. Dad used to NOT be a chatty person. Now? Totally different.

"She's great," he said. "Well, she's not great, she's on bedrest, but we've been having the greatest time hanging out in bed, eating popcorn and watching all our old favourite movies, like *The Breakfast Club*. Man, she just loves that movie!"

"Me too," I said. A tear escaped from my eye. That used to be our favourite movie to watch together. Now he doesn't need me anymore, he needs MMMMelody. I could hear The New Bird in the background, tweeting like no tomorrow. I could imagine what it was like in the house. Melody had probably turned my room into a nursery already. Suddenly, I was totally sorry for myself.

I hung up and slumped back to the table. Honestly, how could it be SNOWING on my trip to California?

This was The Worst Idea Of My Life (TWIOML).

Hey, maybe that's what I should call the book!

That I haven't written.

Maybe should write book.

Nah. Maybe should order another chocolate milkshake.

Nah. Have already blown healthy eating road-trip diet out the window by subsisting entirely on club sandwiches and fries.

Sigh.

Totally Izzy!
Date: December 11
Mood: Crazy!
Weather: The Worst Ever
Haley: Most Depressing Girl I've Ever Met!

So, My Bloggy Peeps, guess what? I'm stuck in the snow in No Place, Oregon with Haley the Hippie. It's crazy — or maybe it's just driving me crazy!

I should tell you, she has this picture of her and Brad (sigh!) taped to the inside of her computer. He's so dreamy! I keep looking at the picture to remind me what I'm here for! And that's LOVE, not this crazy trip! I don't even think she's written any more of her dumb book. In any event, she kicked me off the project. Apparently because I like Diet Coke better than Diet Pepsi, she can't stand the sight of me! I guess I'll have to try to get along because eventually the snow will recede (or our money will run out!) and we'll be on the road to Dreamboat Brad.

I kind of want her to call him and tell him that we're coming! He's going to be so surprised that I'm here. I wonder what he'll do. I bet he'll be happy because he'll know that I'm The One. I know it sounds like I'm a crazy stalker-girl with a stupid crush, but I'm not! I don't get crushes, totally not like Haley who always has one! Like before we started fighting, Haley admitted to me that she had a crush on JT (Brad's cousin, no less) for, like, ten years! Ha. Like he'd ever look at her twice! I used to go out with him when we were really young. He was a cutie! We looked good together, but it wasn't "love," you know? More like "luv."

Guess what? Haley's hair is starting to look cute, but don't tell her I said so. Very Natalie Portman, you know? I still think mine's nicer, though, because it's blonde and curly and hey, that's timeless, right? Not totally trendy and lame.

So I don't know but lately I've been thinking about stuff like church and whatnot, maybe because I miss it a bit, but not really. I mean, I'm totally a spiritual person!

It's just that I wonder what Jesus would say if he knew what I was doing (I know I don't talk about church very much on here, but believe me, I've always got it in my heart). Would he think it was wrong and crazy? I doubt it. He'd probably be all like, "You go, girl!"
Peace out, blog (and Izzy!) fans.
More later!
P.S. — It's stopped snowing! Whoo hoo!

The Last Word
Calories consumed: 847
Number of boys flirted with: 0
Number of boys TO flirt with: 0

Friday, December 12
Picture: Weird creepy things in the Enchanted Forest, Salem, OR

The clouds in front of our faces are because it's so cold. The fear in our eyes is because the statues are so creepy. And don't get me started on how claustrophobic I got in the tunnels. I had to breathe into a paper bag. But only for a few minutes.

Picture: Giant black crow statue (unclothed), Medford, OR

Apparently they dress this thing and then people steal its clothes? Go figure. Not much more to say about that. I guess it's more interesting than a giant ball of string or the like.

Saturday, December 13
11:11 a.m.

Izzy and I have come up with a peace pact. It went something like this.

Me: Look, I'm sorry if I've been weird or something. I'm just kind of worried about seeing Brad and stuff and I'm not good at being trapped in the snow and I feel bad about lying to my dad and I miss Jules and Kiki and I'm feeling really ... unquirky. Which is dumb because I'm supposed to be "quirky." Being "quirky" is harder than you might think.

Izzy: Yeah, me too. I mean, I'm sorry. I'm not "quirky." I don't even like the word "quirky." It's too nerdy.

Me: OK, fine. Let's not have a fight about it.

Izzy: Let's start over.

Me: OK.

Izzy: But I'm driving.

Me: No. I'm healed enough to drive and you aren't allowed. It's stupid and illegal.

Izzy: You didn't mind before!

Me: That was when I was in pain and on painkillers and out of it.

Izzy: So?

Me: I'm healed now! We've been in a motel for days. I'm fine!

Izzy: Whatever.

The sad thing is that Izzy, in all her horrible annoyingness, is probably the best friend I have right now.

And that's really depressing.

Izzy started singing along with Duran Duran and bopping her head around, so naturally I tried to tune her out and to write in my head. A great deal of writing books takes place in your brain, after all. There's no reason why I can't think and drive at the same time.

Procrastination is all very well and good, but it only gets you so far. Finally, you have to write something. I sat up straight (well, as straight as I could comfortably without putting too much pressure on my tailbone), which made my coccyx ache. I closed my eyes and felt my pulse in my knee. It was weirdly compelling, except it made me over-aware of my heartbeat, which made me wonder what would happen if it suddenly stopped or something.

"Argh!" screamed Izzy.

"WHAT?" I said.

"YOU CAN'T DRIVE WITH YOUR EYES CLOSED, YOU'LL KILL US!"

"Sorry," I said. I don't know what I was thinking. The thing is, that driving is very hypnotic, especially on long straight stretches. It starts to seem reasonable to close your eyes, you know?

"Concentrate!" I said out loud.

"What?" she yelled, over the music. I honestly can't see how she can still be liking this tape, but whatever. I guess it's better than having to make conversation. Besides, I will treat the background music like a mantra and let it help me think-write.

Hmmm. Thinking makes me think of HBG. I wonder what he's doing right now? The thing is that it would make so much more sense for me to end up with HBG than with Brad. HBG has a bookstore, and I'm going to be a famous writer. What could be a better match? And Brad, well, he's going to be a hockey star, which is great, but he'll be away a lot (like he has been already) and we'd never see each other.

I bet HBG is secretly rich. His accent makes me think that maybe he lives in a glamorous mansion and only runs a shabby mall bookstore as a hobby because he's passionate about books (ergo, also about writers).

I wonder if his mansion has an office in it that I could take over and make into my writing office. I saw Judy Blume on TV once and she has about eighteen houses, all of which have glamorous writer's offices in them.

Wonder if HBG has multiple houses. Not that wealth is important to me. I honestly totally believe that it's what's inside that counts.

But a nice room would probably help me write.

I closed my eyes.

"HALEY!" Izzy yelled.

"OK!" I said, and took the next exit, which luckily was a rest stop. I kind of scared myself, to tell you the truth. I could never be a long-distance trucker because my mind is too wandery for that. "I have to stop," I explained. "I'm inspired."

"Huh," she said, and slammed the door behind her and huffed off toward the coffee shop.

I started to type.

It was weird, but it sort of worked. I typed for a whole hour without stopping, after which I had about twenty pages. TWENTY! I couldn't believe it. I made myself not reread it. Because, you know how when you reread things? Sometimes you get freaked out that you wrote it? Because it doesn't sound like you? It was like that for me.

I fell asleep after that for a while. But I password-locked my entry first. I don't want Izzy reading it. Somehow, that would just wreck it.

Besides, she'd probably delete it if she found it.

Sunday, December 14

Picture: Palm Tree, near Yreka, CA

This really doesn't look like what I thought California would look like. Picture is taken through Van window. Note the weird cloud of smoke hovering in the air near the exhaust. Hopefully not a sign of impending car trouble.

"Come on," Izzy pleaded. "Let me read it."

"No way," I said. "Hey, look, a palm tree!"

She swung around, somehow grabbing the wheel in the process and nearly forcing us onto the shoulder of the road. It was a pretty grey day and kind of raining a bit (which was so much better than snow, it didn't bother me at all), and there in the haze was a palm tree.

"Whooo!" she yelled, in her cheerleader voice. Frankly, I think that cheers can be left behind once you graduate, but I gave her a high-five anyway in the interest of getting along.

"We're in California!" I said. Somehow it wasn't what I would have pictured. For some reason, apart from L.A., Hollywood, Disneyland and surfing spots, I hadn't really pictured northern California at all. And this seemed so ... grey.

"I'm going to call Brad now," I decided out loud. It just inexplicably felt right.

Conversation with Brad:

Me: So, it's me!

Brad: Uh.

Me: Haley!

Brad: Uh, wow. Huh. I was sleeping.

Me: Sorry, I woke you up.

Brad: No! That's OK! I mean, why are you calling me?

Me: I'm coming to see you.

Brad: ...

Me: To San Diego!

Brad: But I'm in Washington.

Me: What? I thought I heard you say you were in Washington.

Brad: I AM in Washington. But I'll be back in time for Christmas, and then I was going to go home. We're on the road. Playing, uh, hockey. You know.

Me: Oh.

Brad: Why are you coming to see me?

Me: Oh, look at the time! I have to go! See ya!

"Haley!" said Izzy. She was totally hovering over me and making me nervous. "What did he say?"

"Nothing!" I said, breezily. "No big deal."

"HALEY," she said. "What is it? I can totally tell that you're bummed."

"Fine," I said. "I didn't think that ... I mean, I ..."

"Haley," she said. "Tell me what he said!"

"He's in Washington," I said. I sort of laughed. I mean, of course he'd be away. Why wouldn't he? That's the whole point of hockey, that they travel all the time! They never stay in one place! That's why we had such a hard time back home! Because he was away so much!

"Washington," she said. She sat down with a thunk, which probably hurt because she's thin enough that sitting down hard might cause bruising. We were parked in yet another rest stop. I'm starting to think I should call this book *The Cool Girls' Guide to Rest Stops*.

I should say that the rest stops in California were totally different than in the other states. They were really nice. This one had showers and a souvenir shop attached. Both of us had wet hair from the shower. (Hers looking lovely and curly and mine just looking wet, natch.)

"We could go back!" she said.

"No way," I said. "No. Let's keep going. How much money do we have left?"

"I don't know," she said, waving her hands around. "Let's go back!"

"No," I said more firmly. I mean, the point of the trip was to see Brad, of course, but it was also to write my book. And it was starting to flow so well that I didn't want to wreck it. It would be pretty lame to have a book where we drove part of the way to San Diego and then went back. It would be like half a book! Not even a book! It would be an essay!

"I don't want to go to San Diego if Brad's not there," she said firmly.

I looked at her. "What?" I said.

"I mean," she said, looking flustered, "I want you two to get back together!"

"Whatever," I said, loftily. Suddenly, I didn't care that much if we did or didn't get back together. This trip was for me. Oh, and Izzy, I guess.

What WAS Izzy doing here anyway? I couldn't even remember.

"Why are you here?" I said suddenly.

"What?" she said.

"Why did you come with me?" I repeated. "I thought you wanted to get to San Diego for some reason." I searched my memory but couldn't remember what her reason was. "Do you have a reason?"

Her eyes filled with tears. "Whatever, Haley," she said, and stomped back into The Van, slamming the door so hard behind her that rust fell off the bottom.

Great, now The Van was falling apart.

I mean, I'm sorry I made her cry, but you know what? I don't even like her. I don't have to like everyone, do I? Just because she was nice to me for ten seconds does not make us best friends.

I took my shoes off and put my feet on the pavement. It was cold and raining and maybe that seems like a weird thing to do, but for some reason I just wanted to touch California. I sat there for a while before I hopped back into The Van.

Then I started driving south. Hey, this was MY road trip after all. It's not my fault she insisted on coming along.

What Am I Really Doing? (List Made by Haley while Izzy Snores at 4:00 a.m. Somewhere outside of San Francisco)

1. Finding Myself!!!!
2. Going to make up with Brad (see Part 2 of List).
3. Proving something (see Part 3 of List).
4. Writing book.

Part 2 — Reasons to Make Up with Brad

1. Was sweet and considerate boyfriend.
2. May be famous one day.
3. Nicer than most boys.
4. First boy I ever loved.
5. Maybe is love of life!
6. Or maybe not (see Part 2b).
7. Gives me a reason to take a trip, at least.
8. Really likes me (or used to).
9. Says that I'm pretty.
10. Does not make me nervous (very often).

Part 2b — Reasons to Not Make Up with Brad

1. Spent most of relationship figuring out how to break up with Brad.
2. Find other boys interesting when attached to Brad.
3. Don't have all that much in common.
4. Don't like hockey all that much.
5. Like him better when he isn't around.
6. Don't really miss him when he's not around unless no one else is around either.
7. HBG.

Part 3 — What Am I Proving?

1. That I'm grown up, at least enough to go somewhere without telling my dad where I am. Which is weird and I feel guilty about it, but say I am grown up, will he always know where I am? Well, probably. Maybe I should have told him. Feel sick. What if something happens to me and he doesn't know where I am?

Panicking! Breathing into bag! Will be OK in a minute!

2. Proving to myself that I can do something without being told how (e.g. writing a book).

3. Doing something out of passion (e.g. writing a book, following Brad, etc.).

4. Testing ability to get along with annoying people (e.g. Izzy).

Monday, December 15

2:11 p.m.

San Francisco is nothing like I thought. First of all, you have to take a billion different roads to get there and the signs are very confusing and you can enter and exit in the wrong spot.

Maybe we're in the wrong part of it, but I thought it was fancier and sunnier. It's so foggy! And we can't even find a streetcar.

3:30 p.m.

Picture: The World's Largest Rubber Band Ball, SF, CA Weird that it's all covered up and inside a Superette. The guy got a bit cross with us for trying to take a picture. There was a sign that said "No Pictures" but I thought they were kidding. Why would you bother to have the world's largest rubber band ball if you weren't going to let people take pictures of it?

On the plus side, I found the best pair of vintage Levis at a thrift store. The thrift stores here are AMAZING. It was all designer stuff and so gorgeous. I went crazy, even though we're getting way down in our money supply. The money tin is sort of mostly empty.

I actually bought eight pairs because I'm going to sell them on eBay. We're saving money by living entirely on Diet Coke (which we bought a case of at a Costco we passed on the highway) and Doritos (also by the case) and New Zealand apples (ditto).

Am so sick of Doritos and apples. And Diet Coke.

5:02 p.m.

"I don't know," said Izzy. "I thought there would be more sunshine. And beaches. Pretty stupid, I guess."

"Uh huh," I said. I was trying to sound ambivalent, like I wasn't agreeing about the sunshine, but that she was stupid.

"Let's go shopping!" she said.

"I don't want to," I said. "We don't have any money."

"You just bought a bunch of jeans," she pointed out. "That's not fair."

"Fine," I sighed.

I turned The Van down another street. We'd been driving around for ages to find that big rubber band ball (BIG disappointment) and I was hungry and queasy from the chips.

The Van jittered a little bit on the hill and coughed out some smoke. We'd somehow got into a prettier area of town. We'd been circling around San Francisco for the whole day. I'm telling you, nothing is more terrifying than the five quadrillion lanes of traffic narrowing down to about six on the Golden Gate Bridge when your Van doesn't like going more than fifty. I held my breath for the whole crossing, and then nearly fainted. I don't know why I was holding my breath. When I was little, I used to hold my breath in tunnels and stuff and I guess I was a bit afraid of earthquakes. The whole time we were crossing, I was remembering footage of the last big earthquake here with cars hanging over the edge. Was that even this bridge? I couldn't remember, but I didn't much want to know.

Hence the breath-holding.

Anyway, now that we were here, I think both of us were reluctant to go on.

"Do you know where you're going?" she said. She was holding a map, but upside down. And kind of waving it in my face.

"Stop it," I said. "Sort of. Not really. I don't know."

"We should just park," she said. "We'll find something."

"OK," I said. Mostly because I didn't want to do any more driving. The weird thing is that after you've been driving all day every day for ages (or in our case, getting repeatedly lost by going in the wrong direction and getting trapped by freak weather patterns), your legs just start feeling wobbly on solid ground.

Or else I was getting an inner ear infection. Everything felt wobbly.

Somehow, and I don't know how, she talked me into going into Saks. I wasn't dressed for shopping. I really wasn't. I mean, we had showers a couple of days ago, but my hair was all sticky-uppy and I was wearing a T-shirt that needed to see the inside of a washing machine (we haven't done laundry since the blizzard). I wasn't really paying much attention, in my defence. I was still limping and my knee/hip/ankle on the left were all killing me, not to mention my butt. Well, not killing me, but aching. Possibly my coccyx injury threw my whole body out of alignment. I really needed a chiropractor.

I walked around the racks touching stuff and thinking about how much it sucked. I know it's weird, but really expensive clothes just feel nicer than regular stuff, but at the same time, if you can't afford them, what's the point? I was imagining Jules shopping here and her just grabbing stuff off the racks and buying it all.

Izzy disappeared into the change room, and I wandered and tried to ward off salespeople, who kept looking at me disapprovingly.

I hate salespeople.

Hey, I wanted to say. Don't look at me like that. One day, I'll be a famous writer!

But I didn't. I just kind of stammered that I was waiting for someone. There should be a name for the weird stammering, blushing, bad feeling people get when shopping in fancy stores. Like how the salespeople make you feel horrible. For a minute, I felt like Julia Roberts in *Pretty Woman*, except I didn't have Richard Gere to come in and throw his card down and make me feel good and them horrible.

Finally, I found a little coffee place (cute waiters) and sat down to wait for her. Unfortunately, there were a lot of mirrors in it, which allowed me to see myself awfully clearly for the first time in days.

Reasons to Not Look in Mirror (written on back of napkin):
1. Weird, sticking-out hair belongs on toddler or elderly man.
2. Skin has broken out in bad blemishes over entire T-zone.
3. Unruly brows look longer than ever.
4. Chapped lips give general impression of leprosy.

Things I Miss about Home (flip side of napkin, subsequently used to wipe up spilled milk):
1. Regular haircuts.
2. Access to facial scrubbing stuff.
3. My bed.

Izzy had no idea where I was, but I figured she'd find me. In retrospect, I don't know why I thought this. San Francisco was much bigger than I'd imagined. I don't know what I'd thought before — I guess that all the stuff I'd heard of would all be co-located around a little square or something. But that is not the case, much like in Portland.

I ordered an extra hot latte and sat there for ages. It wasn't very good, but it felt like the right thing to be drinking. People kept coming in and out, I guess they were on their way home from work or whatever. Most of them were really well dressed. I felt pretty cosmopolitan, to tell you the truth. I was pretending that I lived there, by myself, and was just hanging out being a writer, which I was, in my fantasy, anyway.

I mean, I am one, but I don't think you can call yourself a writer until you've actually published something.

I sat there for so long my latte got cold. I can only drink so much coffee in a day before I start to get palpitations. So I kind of swirled it around, but I sat there for long enough that it started to look old.

I took a lot of time to think about stuff, like about Bard, I mean Brad, and NOT about HBG (OK, maybe a little), and about my soon-to-be-brother (all of a sudden I started to panic about Melody being on bedrest — what did that mean, anyway? was the baby OK? and was I an awful person for not panicking about it sooner?), and about the fact that if I'd brought my computer, I could have written chapters and chapters. I'm thinking of using the pictures of the weird tourist stuff to frame the book up. I think they are funny enough on their own.

The guy who owns the shop came over and started talking to me and I told him what I was doing (writing a book featuring weird tourist attractions) and he told me a bunch of other stuff that I just have to see, but it's on the other highway. The I-5 is almost devoid of interesting stuff, as it turns out. He was nice. He reminded me of my dad, in that used-to-be-a-hippie way. I kind of wanted to hug him, but that would have been creepy and wrong.

Then I started worrying about Junior being in The Van and The Van not locking properly, so I went looking for Izzy.

I went back to Saks and looked all over. I couldn't find her (although I did find some great shoes that were on sale, but I didn't buy them because of our dire money situation). Finally, I gave up and made my way back to where The Van was.

Only it wasn't there.

Or I was in the wrong place.

All parking garages, it turns out, look EXACTLY the same.

I started to panic. It was hard walking around with such a sore body. Also, it was crowded with Christmas shoppers. It was weird to have Christmas decorations everywhere and for it not to be very cold. Although a lot of people were dressed as though they might be hit with snow at any second, it was really pretty warm.

Or maybe the fear was keeping me warm.

For some reason, I was really trying to look like I was not panicking, which made me panic more. I walked for what felt like hours. The pavement smelled weird and there were lots of street people asking for change. What if I was lost forever? What if I became a street person accidentally, like Allie in that old episode of *Kate and Allie* where she loses her wallet and has to beg for change and somehow loses her shoes?

I forced myself to sit down. Naturally, I sat on a piece of chewed gum. I've never figured out why it's so much extra trouble for people to just throw their gum in the garbage can two steps away. San Francisco was really very dirty. I scraped as much of it off as I could, using an old newspaper. I could feel myself starting to have a panic attack. My hands were shaking like crazy.

I called Kiki.

"Hi!" I said, trying to sound normal. "How are you?"

"Hi," she said. "How are you?"

"I asked you first," I said, concentrating on breathing in through my mouth and out through my nose.

"I'm fine," she said. "How are you?"

"Good," I said. "I mean, lost! I've lost the car! I can't really breathe! My hands are totally shaking!"

"Haley," she said. "I'm so sorry, but I have to go. I've got a bunch of people waiting for me for study group. Are you OK?"

"No!" I said. "Never mind!" I hung up and put my head between my knees. I tried to breathe. Maybe it was in through my nose and out through my mouth. A burly street guy sat down next to me. He smelled like fish. I gagged a bit, OK, I threw up into my mouth, and got up and jogged down the sidewalk. Which really hurt my knee.

I hate Kiki. She was never a good friend to me anyway.

Forty minutes later

I found The Van! And Junior!

Hi Junior!

I'm sitting inside, well, lying inside, trying to calm down. It was really disconcerting being lost like that and knowing that my dad didn't know where I was. I mean, I know I sound like a big baby and whatnot, but I felt really disoriented. Somehow, when he knows where I am, it makes it OK that I'm lost. Not that I get lost that often, but you know what I mean.

Where IS Izzy anyway? I should wait here for her because at least she'll know to look for me here. If I go look for her, and she's come back here, then what? We'll never find each other.

I wonder what happened to her. I have a sneaking suspicion that she met a boy of some sort and followed him home or something. She's such a ridiculous human being. For the seven billionth time, I contemplated the fact that I have no earthly idea why I brought her with me. WHAT WAS I THINKING?

I hope he's not a serial killer.

What if he is?

My heart started beating really fast. Oh my god! Izzy!

Four hours later

OMG, I fell asleep! Izzy isn't here! Argh!

List of Possible Actions to Take:
1. Call the police!
2. Call Dad and ask for advice!
3. Call Brad and ask for advice!
4. Call anyone and ask for advice!
5. Call Izzy's cell phone! DUH.

Later, sometime after dark

Me: Oh my GOD, where ARE you?

Izzy: Where are YOU?

Me: I'm in The Van! Waiting for you! I'm freaking out! I think the parking garage is locked and I'll have to stay in here all night! There are probably thugs!

Izzy: Calm down!

Me: I am calm!

Izzy: No, you aren't!

Me: Where ARE you?

Izzy: I'm in jail! They're taking my phone away. Hey, give
      that back ...

Me: Izzy? Izzy?

One minute later

OK, must get it together. Obviously, by "jail," she meant

...

...

...

I don't think there are too many other meanings for
jail. Unless jail is one of those words like "sick," which
suddenly means the opposite. But what's the opposite of
"jail"?

   "Home"?

   I have no idea.

   Who would know this?

Three minutes later

Me: Jules, you have to help me!

Jules: Haley? It's the middle of the night. Why are you
       calling? You won't believe it. Todd's broken up with
       me! He said he thought I was a real model and not
       just some *catalogue* girl. [crying] I am a real model!

Me: What's the opposite of jail?

Jules: Are you drunk?

Me: No!

Jules: I can't believe he'd dump ME. What's that all about?
       I think he was just a player. You know, a guy who

just dates models for status. I'm so embarrassed! I told him I loved him!

Me: What?

Jules: I know, it sounded stupid when I was saying it too. I want to go home!

Me: Really?

Jules: No, I was just saying that for dramatic effect.

Me: This is important, Jules. I need to know if "jail" means anything.

Jules: What are you talking about? I have a broken heart.

Me: Like, sick.

Jules: Heartsick, yeah.

Me: Never mind.

Jules: It's four in the morning!

She hung up. Fat lot of help she was. I'm a little worried about how much my cellphone bill is going to be, but not to worry, my book advance will pay it off.

Right?

Or, more likely, I'll have to work at Hefty's for sixty years just to pay it off.

No, I can't think like that. My book will be wildly successful and I'll have plenty of money. Maybe I'll get one of those phones with the camera in it or even one that's got a built-in iPod.

Izzy!

OK, I must be grown up about this. Jail must mean "jail." Am sure she'll call again. Will just crawl into bed until she does. Am strangely cold but also exhausted. Hope I'm not coming down with the Asian bird flu, which

I just read about in the newspaper and is transmitted via chickens.

Will just layer up in clothes and hide, I mean "sleep," under this blanket.

Tuesday, December 16
7:15 a.m.
Dear Junior:

That was the most terrifying night of my life. There are reasons to not sleep in parking garages. Where do all these people come from? There were people around all night, banging on The Van and such, with what sounded like knives and forks. They were probably cannibals.

Seriously, you never know.

I was so scared that someone would try the broken door and it would open and they would come in and kill me and eat me. It's not an unrealistic fear, if you think about it. I'm guessing that the kind of people who hang out for fun in parking garages are not the kind of people who would opt to Not Kill (and eat) someone they found sleeping in her Van.

Have not heard from Izzy again.

And it cost me $40 to get my car out of the garage.

Love,
Nearly Broke and Alone Girl

3:17 p.m.
Hallelujah! I've found Izzy.

Or she found me. I was just sitting in the park, with my phone and typing away at my book. It's unbelievable how well it's going all of a sudden, it's like Kiki once told me — sometimes when you really get typing, it's like it's not even you doing the work. It's like you're channelling someone else. Not that I believe in that kind of thing, but I do. Kind of. I mean, I believe in the Ouija board and in ghosts, so why wouldn't I believe that I was channelling some dead travel writer? I only hope that I'm channelling a GOOD dead travel writer. And that it's not some kind of cosmic joke.

I'm scared to reread what I've written though, just in case.

I've typed fifty pages about Washington and Oregon already. Then I found this guide to California at this tourist place and it's helping me figure out the California parts. For one thing, I plan to see more of California than I did of the other two states. We kind of missed those altogether, except for the really big egg and the crow with the stolen clothes. And that tiny park.

And the inside of the motel room.

And the scary abandoned gas station.

I'm also seriously thinking of going back to my other great idea that I'm going to review all the rest stops that we visit at each exit. Oh, and on the way back, I'm going to take the coast highway because it's apparently way prettier. I don't know why we took the I-5. We should have known that it would all look the same.

Anyway.

Izzy called about half an hour ago. She sounded perky, as usual, and not a bit embarrassed. Any normal human would have been, but I forget sometimes how subhuman she is.

The story is that she was caught shoplifting in Saks and she tried to call me (I guess my phone wasn't working?) when she got busted.

"What were you stealing?" I said.

"I wasn't!" she said. "It was just a mistake!"

"Uh huh," I said.

"I was totally set up!" she said. She sounded almost unbearably cheerful about this. Maybe she was a clone. A clone programmed with only a "happy" chip and "perky" chip.

She did have freakily good skin.

Hmmm.

In a way, it made her more interesting to me. Not her clone-ishness, but the shoplifting. Not that I think that's cool, I think it's stupid. But I mean, I thought of her as this prissy, perfect-life, pointless person and maybe there is a bit more to her. Look at Winona Ryder! Not that shoplifting made her deep or anything. It just made her more interesting, in the way that screwed-up people are more interesting than happy-go-lucky perky cheerleaders.

Shoplifting itself freaks me out. I took a chocolate bar from 7-11 once and I still have bad dreams about it. I'm not kidding. I wake up at night in a cold sweat. I've never been able to look at Reese's peanut butter cups the same way. In a way, I think I'm pretty lame. What's the big deal? Everyone does it, right? Except I don't. When I did it, I didn't feel like me. I felt so awful. I was sick about it. It was disproportionate and didn't make sense, but there you go. It was what it was.

It took me ages to find Izzy when I went to pick her up. For a few minutes, I thought about driving away and just leaving her there, but I couldn't do it. That would be way too mean.

Or would it?

I guess I'm feeling strong? I mean, I made it through the night by myself and it was terrifying, yes, but I didn't die.

What do I need her for?

Totally Izzy!
Date: December 16
Mood: Ashamed!!!!!
Weather: Foggy
Haley: My saviour!!! (But still a freak!)!
So y'all aren't even going to believe what happened. I thought about not telling you (or anyone!) but then I figured, hey, it's good for people to see that I'm not perfect. (NOT that I think I'm perfect! I totally don't!) And this is like confession, or like what I think confession is like because I'm not a Catholic so I really have no idea. I think Jesus is very forgiving and whatever! I'm sure he'd forgive me. The thing is, we spent SOOO much money on the motel when it was snowing in Oregon (weird to think about! that we were just in the snow and now it's not snowing at all!) and there was this really cute pair of jeans at Saks and I just took them! I don't know what's wrong with me, really! I saw on TV once a show about regular people shoplifting and how horrible they felt, etc. etc. and they also talked

about how they did it and so I did it! I went into the change room and put on jeans under my regular clothes. I figured no one would notice, but boy was I WRONG. As soon as that guy put his hand on my arm, I knew he'd caught me and not that he was flirting with me, like I'd previously thought! I mean, he was follow-ing me around, duh. I thought he was majorly into me. Anyway, because I'm Canadian and said I was an orphan (sorry, mom and dad!), they didn't know what to do with me and I actually got held just in the weird jail thing in the police station, so it wasn't actual jail. And then they let me go this morning. I guess it was supposed to scare me or whatever but really it just freaked me out because it was so gross and smelly and I thought maybe Hippie Haley was going to take off without me and then where would I be? Stuck in San Francisco? I'm sure I could, like, figure out a way to get home, but never mind that. I NEED to get to San Diego with Haley. San Diego is like, SO close to here, we could totally drive it in a half day but Haley wants to drive around and sleep in The Van more and stink it up because Brad won't be back for another week or what-ever. So we're looking for beaches! How hard can that be? And I have a totally cute bikini to wear.

So what I was saying is Don't Shoplift! It's super-embarrassing and of course it's wrong because it costs other shoppers, etc. etc. I'm sure you saw those PSAs on TV yourself so I won't bother repeating them. Haley's giving me the stink-eye now for taking too long, so peace out, kidniks.

Oh, the punchline? They didn't take the jeans back!
So I totally got some rippin' jeans. I guess I should feel
bad about that, but I really don't.
The Last Word
Flirters: *4! (I'm sure that cop was flirting!)*
Flirtees: *3 (he wasn't worth flirting back with!)*
Calories: *none!*

Picture: Mystery Spot, Santa Cruz, CA
OK, so it was miles out of our way and hard to find, but
so what? BALLS ROLL UPHILL! There is no explanation
for this. We asked our guide, but he was about twelve
and didn't have a clue. There was an old guy on the
tour who was convinced that it was the work of the
Devil. Which started out as funny and then turned
scary.

Things That Scare Me, written on postcard of Mystery Spot:
1. Mystery Spots.
2. Demon possession movies.
3. The Ouija board.
4. Sharks.
5. Serial killers.

Wednesday, December 17
Dear Junior:
Now we have some time to fill up in California, I'm determined to see a bunch of different stuff so that I have more
to write about. I figure if I just take lots of regular journal-
type notes every day, I'll be able to write (or channel) the

book really easily when I get home. I've got such a good start on it, it's amazing.

I think maybe I can actually do this after all.

I've been thinking about it and I think maybe I'll dedicate the book to Bard, I mean Brad, even if we don't get back together (and I'm not even sure that I want to, I mean, I hardly even think of him anymore, so why do I think it's important that he's my boyfriend?). He's sort of the inspiration, if you think about it.

And I can't dedicate it to HBG, because that would be wrong and stalker-ish and I would die of embarrassment if he found out I had a crush on him. Because I don't. I think the thing is that when I don't have anything else to think about, my brain just fills in with extraneous stuff. Like inappropriate and unreciprocated crushes.

The funny thing is that if I'd been spending less time thinking about HBG and Brad and even JT, I could have spent more time researching this trip. For example, I didn't realize it would take such a short time to drive to San Diego. I mean, I thought it would take weeks! If we hadn't hit that blizzard in Oregon, we would have been there ages ago.

Clearly, I have no sense of time or distance. That's probably a special kind of brain tumour wherein you lose that kind of perspective, but I'm determined not to check on the internet, even though we seem to visit internet cafés more than any other place. Izzy is writing some of her entries there now, so they aren't on Junior. She types with three fingers. This is very irritating. She also types loudly. I've never known anyone to hit the keyboard so hard when she types. I'm seriously accumulating a very long list of things about Izzy that drive me insane.

Still, I have this idea that I'll crack her password and see what she's writing, but I haven't yet. How hard can it be? She has the IQ of a gnat. On the other hand, I'm not sure I want to know.

Anyway, now we can explore California properly, although I won't be able to let Izzy out of my sight. (She'll probably steal something. Is it a cry for help? After hearing her talk about it now for what seems like days, I don't even CARE.) I want to find some beaches and go to L.A. and see stuff. Like the Hollywood sign. The Chinese Theater. Hollywood Boulevard. The Starbucks where Jennifer Aniston goes.

I know it's cheesy, but it's what you do here, right? It's starting to get warmer as we go farther south. Somehow, The Van seems to only know two temperatures — bitter cold and boiling heat. It seems like just a few days ago (actually, it was) that we were nearly dying of hypothermia and/or exposure. Now we'll be lucky to not get heatstroke.

The really funny part is that the people who live here seem to think it's really really cold. It's winter! Only it's not cold at all. I'm wearing a short-sleeved T-shirt. At home, I'd be in a parka by now.

I don't want to think about home, though. I'm getting the strangest feeling in the pit of my stomach about my brother (or sister). I feel ... I guess, I feel guilty. Like I should be there when he (or she) comes into the world, especially now that he's almost ready to arrive.

I should be there.

But I can't be. Because this is a hugely important part of my life too. It's the part that starts the rest. It's like college, but different. It's my choice and I'm following the path I'm supposed to be on. (Obviously my dad's hippiness is rubbing off on me because that sounds exactly like what he would say. Come to think of it, he did say that. Yesterday, on the phone.)

I'm so excited about this part of the trip. I can't explain why. It's sort of like now that I know Brad isn't there anyway, I'm free to just relax and do things without having it in the back of my head that I'm supposed to hurry.

Oh, hang on. The phone is ringing.

Oh my God.

Melody called to say that she was in labour! I'm kind of freaking out, but I can't do anything about it. I told her it was snowing a lot and I wouldn't be able to come down, but I want to see the baby, and of course, I don't even know if it's snowing in the place I said I was, wherever that is, and now I'm hyperventilating because what if all my lying leads to bad karma for the baby and something goes wrong and in a roundabout way, it's my fault?

What DO I DO?

It's my BROTHER! (Or sister).

Oh my god, oh my god, oh my god.

But even if we turned around right now and went home, it wouldn't matter, we'd still miss it.

I don't know how I feel about that.

I have to think about it.

Love,

Soon-to-Be Big Sister Haley

3:20 p.m.

"I think you should go home," said Izzy. "And don't you want to go home for Christmas anyway?" She tapped the steering wheel to the beat with her foot, which I batted out of the way.

"That's dangerous," I said. "Stop it."

I don't know how she can stand this music anyway. If I hear one more bar of Duran Duran, I'm going to have to poke my eardrum out with a hot stick.

"Argh!" I said. "I don't want to be home for Christmas. I mean, I don't care. Do you care?"

"We don't celebrate Christmas," she said. "It's not in our religion."

"What religion are you?" I said.

"I can't tell you," she said. "It's a secret."

"You have a secret religion?" I asked. "Seriously?"

"It's only a secret from you because, you, like, wouldn't understand it," she said. "I don't want to talk about it."

"Huh," I said.

"What I was saying, Hale, is that it's not every day that your brother is born," she said.

"I know," I said. "It's not like I could get there very quickly, though, and then what would I do when I got there? Don't call me 'Hale.' That's creepy."

"Um, be supportive to your stepmom? Hasn't she been in labour for like hours?" she said. "HALE."

"Whatever," I said. I rearranged an ice pack (i.e. pack of frozen peas) on my knee, which, for some mysterious reason, had swollen up in the night. "Where are we going?"

I'd been eating them too. Frozen peas aren't half-bad, really.

"Wherever you're driving," she said.

"I'm just following the traffic," I said. "I have no idea, you're supposed to navigate."

I looked at her dubiously. So far today, I'd hit the curb three times and the meridian twice. It really irritated me that she couldn't do the driving, but I didn't want her to drive my Van without a licence again. My knee was suddenly hurting so much I felt like crying. Secretly, I was starting to worry that something worse was happening to it than we previously thought and I should go home for medical attention. But that would be too much like giving up.

The Van wobbled off another curb. I doubted that there was much more the tires on The Van could stand. I was almost hoping to be pulled over by the California Highway Patrol, a.k.a. CHiPs. Preferably by an Erik Estrada look-alike. Not that Izzy would know who that was. *Her* dad probably did not have the entire series of *CHiPs* on DVD.

I stared out the window. California was starting to look like just a mass of highways to me. I wanted to go to the beach and look at the sea. Somehow looking at the ocean calmed me down and I was feeling very uncalm.

I called my dad again from the cellphone.

"How's it going?" I said.

"The midwife just came back," he said. "She'd stepped out for some meditation. Nothing much has changed, but we're setting up the wading pool."

"Cool," I said. "Shouldn't she go to the hospital, though?"

"No," said Dad. "Do you know how germy hospitals are?"

"Um," I said. "I hope you cleaned the pool."

"Yup," he said. "I wish you were here."

"I wish I was too," I said, although I have to say that I was a little relieved not to be. I'm happy (somewhat) to be having a brother (or sister), but watching Melody squatting in a filthy wading pool and squirting him (or her) out was not on my list of top entertainment. "Say 'hi' to Melody," I added.

"Love you," said Dad. In the background, I heard a horrible howling noise.

"Was that MELODY?" I asked.

"No," he said. "It was The Cat."

"Ah," I said. Was The Cat going to share in the experience? I mean, I love The Cat and everything, but there is something inherently unsanitary about cats, no?

"OK," I said. "I gotta go."

"We'll keep you updated," he said. "We're just waiting and mellowing out."

"Yeah," I said. "Well, good luck."

"Thanks," he said. "Wish you were here."

"You said," I said. "I gotta go, Dad. Bye."

"You should totally be there," said Izzy. "I could take The Van to San Diego and explain to Brad."

"Explain WHAT to Brad?" I asked irritably. "YOU DON'T HAVE A LICENCE SO YOU CAN'T DRIVE."

"You know," she said. "Whatever."

"Whatever isn't a word," I said. "I mean, it is, but without context it has no meaning."

"Whatever," she said, shrugging. She pulled the mirror back and started inspecting her teeth. Which was all very well, except for the part where I needed to see in the mirror to DRIVE.

"Watch OUT!" I said. "You're going to kill us!"

She laughed. "No, I won't!" She kept laughing like I'd said something really hilarious. I, for one, do not consider being killed to be very funny. I glared at her.

"Ohh, that was your exit!" she said, grabbing the wheel so quickly The Van all but turned over.

"Argh!" I screamed, wrestling it back. "That really isn't funny!"

"Honestly, Haley," she said. "You don't have to be so dramatic about everything."

"Whatever," I said.

Picture: My Swollen Knee, 7-11 Parking Lot, somewhere in CA
Notice the black and blue patterning, which could indicate clotting beneath the skin.

Picture: Giant Chessboard, Morro Bay, CA
Not nearly as interesting (or as giant) as the guidebook led us to believe.

Picture: THE OCEAN, Morro Bay, CA
Oh, finally, after days of highways, the SEA. You can just see it there through the fog.

Picture: My foot in The Ocean, Morro Bay, CA
It's my foot, it's the ocean. I really love the sea. Maybe should consider doing something for a living that involves the sea, such as becoming famous marine biologist in the style of Bill Murray in that weird movie with the title I can't remember.

Picture: Me, soaking wet, after being doused by surf at Morro Bay, CA
OK, now I'm freezing cold.

Totally Izzy!
Date: December 17
Mood: Refreshed
Weather: Mostly foggy
Haley: In a weird mood
Hey blog fans, my homies, my peeps, what's up?

We're in Marrow Bay, CA, or something like that! Which I had never heard of before, but we had to come here to see some lame chessboard that Haley thought was going to be cool and "quirky" for her book. I think that she has a weird idea of what is interesting! The chessboard sucked, but the bay itself is wicked cool. All rolling surf and wide sand. Much colder than I would have thought! No bikini for me yet! We met some boys at this little coffee shop/ice cream parlour and they totally talked us into coming to a beach party tonight! Now we're just hanging out in The Van. Haley is napping while I'm here in the internet café. She sleeps a lot! I think she's freaked out because her stepmother is having a baby, probably as we speak.

How much of a bitch is she for not being there? She's a weirdo.

Her dad e-mailed a picture of the wading pool. YIKES. These people are so weird! I can't imagine my dad even knowing what a wading pool was! Much less using one as a birthing pond in the middle of the house!

I'm getting tired of driving around and looking at weird things. As soon as we're done here, I'm going to try to talk Haley into heading south to San Diego, where You Know Who lives. Even if he isn't back yet, at least we'll be there! I'm a little worried that The Van will break down. It keeps making strange lurching sounds and Haley keeps taping things in the engine with duct tape. I'm not sure she knows what she's doing. I know she took auto mechanics in high school, but ... well, you know Haley! Flaky as always. And her knee looks really gross.

She's not getting on my nerves as much as I thought she would, though. I mean the week in Oregon in the motel was enough to drive me over the edge, but she's been OK (pretty quiet) for the last little bit. She's always typing! Hey, maybe she'll really write her book. Probably she'll dedicate it to me!

Peace out, kids.

The Last Word

Flirters: *5*

Flirtees: *3*

Number of times I made Brad's name out of licence plates: *16!!!!*

5:17 p.m.

Dear Junior:

This is such a pretty town. I could live here forever.

Love,

Haley, Beach Girl

Thursday, December 18

Reasons Why I Will Never Go to Another Beach Party:

1. They always sound like MUCH more fun than they are.
2. Sand gets everywhere.
3. Sand fleas.
4. It's always cold by the water.
5. Someone always tries to get everyone wet.
6. Smoke from the fire always follows me around.

What was I thinking to let Izzy talk me into anything? The beach party (oh, excuse me, the CHRISTMAS party) was ... well, seriously disturbing, to say the least. What are all these people taking? I hate drugs! Drugs make me anxious. Stoned people make me anxious. Everything about that beach party made me anxious, especially the guy dressed up like Santa who looked about forty-five years old.

Izzy makes me anxious.

Conclusion: I'm very anxious.

What is WRONG with her? She'll do anything that a cute boy suggests.

The last time I saw her, she was about to dive into the water, which reminded me an awful lot of the opening scene from *Jaws* where the couple go skinny-dipping and the next thing you know, they are shark snacks.

I almost wished it on her, but not quite.

I've stormed back to The Van, but there is a fire right near it, and The Van is pretty smoky inside. Can't you get carbon monoxide poisoning from that? Am I feeling light-headed?

What if she drowns?

I hate this.

An hour later

Still no sign of Izzy. I'm going to sleep. I refuse to worry about her.

I refuse.

She's irresponsible and irritating. She makes Jules seem normal and well-balanced (sort of).

I'm not worried.

I'm NOT.

OK, I am.

Will just go see if I can find her.

Two hours later

Am freezing to death. Isn't it supposed to be hot in California? Why didn't anyone tell me how cold it was here at night? I wish I had a scarf. Have layered up and crawled under the blankets and am typing this with one finger. My other fingers are huddled together for warmth.

Maybe there's something wrong with my thyroid.

Oh, for the record, I found Izzy. She'd passed out on a blanket in this grassy hilly area behind the beach. I hope she's OK. I dragged her over to some logs and left her with some people (total hippies, btw, who seemed nice and harmless) who were camping out there. I think they'll take care of her. And it serves her right.

It's not like I could have dragged her all the way back here again. She might weigh only 110 pounds (EXACTLY, according to her) but she's hard to drag.

Also, she stank like beer and smoke. Yuck.

Wish I was travelling alone.

Friday, December 19
2:41 p.m.

Am so glad I'm not travelling alone. The highway system here is freaking me out. What's wrong with me? We were just driving along (Izzy was sleeping, a.k.a. SNORING) and I looked out the window and everywhere I looked, all I could see were cars and more cars and lanes and lanes of cars. Don't ask me why, but I suddenly started thinking, What if I had a heart attack? Who would rescue me? How would the ambulance get through all these lanes of cars? It was like claustrophobia, only different. I'd look up the name for it (I'm sure there is one) but I don't have the internet handy.

In other news, Melody's labour apparently stopped.

Who knew that could happen?

Maybe I should go home.

Maybe I shouldn't.

Sigh.

Note to Self: Invest in satellite connection for laptop as soon as they become affordable.

2:49 p.m.

Gridlock! I hate gridlock. Is this for real? When I think about being at home and people complaining about it taking twenty minutes to get home in rush hour, I think, HA. This is insane.

4:49 p.m.

Oh my God! Oh my God! My brother is a sister! Melody's labour started again!

As it turned out, the whole wading pool thing went by the wayside as soon as the real pain started. Apparently Melody was screaming her head off for drugs, which makes me like her more. It's probably a good thing because if she'd managed to deliver the baby into a puddle with a beatific smile on her face, I'd have had to hate her a great deal. Anyway, she made them take her to the hospital, where the baby GIRL was born.

Also, the baby weighed ten pounds.

TEN pounds.

Think about how horribly painful that must have been.

They are naming her Galaxy. I know. Don't get me started.

P.S. — I had a feeling this whole time that my "brother" was a "sister."

5:30 p.m.

Picture: Madonna Inn, San Luis Obispo, CA
This is the neatest inn I've ever seen. It somehow reminds me of home. My dad would love it. It's. Just. So. Ugly.

Picture: Dunes at Grover Beach, CA
Cool sand dunes, hard to walk on with a wrecked knee. Also, when you try to pee on a sand dune you must be very careful not to pee in your own shoe. I'm just saying.

9:45 p.m.

I'm a sister! It's the weirdest thing. I can't stop thinking about it. I've always wanted to have more of a family. I mean, I have a family, and I love my family, but I have an Absentee Mom (who I've seen about ten times in my whole life) and my dad is, well, he's great. He's my dad.

But Melody isn't related to me and there isn't anyone else. I don't have cousins and aunts and uncles or anything. In a way, it's a bit like being an orphan, only not exactly.

But now that I have a sister, it's different. It's like she's the anchor or something like that. Like she's the glue that will make us all real? I know that doesn't make sense.

I cried a little bit. I'm really happy.

Dad e-mailed a picture and she looks exactly like a cone-headed pink mouse. She's the most beautiful thing I've ever seen.

Saturday, December 20
7:20 a.m.

To distract myself from thinking about the fact that I really should be somewhere else (i.e. at home), I convinced myself that I was excited to get to L.A. I woke up at five and woke Izzy up by kicking her sharply in the shin. It only stopped her snoring for a tenth of a second. Needless to say, she's still in her pyjamas, which look just perfectly fine.

If I was still in my pyjamas, we'd probably be arrested for public indecency.

In any event, we got started early and came into town at dawn in an effort to avoid rush hour traffic.

Ha.

As if it's possible to avoid. It's busier than I've ever seen any highway at any time.

And I was having such a good sleep too, when I startled awake at five dreaming I was at home and could hear a baby crying. I sat up really fast and hit my head on the corner of the cupboard, which still hurts.

Once again, I fell in love with one of California's rest stops. So great. There were Band-Aids in the first-aid cupboard in the washroom (how is it possible that they haven't been stolen?), so now I have a Band-Aid on my temple. Dignified, no, but at least I don't have blood running down to my chin.

I'd like to point out that L.A. is NOTHING like what I imagined or like what I've seen on TV. Granted, I was only here once before, and thought something similar. But I was with Jules, when she auditioned for the TV show *Who Is the Prettiest of Them All*, and the whole TV show thing (and Jules herself) made L.A. seem at least marginally glamorous. But that time, we flew. It was a completely different perspective from the highway. For one thing, I had no idea that so many people would have old mattresses on the roofs of their cars that apparently they sporadically dropped off on the shoulder of the road. Why would you do that? Was it a conscious decision to dump your mattress? Did you take a special trip for mattress dumping? Or was it an accident?

It was also impossible to keep up with traffic, which went so quickly it made me dizzy. The cars whipped all over the place and exits randomly popped up in the middle of the road.

The sky was all dark and smoggy, which was gross, but I knew it would be like that.

Izzy was all excited, now that she was awake.

"I've been here before," I kept saying. "I know what I'm doing." I don't know why I said that, because having been here before, I pretty much just saw the inside of the hotel room. (I had a broken leg from a running accident.) (Which totally wasn't my own fault.)

Luckily, this time I wasn't on crutches. (Although I had them if I needed them and my knee was hurting more than it did when I injured it. It was black and blue and my tailbone was still aching and making me grouchy.)

"DON'T TURN HERE!" she suddenly screamed. "It's the wrong exit!"

"It's the right exit!" I yelled. Izzy was frantically flipping maps around. I have no idea why. We weren't even looking for anything in particular! We were just driving, to see what we could see. I mean, I kind of wanted to find the California Science Center because I heard that there was a fifty-foot-tall transparent woman there (a model of a woman, not a real woman), which would be a good picture for the Quirky Guide.

I nearly took the side of The Van off on the guardrail on the exit ramp. Even on the ramp, people were driving at about 100 km/h (i.e. some unknown number of miles/hour). I'm sure my blood pressure was going up. I saw a show once where people wore blood pressure monitors all over the place, like to work, and when they were in traffic, the monitors went crazy. My ears were ringing a little bit too. Frankly, looking for the fifty-foot-tall woman was becoming a low priority.

"Where are we *going?*" Izzy whined. "We should get breakfast." She was tapping her knees on the dashboard and it was bending in under the pressure of her legs.

"Don't break the dashboard," I said irritably. I cut over a

couple of lanes and people started honking. I gave everyone the finger.

"Don't do that!" she said. "Someone will probably shoot us!"

"No, they won't," I said.

"You're the one who's always going on and on and on about getting shot in a rest stop," she snapped. "You're much more likely to be killed in a car accident. You're the worst driver in the world!"

"I am not," I said. "You're worse."

"But I don't even have a licence!" she said. She sounded all surprised.

"So?" I said.

"So I must be good because I know how to do it and no one ever taught me."

"No one taught you how to drive?" I said. "I thought you said that you knew how, you just didn't have a licence."

"I've never driven before!" she said. "I watched you do it and thought, 'How hard can it be?' I mean, if Haley Harmony can do it, anyone can do it!"

"You drove my Van and you don't know how?" I yelled.

"Don't get all excited!" she said. "You're going to hit something!"

"No, I'm not!" I said, and took another exit, which was very disconcerting as we'd already exited, although apparently the first exit just led to another highway. We rolled down into an area that looked, frankly, completely deserted, which was incredibly startling after the mayhem we'd just encountered. There wasn't a person in sight. It was very weird to go from the mad, frantic traffic to ... nothing.

There were a lot of old dilapidated buildings. And some more mattresses. Actually, quite a few more mattresses. The mattresses really are a mystery to me.

I was thinking about that when Izzy said, "Stop, there's a 7-11."

It's a peculiar thing when you're travelling, but when you see something even remotely familiar, it makes you feel better.

"I want a Slurpee," I said. "Coke, please. Mixed with cherry if they have it."

"OK," she said, bouncing out of The Van. I wanted to tell her she should change first, but then I actually kind of wouldn't have minded if she'd embarrassed herself. I threw the mushy peas in the garbage and when she didn't come out for twenty minutes, I went in after her.

No surprise. She was very VERY busy. Flirting with the boy behind the counter, natch. He was Spanish and I must say he did look a bit like Antonio Banderas. He was cute-ish. I kind of smiled at him and he turned to me and started telling me how to get to Hollywood and what we should see. I was about to ask him about all the mattresses, but I could feel Izzy's eyes burning through my head. The boy wrote directions on my arm with a felt-tipped pen, which was weird but also kind of flirty. At least it was until he saw my tattoo.

"What is Bard?" he said. "Is it a band? It's very cool, your tattoo."

Izzy started giggling like mad.

"What is funny?" he said, which made me like him better.

"It says 'Brad'!" she shrieked.

He looked at it again. "I'm sorry," he said. "I think you spelled it wrong."

"Ha ha," I said. My face was about a billion shades of red. Izzy laughed so hard she got the hiccups, which made her sound perkier than ever. I swear, sometimes I wished I had a pom pom available that I could pummel her with.

"Shut up," I said.

"Don't be so, like, upset!" she laughed.

I stormed out. I was really mad. But when we got back to the car, Izzy was furious. "He was mine!" she said. "I saw him first!"

"What does that even mean?" I said. "That's ridiculous. I only SMILED at him. Whatever. I'm the one who's mad at YOU. YOU are the one that got this stupid tattoo spelled wrong! You were laughing at me! What kind of friend are you?"

"You are so competitive," she said. "It's disgusting. Get hold of yourself. I'm mad at YOU."

"What are you TALKING about?" I said. "I am hold of myself."

"Shut up," she said. "Just drive."

"OK," I said. Secretly, I was feeling pretty proud of myself. I mean, Izzy might be annoying, but she is really pretty. And the boy in 7-11 was definitely flirting with me.

Maybe I AM pretty.

Just a little bit.

Imagined Scenarios That Could Happen While in L.A.
1. Could run into Ryan Phillippe at Starbucks.
2. Could run into Jennifer Aniston walking her dog on the beach.
3. Could run into cast of *The O.C.* shopping at Macy's.
4. Could run into nobody and see nothing.
5. Could run into scouting agent who decides I would be a perfect character actress and casts me in his next quirky independent film, launching me to fame and stardom.
6. Could run into scouting agent who thinks I'm pretty and casts me as romantic lead opposite Orlando Bloom in blockbuster romantic comedy, launching me to fame and stardom.

Actual Events That Happened in Los Angeles
1. Ran into parked car on Hollywood Boulevard (not nearly as glamorous as it sounds, by the way).
2. Panicked and backed away from parked car into traffic and was hit from behind by pickup truck full of scary-looking teenage boys who all started yelling and jumping around like they were going to kill us with their bare hands.
3. Freaked out.
4. Boys tipped Van over.
5. Crawled out of Van before oncoming car hit Van.
6. VAN TOTALLED.

Injuries: None to me, none to Izzy, Junior's screen cracked.
Situation: PANIC.

2:12 p.m.

"Stop ASKING me!" yelled Izzy. "I don't know either! Maybe you can flirt your way out of it!"

"Hey," I said. "YOU'RE the flirt."

"You should talk!" she said. "Flirter!"

I glared at her and sat down on the sidewalk. At least it was warm. The sidewalk was filthy, but it hardly mattered. In my hand was the card of the guy who towed The Van away, whose name was Brock McRock. I wondered if that was made up. It didn't sound real. My heart was still beating at about a billion beats per second and I was kind of crying. The accident was terrifying. It was. I thought we were going to die.

I was sure of it.

And the worst thing in the world would be to die with Izzy Archibaud. I don't care what she thinks, she's still my arch-enemy. I don't even like her. I don't want to die with someone I don't even like.

I don't want to die at all.

Granted, we didn't die, but we could have. I looked around. Beside us was a heap of all our stuff. All of it. Clothes stuffed into garbage bags. A stupid amount of ski equipment. I was holding Junior like a baby, which made me think of Galaxy and how I'd never even met her.

"What are we going to do?" I wailed.

"Haley," she said. "I. Don't. Know."

"Argh," I said. I stood up and felt something snap and hit my back. Great. My bra was broken. I tried to pull it out the sleeve of my shirt, but it didn't work. At least, I didn't do it quickly enough to not have it witnessed by a family of Japanese tourists. I left it dangling there. What difference did it make?

I kicked one of the bags, and of course, it split open and my socks and underwear tumbled out onto the ground next to the fancy skis. Great. Now all of Hollywood can see my ugly panties. I wrenched the bra out of my sleeve and threw it in the pile. I felt naked, but who cared? Could it get any worse?

"Buck up!" said Izzy.

"Did you seriously just say that to me?" I said. "BUCK UP? Who says that?"

"I do," she said. She sat down beside me and patted my back, which made me even madder.

I lay down. There were about a thousand pieces of chewed gum smeared all over the sidewalk and now, no doubt, stuck in my hair.

Wasn't someone supposed to help you after an accident? The police came and went and The Van was taken away and now we were just HERE.

"We could call Brad," she said. "I bet he'd know what to do!"

How she could continue to sound upbeat, I had no idea. I snarled at her as well as I could from my prone position.

"You've got gum in your hair," she said helpfully.

I made a whimpering sound. My hair, as was to be expected, was stuck to the ground. How could it get any worse?

"We can't call Brad," I said through clenched teeth. "For one thing, he's in *Washington* and we are in *Los Angeles*.

For another thing, he wouldn't know what to do either. How could he know what to do? It's not like anything like this ever happens to him."

"Well, we have to call someone," she said. She was twirling her phone around like it was a baton. I squinted at her. I couldn't summon up the energy to comment.

"No one knows where we are," I finally said, very slowly, like I was talking to someone who didn't speak the language. "We can't very well call home and say, 'We are on Hollywood Boulevard and have wrecked our van, please help!' when they think we are working in a ski lodge UP NORTH."

"We're going to have to," she said. She squatted down next to me. "We don't have any money left."

"How much money DO we have?" I asked.

"Um," she said. She dug through the bags to find the cookie tin. "Forty-seven dollars!"

"Great," I said. I was starting to get a headache. Little twinkling lights kept floating past my eyes. At first, I thought I was finally going to lose my retinas and then I realized it was just the headlights on passing cars. It was getting dark.

"I don't know what to do," I said, for the billionth time.

"Is that Tom Cruise?" she said, pointing down the street.

I jumped up, which hurt a lot, considering the whole hair-stuck-to-ground problem. "No," I said. "That's just some guy." He didn't even look like Tom Cruise. He had blond hair and a beer belly. Actually, he looked a little bit like JT, not that I ever think about him anymore.

I wonder what he's doing right now? And who he's doing it with?

Note to Self: Stop thinking about JT. How crazy are you? JT is a part of the distant past and escaping into random crush-territory can't help you now. In fact, has never helped you.

I took a deep breath and let it out slowly. I tried closing my eyes and visualizing my happy place, but I couldn't think of one. For some reason, the only thing that came into my head was The Van, and thinking about The Van made me anxious. My happy place was now my anxious place. My heart was flipping around in my chest like a dying seal on an ice floe. It was likely I was having some kind of ventricular failure.

"Stop gasping like that," said Izzy. "It's so weird. Do you have to be weird all the time? Maybe I should call MY dad. He won't be mad, he doesn't care where I am. And he could wire us money."

"Would he *do* that?" I said.

"No," she said. "Probably not. But it's worth a try."

"We could ask Jules," I said suddenly. "Jules could wire us money!"

"Jules?" she said. "She wouldn't know how."

"How hard can it be?" I said. I felt a bit defensive. "She's not stupid, you know."

"Besides," said Izzy. "It's the middle of the night there."

"I wish we were in San Diego already," I said.

"Me too," she said. "Brad would totally help us out!"

"Brad. Isn't. There," I said again.

It really bugged me for no discernible reason that she was making Brad out to be some kind of hero. I mean, he was a really nice guy and everything, but he was hardly the type to lift a car off a baby or anything.

JT was more the hero type, not that he'd ever done anything heroic either.

HBG was probably even more of a hero, in a skinny, non-participatory way. I mean, he wouldn't exactly be of much use in a baby–car situation, but he might have clever ideas about how to get out of this mess. British men always seem cleverer than they probably are, though. Not that I personally know any British men. Except HBG, of course.

Not that I know him very well.

JT would be able to carry our stuff, at least.

Sigh.

I just drove all the way through Washington and Oregon and a good portion of California without thinking about JT at all, really, and now I was thinking of him again? This is because I'm totally over what was a stupid, misguided crush.

Oddly enough, I hadn't spent too much time thinking about Brad either. Before I left, I couldn't stop thinking about him.

Hmmm.

I stuffed my assorted underwear back into the bag and tied it shut in a knot. We basically had our purses, backpacks, useless ski gear, and five garbage bags full of clothes. The exhaust from the traffic was starting to make me nauseated.[8]

"I'm nauseous," said Izzy. "These cars stink."

"It's nauseated," I said.

"Me too," she said. "That's what I just said."

I rolled my eyes and let it go. Because, really, let's face it, it wasn't the time for a grammar lesson.

Our immediate problems were:

1. No place to go.
2. Not much money.
3. No food.

"I'm hungry," she whined.

"OK," I sighed. "Look, we have to figure this out. We need to buy something to eat. Or something."

"Fine," she said. She reached down as if to help me up and then changed her mind.

"You're dirty," she said, wrinkling her nose.

"Hrmmmph," I growled and got up. We divvied up the stuff and started walking down the street. Izzy had the skis, which she repeatedly nearly decapitated me with. I think she was doing it on purpose. In order to survive, I had to walk about five hundred feet behind her, which nearly ended up in us getting separated. Finally, we stashed them in some pretty bushes, which on close inspection were also housing a bunch of broken bottles and a MATTRESS.

---

8 Not "nauseous." This is my pet peeve. "Nauseous" means "makes people sick."

It made me feel bad to do it. They looked expensive, especially amongst all the garbage. I hoped someone nice would find them. But who? And who would need skis in L.A.? Probably they'd show up on eBay for thousands of dollars.

But we just couldn't carry them. Frankly, I was starting to wonder if we'd survive the ordeal at all. It was starting to be totally overwhelming and it made me think of how people were always going back into burning buildings for their purses and stuff. I didn't want to sacrifice *myself* for the skis.

Besides which, I hate skiing.

And what else could we do? We were weak from hunger. We couldn't carry them.

We walked for about a billion miles (which is 2 billion kilometres more or less) with the remaining garbage bags of stuff and our backpacks and purses. And Junior, of course. Finally, we found a bus stop and an actual bus. Getting on the bus, in retrospect, was not that smart, as we had no idea where it was going.

It seemed like a good idea at the time. What can I tell you?

I don't even know where we ended up. I wish I could tell you, but I can't. All I know is that it was dark by the time we got there, and scary. Granted, everything is scary in the dark. But somehow L.A. was more scary.

Summary: We are lost in L.A. It's dark. It's scary.

Crap.

Probably around midnight

Phone Call with Jules:

Me: Jules, do you know how to wire money?

Jules: Haley, why are you always calling me at weird times? It's three in the morning! I'm not wiring you money! How do you do that, anyway?

Me: I don't know! We were in a car accident.

Jules: I thought you took The Van?

Me: Same thing!

Jules: What?

Me: The Van was in an accident.

Jules: By itself?

Me: What?

Jules: Haley, I can't talk to you right now, you're hurting my head. I'll be home tomorrow, though. I'm coming home for Christmas! I'll call you. I got you a really great present. You'll love it. Do you want to know what it is?

Me: Is it money that you're wiring me?

Jules: It's pretty tacky to ask for money, don't you think?

Me: JULES.

Jules: It's a surprise! I'm not going to tell you. That would just wreck it.

Me: Can you focus, please?.

Jules: I'm not even wearing my contacts. God. I'm so tired. I should go back to sleep. I've got a go-see tomorrow for Prada.

Me: That's great!

Jules: Thanks. Well, I'll let you go! Bye!

Me: Don't let me go!

It was too late, she'd already hung up.

Of course.

Phone Call with Brad:

Me: I'm such an idiot.

Brad: That could be true.

Me: You're not supposed to agree!

Brad: Why are you calling me?

Me: We were in an accident!

Brad: God, Haley, why didn't you say so? Are you OK?

Me: Yes, but The Van is wrecked. We're lost in L.A.

Brad: Oh.

Me: I thought you might be able to help us!

Brad: HOW CAN I HELP YOU? I'm in Washington. I should be sleeping. We've got early practice tomorrow.

Me: Don't you CARE that we're lost in L.A.?

Brad: Of course I do. But I can't help you. Get on a bus or something and go to San Diego. I'll be there on the 22nd at, like midnight, I think. Although I'm leaving again on the 24th. Or go home. Call your dad.

Me: We don't have any money!

Brad: Haley, calm down.

Me: I can't calm down!

Brad: I have to go, Haley. Call me tomorrow and let me know you're OK.

Me: We'll probably be dead by tomorrow!

I was only slightly kidding. I mean, people get killed in big cities all the time. I don't know what the murder statistics are, but I'm sure they're pretty high. Not to mention the air quality. The air alone could kill a person. I wheezed and coughed.

I had one last resort.

Phone Call with Kiki:

Me: Hi, it's me.

Kiki: [sobbing] Haley, how did you know?

Me: How did I know what?

Kiki: To call me here.

Me: Where are you?

Kiki: At home.

Me: Harvard?

Kiki: NO, home. Where you called me.

Me: I called your cell.

Kiki: Oh … right.

Me: Why are you at home?

Kiki: I dropped out of Harvard.

Me: What?

Kiki: I can't talk about it now.

Me: WHAT?

Kiki: I've got to go.

Kiki dropped out of Harvard? I wouldn't be more surprised if, say, that owl over there flew over and started pecking my eyes out.

"HALEY!" Izzy yelled. She was standing in the middle of the road. Somehow, we were in a totally residential area. There weren't even any street lights. How did this happen?

I have to admit that it was kind of pretty in a help-we're-lost kind of way. "I really have to pee!" she said.

"I don't care," I said. I felt numb and weird. Brad sounded sort of like he didn't care. Maybe he doesn't care. What was I doing going all the way to San Diego to visit him anyway?

"I'm going to pee behind this plant!" she yelled. "Warn me if someone's coming."

"Sure," I said. I was trying to figure out which way was north from the stars. I saw this on a show once. Not that going north would help us or anything, it just seemed like the right thing to do.

I sat down and started imagining all the things I'd rather be doing.

Things I'd Rather Be Doing:
1. Sleeping.
2. Watching TV with my dad.
3. Running with Kiki.
4. Shopping with Jules.
5. Bungee jumping.
6. Having wisdom tooth surgery.
7. Having my appendix removed.
8. Cleaning table bases at Hefty's.

I should have been paying attention, but next thing you know, there was a tremendously loud dog barking and growling and Izzy shot out from behind the plant screaming.

"Help!" she yelled.

"I can't help you!" I yelled back. I started to run, with Junior clutched under one arm and my backpack over the other — the rest of the stuff I couldn't have cared less about. I mean, it was just clothes, right?

We're talking MAD DOG here.

"Wait!" she yelled. She ran after me, dragging a garbage bag.

I don't know how long we ran. A long time.

The dog didn't follow us.

What is it with us and dogs anyway?

Sunday, December 21

Dear Junior:

We have escaped from L.A. It's a long story. For one thing, we lost almost all of our clothes and, well, everything, except for you (Junior) and our tin of money and my backpack and one half-empty garbage bag.

At least we have ID and credit cards. Yes, cardS. Plural.

All this time, I'd been putting everything extra on my Visa card because Izzy didn't have one. What she "forgot" (so that I would pay for everything?) was that she had an "emergency" MasterCard hidden in her wallet.

She's so manipulative, seriously, I have no idea why I don't just walk away and leave her here in L.A. forever. I don't think she could survive without me.

But then again, I don't think I could survive without her MasterCard. She bought me some clothes at the Gap. Off the sale rack. She bought herself about ten outfits from the regular priced stuff. Not that I'm bitter.

OK, maybe a bit.

"You can pay me back later, totally!" she said. I just glared at her. I'd paid for everything else! She spent $150 and I had to pay her back?

I mean, seriously?

I glared but didn't freak out. I needed her, sad as that seems.

Needless to say, we are now holed up in a Howard Johnson.

I love you, HoJo.

I love showers. I love beds. I love everything about this place.

We're saved! By MasterCard. At least, sort of.

We've thought about it a lot (I say "we," but I mean "I" because "thinking" doesn't seem to be Izzy's strong suit — although her constant, daunting cheerfulness gives her an aura of capability, I've discovered that she's actually pretty helpless) and decided to keep going. I just want to see Brad now, anyway. I've come all this way. Probably when I see him I'll remember how much I love him and stuff and we'll fall into each other's arms (only it bugs me when he touches me) and everything will be OK.

That's The Plan, anyway.

And if we go home now, the book will never get done. So now I'm sort of changing the book a bit. It will be about taking a bus from L.A. to San Diego. I'm sure we'll meet all kinds of interesting characters. I keep trying to talk to people on the street to find out if they are actually interesting characters themselves, and as it turns out, most people don't want to talk to strangers on the street.

"Leave me alone," does not make someone an interesting character.

But, damn it, I'm determined to find some interesting characters at some point in this trip, and I don't mean "characters" like Donald Duck or any other full-sized adult dressed up as a creepy stuffed toy in a theme park. Even though we've decided to go to Disneyland first. I don't know why. It just seemed like the right thing to do.

On Izzy's credit card, of course.

I mean, she owes me, no? I BROUGHT HER HERE AT GREAT PERIL.

Love,

Haley, Girl Adventurer

4:04 p.m.

Talked to Kiki. Turns out that she's happy now that she's home but she wasn't happy at Harvard. Very confused by the conversation and have no idea what she's talking about. Maybe she has had some kind of nervous breakdown. Wish I was at home to comfort her but she says she wants to be alone. Hope she's OK.

Kiki is always OK.

Mustn't worry about Kiki.

Talked to Melody. She sounds really happy. Like, REALLY psychotically happy. I'm a little concerned that she's still on drugs, you know? The baby was crying and screaming in the background and I could hear Dad singing to her, and I felt just the tiniest bit jealous.

I mean, not that I want Dad singing to me or anything. God.

Galaxy. I'm sorry, but "Galaxy" is just a stupid name for a baby. What do you call her for short? "Gal"? "Laxy"? Pfft.

Oh, and Melody has apparently decided that The Wedding is going to take place in the backyard. Next summer. Has she seen the backyard? Is she serious? WHO IN THEIR RIGHT MIND GETS MARRIED ON A PATCH OF DEAD GRASS? Worse than that, she wants me to be her maid of honour. Ha.

I mean, I guess I am sort of touched a bit. But I shudder to think what she'll make me wear. Come to think of it, she probably only asked me so that I'll hold The Baby (sorry, I mean "Laxy" — it's just hard to get used to calling him, I mean her, anything other than The Baby) while she cavorts around doing her pagan ritual, which no doubt involves dancing barefoot on flower buds or river rocks or something.

Anyway, I guess I'll worry about that later.

Much, much, much later.

Totally Izzy!
Date: December 21
Mood: Freaked out
Weather: Dark but sunny
Haley: Worst Driver of All Time, totally

Hey, all of you out there in blog land! So you won't believe what happened to us. I'm happy to tell you, the ugly green van is wrecked! It stunk anyway. It was such a hippie-mobile. It was gross! But we had a minor car accident and it was accidentally totalled. I feel bad for

Haley, a bit. She's still, like, TOTALLY annoying, but I pity her because she totally loved The Van.

We survived the wreck, which is probably like a miracle, you know?

Haley's growing on me a bit. I don't really like her, but she did figure out how to get us to the HoJo. I mean, DUH. How could we forget the emergency credit card of mine? We're so stupid. Now we're going by bus, or whatever, but first ... Disneyland!

I love Disneyland. It's like, my favourite place on earth.

You know, I'm feeling a bit bad about going to San Diego to steal Haley's boyfriend out from under her. But he's not actually her boyfriend, because they broke up. I don't even think he still likes her (although she looks totally cute right now — I might talk her into a haircut or something so she doesn't look so good when we get there), because he totally blew her off when she called him for help.

And he didn't even ask after me!

But he must have been totally distracted with his important hockey stuff. I'm SO excited to see him. But first, Disneyland!

Peace out, my loyal fans.

Monday, December 22 (a.k.a. Bard Day) (I mean, Brad Day)
Noon

Pictures: Disneyland, Anaheim, CA

- assorted creepy large stuffed animals.
- assorted tourists eating massive amounts of food.

- assorted terrifying rides.
- assorted pictures of benches.
- assorted snaps of Izzy, taken by Izzy, being annoying.

When I was here with Jules, we stayed right across the street from Disneyland. Seriously. And we didn't go. It seems like that was a lifetime ago, frankly.

I never thought that I'd miss Jules, but I do. She thought Disneyland was childish and so on, but at least she wouldn't have made me go on rides. Think about it, if every ride has to have a six-foot-high poster warning of the dangers of the ride, then maybe, just maybe, rides are dangerous.

Also, Disneyland is madly expensive. I'm glad we have this credit card, but I don't know how we're going to pay it off when we get home.

Not to worry, though.

The book advance will take care of it. Book advances are usually a lot, right? I heard that J.K. Rowling bought a house with hers, so I'm just going to go ahead and assume I'll have enough to pay off my credit card.

And, apparently, Izzy's. Though we'll cross that bridge when we come to it. I mean, she's been using MINE for this whole trip! Who paid for the Motel 6 in the blizzard?

I did, that's who.

No surprise here, but Izzy really loves Disneyland. Like she REALLY loves it, in the pathological way that some people love Elvis Presley or faint when they see movie stars. Frankly, she's beginning to frighten me. The scarier part is that almost all of the Happiest Staff on Earth reminded me of her. Kind of fake-happy. Over-the-top perky. I find it really depressing, not to mention terrifying. Maybe the Happiest Place on Earth isn't the right spot for the Most Neurotic Girl on Earth, know what I mean?

Amongst other things, I've been obsessively thinking about my sister, which is weird because I wasn't that excited about the fact that she was going to be born. I was, but also I wasn't. Now I keep flashing to her in my mind and thinking, "What is she doing now?" I know new babies don't actually DO anything, but what am I missing?

There are lots of babies at Disneyland (although why anyone would bring their baby here, I have no idea, because it's not like they can go on rides or anything) and each time I see one, I wonder if that's what she's like. Galaxy. If that's what Galaxy is like.

God, Galaxy has to be The Worst Name on Earth. Poor kid. It's even worse than Haley. GALAXY HARMONY? I mean, seriously, that poor little girl.

I liked the Pirates of the Caribbean ride. I went on it about twenty-seven times. The twentieth time, I was sitting next to a couple who I swear were groping each other's laps the whole time.

Barf.

It's a kids' ride! I was so mad.

Other people's gropy happiness gives me angst.

Also, isn't there a rule about fondling in public in Disneyland? It just doesn't seem like the kind of place that would allow it. I'm surprised that the Happiest Police on Earth didn't arrest them and throw them in the Happiest Jail on Earth.

Izzy went on every single ride. Every. Single. One. Did I mention that it was hot? Well, it was. My sweat was sweating and I was getting light-headed from the heat.

I was starting to feel like her crotchety old mother or something, waiting for her to get through the lineup and finish with the ride. I stubbornly refused to go on any ride that went round and round in circles because I knew they would make me dizzy like crazy and I hate being dizzy. I think there may be something wrong with my inner ear because I've never been able to handle even the Tilt-a-Whirl at the fall fair. Even watching Izzy on the rides that went in circles was making me nauseated.

I did a lot of waiting.

Places I Waited in Disneyland:
1. Benches.
2. Little cement walls.
3. Sitting on the ground because there was nowhere else to sit.
4. Gift stores.
5. Public washrooms.
6. Water fountain areas.

Rides Izzy Talked Me into Going on against My Better Judgement:
1. Big Thunder Mountain
2. River Run
3. Splash Mountain

Note to Self: Any ride with the word "mountain" in it is
  terrifying. Do not go on one under any circumstances.
  YOU WILL NEVER RECOVER.

Note to Self 2: Any ride involving water in any way WILL
  drench you (and only you) and you will have to walk
  around for the rest of the day looking like you're audi-
  tioning for some kind of sick wet T-shirt event.

"Don't be such a spoilsport," Izzy whined.

"I can't!" I said. For one thing, my clothes were totally
soaked from that river-rafting ride, which wasn't scary, it
was just wet. I swear, every time it went around a bend,
it dumped a whole garbage bucket's worth of water
over me. No one else in my little cart-thing was even
splashed.

Just me.

Naturally, I was wearing white.

"I'm freezing," I added.

"Just stand in the sun!" she said helpfully. "You'll dry
out!"

"I won't do it," I said.

"It's just a RIDE," she said. "Come on, I've always
wanted to go on this one! Since I was a little kid!
Pleeeease. I went on that stupid pirate ride with you a billion times."

"Go by yourself!" I said.

"It's not scary," she said. "I swear!"

"Of course it is," I said. "It's got MOUNTAIN in it!"

"What does that mean?" she said.

"Mountain!" I said. Somehow we'd got ourselves in line. In front of us, a really obnoxious guy was yelling into his cellphone. He was obviously in the middle of a Very Important Business deal. Honestly, who conducts business in line at Disneyland? He had some little kids with him. I felt sorry for them. He was completely ignoring them.

"Hi," I said. "Are you twins?" I mean, obviously they were, they looked exactly the same.

One of them stomped on my foot and the other one flipped me the bird. They were about five years old! I was so horrified, I didn't know how to respond.

"OK," I said in this really fake, sweet voice. "You have fun now!"

Izzy was laughing like a hyena. Her laugh was starting to get on my nerves. It had a rat-a-tat quality that I can't even describe.

"I'm going on the ride, OK?" I said. "Just don't bug me."

"You're so friendly," she said. "Who knew?"

The obnoxious guy hung up his phone and glared at me. "Please don't bother the girls," he said.

"Sorry," I said.

"Don't do it again," he said. He flipped open his phone and proceeded to start shouting into it again. My head was starting to throb. By the time we got to the front of the lineup, I had about the worst headache I'd ever had in my life.

Probable Causes of Worst Headache Ever:

1. Fear of insane ride.
2. Brain tumour.

3. Aneurysm.
4. Migraine.
5. Bleeding in the brain.
6. Meningitis (again).
7. Tiny stroke.
8. Big stroke.
9. Brad-related stress.

I have to say that Splash Mountain is the most sadistic ride I've ever even heard of. For one thing, all those little fluffy bunnies? The sing-songs? THE GIANT CLIFF THAT YOU FALL OVER?

By the time we finished, my heart was beating about a billion times per minute. I read once, somewhere, that if you're really scared your heart can actually explode. I lay down on the first available bench with my hand on my chest. I mean, if your heart is going to explode, you want to be lying down for it, at least.

"Get up!" said Izzy. "Let's go on something else!"

"I'm never getting up off this bench," I said. "My heart!"

"You're such a drama queen," she said. "Look, there's Orlando Bloom!"

"I don't believe you," I said.

"Seriously," she said.

"I'm not going to look," I said. "I won't fall for that."

Picture: Orlando Bloom, taken at Disneyland, Anaheim, CA
OK, it WAS really him. I was wrong. Don't think I'm

not beating myself up for it on a daily basis, because I am.

"Why didn't you tell me?" I asked for the billionth time.

"I did," Izzy said. "You weren't listening. Isn't that your phone?"

"What?" I said. For some reason, ever since my horrible headache and Splash Mountain, I was having trouble hearing things. Likely my hearing was permanently damaged by the tiny stroke I had from fear on the way onto the ride, exacerbated by the plummeting fall at the end.

"Your phone!" she said.

"Oh!" I said. I flipped it open.

"Hello?" I said.

"Haley, it's Dad," said Dad. I think it's funny when he does this. Like I wouldn't recognize my own dad's voice?

"I know," I said.

"Look," he said, "there's just a small problem with Galaxy."

At first I didn't hear him properly. I thought he meant there was a problem with THE galaxy, like the Milky Way. It took me a second.

"Galaxy?" I said. "That's a terrible name, you know. You mean, The Baby?"

"Yes," he said. "It's nothing to worry about. She's in the hospital. She has a minor heart thing. Apparently, it happens all the time."

"What?" I said. I was having trouble breathing. I put my head between my knees. "What heart thing? What happened?"

"She'll be fine," he said. "I just thought you should know."

"What?" I said.

"Stop saying that, Haley," he said. "I shouldn't have called. Don't panic."

"I'm not panicking," I lied.

"What's that in the background?" he said. "Sounds like you're at a zoo."

"Yeah," I said. "I mean, it's busy here at the lodge! I have to go!"

I'm a horrible person for lying to my own father.

A horrible person.

And because I'm a horrible person, fate has given my sister some kind of horrible disease and I've never even met her.

It's my fault.

Argh!

5:16 p.m.

"We should totally get going," said Izzy, appearing out of thin air, like she always does. She patted her stomach. "I've eaten way too much today! I hope Brad doesn't mind my pot-belly!"

I snarled. For one thing, her belly was totally flat. And for another thing, why would Brad care about her belly?

"Why would Brad care about your belly?" I asked.

"No!" she said. "That's not what I said."

"What did you say?" I said.

"Nothing!" she said. "You totally misheard me! Sheesh!"

"What are you talking about?" I said. My head was

pounding. It felt like tiny Disney dwarfs were hammering it with their happy fists. "We should go."

"Gee, you're in a bad mood," she said. She bounced along beside me. It was pretty hot and I was sweating. I didn't want to tell her about Galaxy. It was just too ... private.

"No, I'm not," I said.

"Yes, you are," she said.

"Not," I said.

"Are too," she said.

"Shut up," I said. Granted, this wasn't the cleverest comeback, but she did shut up.

"I'm so excited to see Brad!" she chirped.

"Why?" I said.

"I mean, I'm excited for you two to get back together!" she said. "It's, like, so totally romantic!"

"No, it isn't," I said. Frankly, I just wanted to go home. My legs felt like lead, which could also mean that I have MS or some other incurable degenerative disease. I pinched my skin to make sure I could feel it.

"What are you doing?" she said.

"Izzy," I said. "Seriously, stop."

"Fine," she said. "Be that way, I don't care." She tossed her curls and marched on ahead. We had to be at the bus station by 6:30 and it was already almost 6:00 and we weren't even at the hotel yet. I concentrated on that and not on the fact that I should be at home with my family.

I swear, I didn't see that little kid crouched down by the doorway of the hotel. He was looking for lizards or something, apparently. Anyway, I tripped right over him.

What are the odds of that?

I also don't know why I didn't instinctively protect my face with my hands. I guess I was reaching out to the kid to make sure he was OK, even as I was falling over him.

Onto my face.

Onto the sidewalk.

There was a horrible crunch and blood came pouring out. It was horrible and it hurt. I felt like crying, but I didn't. All I was thinking, to tell the truth, was that it was a lot less bad than whatever my dad and Melody and Galaxy were going through at home.

It took awhile to get me bandaged up. Izzy was hopping up and down, she was so tense. I guess she just doesn't like the sight of blood or horrible, hideous black eyes. We missed the bus, but it was no big deal. There was another one. We'd just be late, that's all. I don't know why she cared so much.

Actually, I don't know why I didn't wonder a bit more about why she cared so much. But I'm sort of skipping ahead.

Midnight

"Brad!" Izzy shouted. I swear she nearly knocked me down the stairs of the bus. It was surreal. I could see him, sort of sleeping on this bench area at the bus terminal. He jumped about a mile when he saw her. She kind of threw herself onto him, which was a little more forward than I was comfortable with. He's MY boyfriend! Or ex-boyfriend. Or whatever.

I tried to smile at him, but that caused the bandages on my nose to tighten and made my eyes water.

"Haley?" he said. He was standing right in front of me.

"Hi," I said, and I kind of fell into his arms. I was light-headed. Probably because my nose had bled so much. He caught me, which sounds romantic, but it really wasn't. If he hadn't caught me, I guess I would have probably crushed him with my huge weight.[9]

"Hi," he said. "Wow, you're heavy."

See what I mean? Not exactly Meg Ryan and Tom Hanks coming together at the top of the Empire State Building in *Sleepless in Seattle*.

"I know," I said, pushing him away. "Sorry."

"Don't BE like that," he said. He squinted at me. His squint was very irritating. From out of nowhere, I suddenly felt like slapping him. I don't know why. "You look ... wounded," he said.

"I am," I said.

"She fell!" chirped Izzy, thrusting her way between us. She reeked of perfume. I've never understood why people overuse perfume. It just makes other people, like me, annoyed.

"IZZY," I said.

"Izzy," said Brad slowly. "What are you doing here?"

Izzy shrugged. "Road trip?" she said.

"Really," he said. "Uh huh."

"Really!" she said.

---

[9] The French diet hadn't been working out too well for me lately.

I had no idea what they were talking about. It was pretty much one too many "reallys" for me.

"Um," I said. I was really tired. So tired that my legs were shaking. Or maybe I was showing early symptoms of ALS, one of the two, anyway. "I could use some food."

"Food!" said Brad. He looked relieved, like instead of "food," I might have said, "Let's run off and get married!"

I was getting a very strange vibe from him that's hard to explain. Usually, I felt like he was pulling me in? But right now I felt like he was pushing me away. Not literally, just his, well, his aura. For lack of a better word.

It was really hot, even though it was the middle of the night. The air was crackling with dryness. I could feel my pores drying up. If nothing else, San Diego would be good for my skin.

We made our way into some kind of diner. I'm sure we looked like idiots with my busted-up face and Brad's bemused expression and Izzy's unbelievable hyperness. She was starting to REALLY get on my nerves. And I wanted to talk to Brad. Wasn't this supposed to be our big reconciliation or whatever?

I ordered fries and a milkshake. Sometimes a milkshake is absolutely necessary for your health. In this case, I was having a hard time chewing and breathing at the same time. If I went to chew with my mouth closed, I couldn't breathe. I was concentrating on eating without showing everyone my chewed food, so I didn't notice so much that Brad and Izzy were talking up a storm. OK, that's not exactly true. But IZZY was certainly talking a lot.

Like, I don't think they would have noticed if I got up and walked out.

So I did.

I know that probably sounds weird. But that's what happened. And that was the end of my story with Izzy and Brad. I have no idea what happened to them. And I don't even know if I care.

OK, I'm kind of curious, but that's all.

MY story, on the other hand, got really really good after that.

JANUARY

January 1

Happy New Year!

Dear Junior:

Happy New Year! OK, I know the last little bit of time has been extremely unusual. I haven't been writing my journal and I haven't been writing my book. I just haven't been writing.

And the whole thing about getting back together with Brad? It totally fizzled. It fizzled even while it was happening.

Note to Self: Stop saying "totally." It makes you sound stupid. It makes you sound like Izzy.

I guess I knew the second I stepped off the bus that it was really over. With Brad, that is. I guess it had been over for a long time. His eyes kept drifting off me, if that makes sense. If I really think about it a lot, when he was away my eyes (it's a metaphor, OK?) kept drifting off him. Like I had to force myself to think about him and what I felt was pretty much ... nothing.

And onto HBG.

But HBG ... well, I just don't think it was about him anyway. Not that he's not really cute. He is. But it was just about me needing to start looking around at other people. Other than Brad. And other than JT.

I mean, let's face it, I wasted way too much of my life on JT to begin with and I was in danger of wasting even more time on Brad. Time goes by fast. There really isn't a lot to waste. I remember reading this book once and someone was trying on some clothes and whining because they made her look fat and someone else said to her, "Look, there really isn't enough time for that!" And what she meant was that life is short. Don't waste it worrying about stuff you can't control, like the size of your butt and who feels what for you.

But back to Brad:

It was like he couldn't even get me into focus. I don't blame him, I wasn't looking great. Not that I ever do. But it wasn't the funny short hair or my broken nose or any of those things at all. I mean, let's face it, he's seen me with black eyes before and there was a time when he would have thought that it was cute. It's just not cute to someone when they don't love you anymore. Not that I'm an expert in love.

Not really.

OK, so I am a bit.

I think.

Let me back up to where I was before, when I left the diner, leaving Brad in Izzy's clutches (which must have been scary — I didn't really get the fact that she was crazy about him and he wasn't crazy about her, I was too wrapped up in my own stuff to even notice or care).

I just got up and grabbed my backpack and Junior and the one last garbage bag, which somehow had survived. I left all the other stuff — all Izzy's clothes and probably most of mine (that she bought me), which were in these cute suitcases that she'd also bought.

I knew the garbage bag was mine anyway, because my socks were sticking out through a hole in the side (and her stuff was all in the new suitcases, no doubt). They were socks that I remember getting mad at my dad for wearing, and it made me feel sad and weird. There I was in San Diego and my dad was going through all this stuff at home, and I was feeling ... I can't explain it. It was like my heart was too big for my chest, but not in a panic attack kind of way, and not in a good way either. I just had to get outside.

I stood there on the sidewalk for a bit. The wind was hot and dry and made it feel even more like I was on the wrong planet. I flipped open my phone and I called home.

As it turned out, Galaxy was OK. I think that's when I started crying for real. Really hard, and not prettily. So I told him where I was and what I was doing. I think he was kind of shocked because there was a silence. Or maybe he was so mad he couldn't speak. Hard to say, really.

Then he said, "You should have told us. We'll get you home. We'll figure it out, borrow some money or something. Don't worry." It was impossible to say what his tone was. If I didn't know him and didn't know that he never got mad, I would have pegged him as "furious."

"I'm not worried," I said. And the weird thing was, that was true. "Don't bother. I'll find my own way."

"Haley," he started to say, but I'd already hung up. He phoned back right away, but I didn't answer. Maybe that was really irresponsible, but I didn't want him to help me, I wanted to do it on my own.

I opened up my wallet and I had about four dollars in change in it and not much else. So I walked into 7-11 and bought a chocolate bar. It took me a long time to choose which one to buy, and finally I chose a Hershey Bar with almonds. I figured almonds, being nuts, were a good source of protein. Also Hershey bars seemed like something a French woman might choose. Kind of pure. You know? Pure chocolate, some almonds. I don't know why I was choosing the chocolate bar like it was the last thing in the world I was ever going to eat, but I was.

Anyway, I took it up to the till and paid for it and as I was leaving, someone yelled, "Hey, you dropped your socks."

He was standing there in front of me, with my stupid ugly socks in his hand and I felt all the colour just drain out of my face. I can't even tell you what I felt. I just knew.

God, that sounds so lame, doesn't it? Jules would throw up if I told her that. And Kiki? I don't know. When I did finally tell her, she was pretty happy for me. She's kind of spiritual and stuff, so I guess it sounded real to her.

His name is Gray. Gray Cloud. I know, I know. He's a total hippie offspring, just like me. Only NOT like me, in that he's kind of a hippie too. Believe it or not, he was on a road trip, just like me. (Except the part where The Van was totalled — his Van — OK, his mom's van — wasn't totalled. It was in the parking lot.)

And I know it sounds beyond crazy ...

He could have killed me! It could have been a ruse! Like Mark Harmon in that old mini-series about Ted Bundy that they keep showing on late-night TV!

But it wasn't. I just joined them. His mom's name is Serendipity. They call her Sara, though. She's kind of like what I would have thought my own mom would have been like. Before I met her, that is. My own mom is nothing like Sara. Sara is just ... easy. No stress, no worries.

She's sort of like someone I could have imagined my dad with, to be honest. Sort of like the person that Melody probably wants to be, you know?

She phoned my dad, which made me feel about eight years old, to ask if it was OK if I went along with them. I'm almost eighteen! I don't need his permission! I guess that conversation went OK because here I am.

And it's exactly where I'm supposed to be.

It gets even better.

Gray looks exactly (OK, except younger) like HBG. Exactly. It makes me believe in the fates again. Like the fates were warming me up to meet him by getting me all interested in HBG. And it not quite being right.

With Gray, it's just ... right. He's a singer. Well, sort of. His mom says he's a poet. I think he's just funny. He sings these songs that aren't songs and he kind of speak-sings them. We spent one perfect night on the beach and he sang (spoke) some of them to me by the fire. It was totally romantic, or would have been if I hadn't been swarmed by these really weird bugs, which stung me all over my left arm, which then got swollen up like a giant, over-stuffed turkey sausage.

I didn't worry, though.

OK, I'm not totally cured or even very different. I did worry. Actually, I was having a hard time breathing and I started gasping a bit and he thought I was choking, and smacked me on the back until I stopped doing it. A paper bag would probably also have worked.

Anyway. It's probably not forever, but they're going my direction (he lives in Seattle, which frankly doesn't seem like the choice of many hippies, but who am I to say?) and I'm going to get a ride with them. Or I should say, I have been riding with them and I'm going to keep going with them. Christmas was ...

Well, it was different.

Gray and Sara are taking The Longest Possible Route (TLPR) back home, which involves winding around the coastline and generally going about a mile a day (or so it feels!). Which is great by me. I'm getting lots of time to write and think. Christmas felt a bit sad, but I'd never tell Gray. Or Sara. It's just that it wasn't home and I felt sad that I missed Galaxy's first Christmas. Not that she'd notice, but I did.

Not that it wasn't amazing to celebrate with Gray and Sara.

It was. We barbecued a turkey. And Gray gave me a really good CD that he made himself. And Sara gave me some books.

It turns out that Sara is a writer. She writes those romance novels that you buy in the drugstore. With guys in them named Bryce and Ashton. She also writes Stephen King type stuff but under a different name. I won't tell you what it is because it might wreck it for you. Somehow it's hard to imagine this funny little hippie woman as a master horror writer. She says writing is a craft and that a good writer can write anything, just like a good carpenter can build anything. She didn't think my book idea was dumb and she looked at what I've written so far. And then she made this awesome suggestion: She suggested that I just stop writing for a while and enjoy the trip. Then, when I get home and I'm looking for a job, I can sit down and write it all. Because at the end of the day, writing the book IS a job. And I can't enjoy the experience if I'm working the whole time.

Yeah, I know. It sounded like something my dad would say. But hey, maybe she's right. I'm not going to argue because the minute she said that, it was like this huge stress was lifted off my shoulders. I could get up and enjoy a day without worrying if the book was going well or if it wasn't going well. I bet this is a bit like how Kiki felt when she dropped out of Harvard. It isn't that she didn't LIKE Harvard, it's just that she liked it but she wasn't liking anything else at the same time. Kind of like she lost herself in it and if she was at Harvard, that was all she was.

I'm rambling now. I don't know what I mean. But I know when I was trying to write and experience stuff at the same time, in my head there was this kind of mantra saying, "I'm a writer, I'm a writer!" which I did sort of like, but it also removed me from everything I was doing.

I was doing some stuff just for the sake of the book. Like all that stuff with the big egg and giant ball of string. I wanted it to be funny. I was going to force it to be funny no matter what, for the sake of the book. I forgot to figure out whether I found it funny or not.

I guess I find it a bit funny that Izzy was using me to get to Brad. He looked kind of scared of her. It was like, as a last punishment to him for being my boyfriend, I presented him with his stalker. I found her blog on-line and I think she might be a little crazy. As in, "completely." But hey, that isn't my problem. I feel a bit bad about it.

But not that bad.

OK, I feel bad.

Brad wasn't a bad guy, he just wasn't the person for me. And maybe Gray isn't, either. But damn, he's CUTE.

And I'm so happy, sitting here at a picnic table waiting for Sara to finish washing out her clothes at the rest stop. This one has a laundromat, for real. Amazing.

Gray's singing some song about his dog's bad breath. I've talked to my dad and Melody and heard Galaxy crying in the background. I almost felt like crying too, because I'm going to meet her soon.

I'm going to meet my SISTER. How often do you get to say that in your life? I'm so ... lucky.

Everything just fell into place, you know?

Almost everything. I wasn't going to say anything, but last night when I was sleeping, I found this lump behind my left ear. Probably it's nothing.

It's nothing.

I'm sure it's nothing.

But I'm just going to sneak into the internet café over there to make sure. Don't tell anyone where I am, Junior.

Like you could.

Anyway, that's all for now. Thanks for listening,

Love,

Haley, Girl Still Travelling

Totally Izzy!

Date: January 2

Mood: Shattered

Weather: Cold

My heart is broken, blog fans. I've totally got to tell you that love totally isn't worth it. For one thing, Brad turned out to be, like, totally a jerk. He bought me a plane ticket for home and I thought he was coming with me. Turns out he was flying home on a different flight and it was all to totally get rid of me. What a bastard. What a jerk. There aren't even words. But I'm not daunted! I guess Brad doesn't get to be with me and that's his loss!

I'm a beautiful person!

I am!

Oh, and y'all can stop sending me hate mail about what I did to Haley. I didn't DO anything. She totally brought it all on herself. And besides, we had some laughs. That big egg thing was pretty funny. And that tiny park.

I don't know where she is now. I wonder if she's writing her stupid book. I'll totally support her in that, you know. I'm not, like, evil. I wonder if she'll give me credit? I can just see us going on tour together to support the book, and like going on Oprah and whatever. It would be the BEST.

Peace out, kids.

The Last Word

Number of hate e-mails received since December 1: 487

Number of dates that resulted from this blog: 0

Number of boys who flirted with me today: 3

ACKNOWLEDGEMENTS

The really funny thing is that I "remembered" writing the acknowledgements to this book already, and very nearly didn't submit any at all. Which is funny because I hadn't written them. What I remembered writing was the acknowledgements for *The Cure for Crushes (and other deadly plagues)*.

Those were really good acknowledgements.

The thing is that in between that book and this book, I had a baby. A lot of things happen when you have a baby, notwithstanding the terrible physical pain of it. One of those things is that you completely, positively and irrevocably lose any ability you ever had to remember any details about anything (except the pain of childbirth, which you'll remember forever). I know that a lot of you, my favourite readers, are not yet even twenty years old and the best piece of advice I will ever give you is to wait to have a baby until you are old like me (i.e. past thirty). When you are well-aged, the sleepless nights and dramatic birth process are blurred by the onset of senility, and you can cope with it much better than when you're, say, eighteen. When you're eighteen, you should be doing things other than having babies, such as dating inappropriate boys and living in youth hostels in Europe while imagining a future where you get to sleep in a real bed every night. This is just my opinion. But seeing as I have this forum in which I can ramble on and on endlessly about my own thoughts, I felt I should tell you that you should wait.

There are a lot of things you stop doing once you've had a baby. Do all those things first. Travel. Relax. Take entire days and watch horrible TV shows. Then go climb a mountain and do some kayaking. Sleep in. Go scuba diving. Audition for *Survivor*. Learn how to rappel down the side of buildings. Spend a day watching the surf in the winter in Tofino. Try that parkour stuff (free running), that looks so cool. I want to do that, but I'm too tired and rickety. Learn how to surf! I'm sure you probably won't be eaten by a shark. (At least, it isn't likely.) Wear fancy clothes and go to parties where champagne is served. Stay up late. Dance. Sing in public. Train for a marathon. Learn how to ice skate. Spend time in remote places and visit cities that are so big they scare you. Teach yourself how to walk in high heels and buy more shoes. Do everything you've ever wanted to do.

Believe me, you won't do any of these things "later." You'll be too tired.

So on to the business of acknowledging!

I must acknowledge my gorgeous giant son, Linden Rivers Stark — or The Bun, as we prefer to call him — for letting me get my work done by blissfully napping away the afternoon on a regular basis since the moment of birth. I'm kidding, he didn't do that. But he's so cute and such a love that I must acknowledge him anyway for just making me so incredibly happy, even though he pulled on my pant leg while I was trying to type and made sounds a lot like "wah wah wah," which made it difficult to concentrate at times.

Then I have to thank my ever loving and patient and very handsome fiancé, Clayton Rhodes Stark, for supporting me and continuing to love me even when it might have been challenging to do so. And for taking care of the ongoing feeding, entertainment and cleansing needs of The Bun and The Boy so that I could write this book. And for so so so many other things, I can't list them here because I'd be writing a whole other book. ILYWM, LOP.

My mum for being my hero and for always taking on The Bun when I'm scrambling to meet a deadline, not finished my work, and generally am freaking out.

My dad for so patiently waiting for me to become famous and for believing that it's just a matter of time.

My sisters for being proud of me and always remembering to ask what I'm writing and for listening to me go on and on and on. And for holding my legs up while I gave birth — that's love. Crazy love.

And all my family, near and far: mad props to my peeps! (I wrote that because they won't know what it means and then they will think I'm very cool and hip.) (Even though truly cool and hip people would probably not say that anymore.)

My publisher, Michelle Benjamin, for believing in me enough to continually buy my books for rapidly increasing sums that will ultimately allow me to fulfill my dad's steadfast, unwavering belief that I'll one day be outlandishly rich, like J.K. Rowling. (No, I've never met her.) (Yes, I DO wish that I'd written *Harry Potter*.)

This is starting to sound like an Oscar acceptance speech! Except it's far too long, of course. I once promised my drama teacher from high school, Mrs. Aitken, that I would thank her in my Oscar acceptance speech and then I accidentally forgot to become a famous actor, so I'll thank her here for making me think that there was an outside chance that I would be making an acceptance speech of any variety for any reason whatsoever. Thanks, Mrs. A.

I wish I was wearing a fancy, designer dress while I wrote this. That would be great. Writers get very little opportunity to wear fancy, designer dresses.

Sigh.

Where was I?

My agent, Carolyn Swayze, whom I'd like to thank in advance for selling this series of books to Hollywood and fulfilling all of our ambitions. And for continuing to hold my hand through the (sometimes arduous) process of writing (fun) and selling (work).

My editor, Elizabeth McLean, for catching all my incredibly odd and random errors and gently helping me fix them.

My girls, far and near, for everything. (Especially for rearranging bookstore shelves to put my stuff front and centre.)

And most of all, to each and every one of you who visited my website (which is now much improved, by the way, thanks to the actual website professionals who built it), www.karenrivers.com, and took the time to write to me and request a sequel. I'm so excited that you did that and so glad that I listened. This book was a tremendous amount of fun to write and I'm so sad that it's the last in the Haley series.

Maybe.

Unless there is popular demand!

I might wait a decade and then revisit her and see what she ended up doing with her life. Hmm, maybe I should write that down so I remember to pitch it in ten years.

Keep writing to me, keep reading, and believe in yourselves. You are the best. And I'm not just saying that. And if any one of you ever wins an Oscar (or America's Next Top Model) (or a Nobel Peace Prize), will you please thank me in your speech?

Thanks!

Karen

ABOUT THE AUTHOR

Karen Rivers has published eight previous YA books, including *Surviving Sam*, which was shortlisted for the 2004 White Pine Award; as well as the first two Haley Harmony books, *The Healing Time of Hickeys* and *The Cure for Crushes*. *The Healing Time of Hickeys* was shortlisted for the 2003 Canadian Library Association's "Young Adult Book of the Year" award, is a Children's Book Centre "Our Choice" selection, and was a featured title for Barnes & Noble and Amazon.ca. She lives in Victoria, British Columbia.

Check out the previous books in the Haley Harmony series:

THE HEALING TIME OF HICKEYS 1-55192-600-8
THE CURE FOR CRUSHES 1-55192-779-9

By printing QUIRKY GIRLS' GUIDE TO REST STOPS AND ROAD TRIPS
on paper made from 100% recycled/40% post-consumer recycled
fibre rather than virgin tree fibre, Raincoast Books has made
the following ecological savings:

- 48 trees
- 4,599 kilograms of greenhouse gases (equivalent to driving
  an average North American car for eleven months)
- 39 million BTUs (equivalent to the power consumption of a
  North American home for over five months)
- 28,176 litres of water (equivalent to nearly one Olympic
  sized pool)
- 1,722 kilograms of solid waste (equivalent to a little less than
  one garbage truck load)